VANISHED

The Nicole Jones series

Karen E. Olson

Severn House

This first world edition published 2017
in Great Britain and the USA by
SEVERN HOUSE PUBLISHERS LTD of
Eardley House, 4 Uxbridge Street, London W8 7SY.
Trade paperback edition first published
in Great Britain and the USA 2019 by
SEVERN HOUSE PUBLISHERS LTD.

British Library Cataloguing in Publication Data
A CIP catalogue record for this title is available from the British Library.

ISBN-13: 978-0-7278-8755-9 (cased)
ISBN-13: 978-1-84751-868-2 (trade paper)
ISBN-13: 978-1-78010-931-2 (e-book)

Typeset by Palimpsest Book Production Ltd.,
Falkirk, Stirlingshire, Scotland.

PROLOGUE

The hacker known as Tracker moves along the sidewalk, a hoodie pulled up over his head, his eyes darting from side to side. He approaches an ATM and pauses for a second. Someone comes up behind him, and he whirls around, but it's only a young woman, maybe in her twenties, a question in her eyes. He knows what she wants, so he steps aside. She nods, her card in her hand. He wants to warn her, but he knows this one is OK. Knows it because he's got the skimmer in his pocket. His hand closes over it, feeling its smooth surface, the tiny motherboard on the other side.

The woman takes her cash from the machine and tucks her card into her pocket. She turns and walks away; he's invisible to her. While the sidewalk is bustling, no one pays attention as he approaches the machine. He hovers over it, shielding it. If anyone notices him, he merely looks as though he's already swiped his card and is trying to figure out how many euros he needs. He could do it now. Right now. He's done it before, but something is stopping him this time. Maybe because it's two years later. Maybe because he's had time to think about it. Maybe because of *her*.

He shakes her out of his head as he makes his decision. In one swift move, he takes out the skimmer. He peels off the tape that covers the glue and affixes it to the machine. He surveys it for a second. No one will be able to tell. No one, unless he looks too closely, will see what he's done.

And the next person who puts his card into the ATM will be compromised.

He tries not to think about what he's doing, careful to stay shrouded as he moves away in the crowd. He doesn't want to linger, see who uses the machine next. He'll know.

He saunters into a nearby hotel, shedding the hoodie in the men's room, stuffing it into a trash can. He's wearing a white button-down shirt and a pullover sweater underneath, and he smooths it down as he takes a look in the mirror. He ignores the worry lines around his eyes as he splashes a little water on his hands and wets his hair back. He pulls out a pair of sunglasses and puts them on. As he walks out of the men's room, he stands up straighter, hands in his pockets. Confident.

A café is to the left, just outside the hotel, and he takes a seat, putting his phone on the table in front of him. He orders a coffee. The air is cooler than he'd like, and he regrets losing the hoodie. His phone vibrates, and he glances at it before picking it up and responding with his own text. He probably shouldn't stay, but he's within sight of the ATM and he's curious, against his better judgment. So far, no one has used it.

The coffee comes, and he sips, relaxing slightly as though he is merely a tourist or a businessman enjoying a few moments of solitude.

His phone vibrates again, interrupting. He looks over at the ATM. It's a young couple, arms around each other. He picks up the phone and touches the icon for the app he's developed just for this purpose. All of the young man's credit card information has downloaded into the app. With just a touch, it will transfer to the server. There isn't supposed to be anything in between the ATM machine and the server, but he's set this up as a safeguard. He's in control. He can decide what gets transferred and what doesn't.

He watches the young couple smiling at each other, and he's envious of them. They stop in front of the fountain and snap a picture of themselves using a phone that's not unlike his. He's never been so close before, never seen the victims. They've always been names and numbers online, no pictures, no videos, no way to feel guilty.

He goes to the menu on the app and hits another button. Again, another safeguard. He only hopes it works as he sends the information to the server.

They brought him in because of what he could do.

The hacker known as Tracker stands, tosses cash onto the table and moves away, disappearing into the crowd.

ONE

Four months later

Sometimes I go to the library just to look at the bank of computers. I pretend to peruse the books, picking them up one by one, but always with an eye toward the machines that have defined me, that lure me with their promise.

I don't touch them. I don't dare.

I've done it before. Stayed away. But it was easier the first time, before my relapse. The withdrawal is all too real. My hands shake; my heart beats so fast I can barely breathe. Beads of sweat form at my temple, and I dab at them, my face flush. I close my eyes and see the code, pinpoint the back doors, navigate my way inside in my head. None of it is real.

I want to find him online. I want to see what's happened to him. However, there's no guarantee that I'd find him there. We went our separate ways; I have a price on my head. I can't afford the risk of exposing myself. While the Internet offers anonymity, it's a false promise. Anyone can be revealed. Anyone can be found.

No, the best way to protect myself is to stay offline. I have no Internet footprint. No social media. No chat-room screen names. No bank account. No phone number.

Only one person knows how to reach me, and he's in as much danger as I am.

Someday I might be able to come out of hiding.

But someone will have to die first.

I sip wine from a small plastic cup, standing in the corner of the gallery, hoping no one will talk to me. Maybe if I act as though I'm merely someone in off the street, they'll leave me alone. No such luck, though, as I see Randy heading my way, his hand under the elbow of an elegant elderly woman with a mass of white curls swept up in the back and held in place with a blue porcelain comb. Her cocktail dress matches the comb; her long fingers are adorned with diamonds.

I won't be able to escape.

A wide smile spreads across Randy's face. 'Tina,' he says with his usual drawl. 'I'd like you to meet Madeline Whittier.'

I force a smile and hope that it's warm, holding out my free hand. Madeline Whittier takes it limply in hers. 'So you are Tina Jones,' she says, her eyes narrowing at me, searching my face for something that I can't make out.

I nod.

'I've been admiring your work,' she says. 'I especially love the beach scenes.'

I glance up at the watercolors across the room: long streaks of blues and pinks and oranges, sunrises, sunsets, the pier, surfers dotting the waves. They are an assault of colors that are a mix of reality and my imagination.

'Thank you,' I say.

'You look so familiar, my dear.'

A small panic rises in my chest. I look like my father, and she looks like she could have been one of his clients – one of the people he conned out of money way back when. But I force the anxiety back down. I have shed the name 'Adler' in favor of something more neutral in the hope that I can keep my anonymity. Randy is convinced he can 'make a local celebrity' out of me: someone who is not a local but who taps into local emotions. I admire his ambitions and it's incredibly flattering, but the threat of exposure frightens me, so I play it down and say that sort of thing is not for me, which frustrates him. I agreed to come to this event with the caveat that I am allowed to keep my privacy otherwise. He does not know where I live, and he pays me in cash.

I am not sure how someone like me manages to attract people like Randy: generous, kind people who seem to only see the good in others. I am the least likely to garner such trust, but I am my own worst enemy. While I want to sequester myself, hide away in a corner, these people find me and feel compelled to draw me out. And I allow myself to be drawn. Just so far, however.

I found my way to Charleston, South Carolina, six months

ago. I cannot stay too far away from the ocean, and it's a charming, relaxed, easy-going kind of place with plentiful art galleries eager to discover a new artist. I had depleted much of my cash before I arrived here, so I found an art supply store on Calhoun Street and made sure to befriend the staff, which eventually led me to Randy Patterson, who is connected to everyone in the art scene in the city. He's lived here twenty-five years, since following his husband to his hometown. Randy's gallery is sought-after by local artists, but when I stumbled on it in the weeks after my arrival, I had no idea who he was. I saw a tall, slender man with a splash of white hair who could be anywhere between forty and sixty-five. He welcomed me in and admired my watercolors over a glass of bourbon. When I lived on Block Island, I was partial to oils, but I had more time there. As a perfectionist, I am embarrassed that I choose watercolors for how quickly I can produce a number of pieces, but money – or lack thereof – is a motivator. I have no idea how long I'll stay here, so I have so far not been tempted to try my hand at oils or even acrylics again, although Randy has been encouraging me.

Madeline Whittier gestures toward one of the watercolors of a salt marsh with her glass of wine, sloshing it slightly. Randy and I pretend not to notice. 'Beautiful.' She steps closer to it, studying it. Randy raises his eyebrows at me, a signal that he's certain he'll make a sale.

I shift a little and set my plastic cup on a small table next to me. I don't like this part of it, the schmoozing. That's Randy's job, and he is so good at it that he doesn't need me. I begin to excuse myself, but he gives a quick shake of his head. Madeline Whittier turns just at that moment, but she doesn't notice. What she does do, however, is give me a wide smile. I notice that the smile doesn't reach her eyes, but it could be more because she's clearly had some work done to smooth out her lines and not because she doesn't want to be warm.

'Where are you from, Ms Jones?' she asks.

I tense up.

Randy intervenes. 'Tina's from Portland,' he offers.

She nods. 'I love Portland,' she says, 'although I love Seattle more.'

I chose Portland because everyone thinks I'm either from Oregon or Maine. I never correct them; I've never been to either city. I run the risk of someone actually asking me something specific about one or the other, but so far no one has. I merely nod back. Rarely do Randy's clients really want to know anything about me. They just want to know that they've bought something beautiful that perhaps their friends haven't discovered yet.

'You do look familiar,' she says again, leaning toward me to study my face. 'You're sure we've never met before?'

'No.' I can hear the tightness in my tone.

'Wouldn't that watercolor look magnificent on your porch, Madeline?' Randy interrupts, and I am grateful to him as he prepares to make his sale.

I excuse myself, heading toward the restroom in the back.

My heart is still pounding, and I pause for a second as I glance inside Randy's office, which is next to the small lavatory. A laptop is perched on the desk.

I hesitate in the doorway, unable to tear my eyes away from it. My need is palpable. In a few keystrokes, I could find out if Madeline Whittier was one of my father's clients, if she will be able to identify me.

I should walk away.

In a split second, I make a decision. I step inside the office and approach the laptop, my fingers tingling. I don't even try to stop myself; I touch one of the keys and the screen comes to life. I tell myself I'm not doing anything to show my hand as I glance back to make sure no one is coming. Randy has not set his laptop up with a password, which is something I would normally point out as dangerous, but he can't know.

I again tell myself I'm not doing anything that can be traced back to me. That I am completely anonymous.

I put Madeline's name and 'Charleston' into the search engine and scroll through the results. I don't dare put in my father's name, but if she was one of his victims, it will probably show up. I'm not exactly fooling myself. Trying to find out about her is just an excuse. A reason to break my fast.

I don't find anything except some society pages from the local newspaper. I am about to erase the search history when

I see one last headline that catches my eye. I click on the story and what I find startles me enough that I gasp out loud.

While I still don't know if Madeline Whittier was one of my father's clients, I do discover that a young man named Ryan Whittier, a student at Charleston College, vanished in Paris four months ago. The last time he was seen was at an ATM near a hotel on rue de Rivoli, not far from the Place de la Concorde. The camera that was trained on the machine captured a stranger installing a skimmer on it just moments before Ryan Whittier took out three hundred euros. While police are quoted as saying there was no indication that Ryan Whittier's disappearance was linked to the stranger or his actions, they are looking for him because he may have seen something that could help them find Ryan.

The article includes a still shot of him, taken by the ATM camera. The stranger's hoodie had fallen down slightly, and from the angle the photograph was taken, it would be hard for anyone to identify him. At least anyone who doesn't know him. But I know who he is.

He's FBI Special Agent Zeke Chapman.

TWO

I skim the story a second time. This was four months ago. Zeke was in Paris. Is he still there? I have no way of knowing. I don't have time to dwell on that, though; someone's coming. I quickly delete the search history – I can't completely erase my presence but there's nothing really incriminating here – close the laptop and move away from the desk, pretending to be intrigued by a small still life in oil.

'Oh, here you are,' Randy says, pursing his lips and shaking his head. 'You are too much of a recluse. I really need to get you out more.'

I give him a small smile, trying to remember how to breathe. 'I don't need to get out more,' I say, but I'm distracted. What was Zeke doing, putting a skimmer on an ATM? Did they ever find him? My fingers itch to get back online, to see if there is an updated story that has more information. It has been four months and since I am more than familiar with trails that grow cold, I am realistic. But at the same time, a surge of adrenaline rushes through me. I have missed him, and I had no idea just how much until I saw that grainy picture.

I am not paying attention. Randy is talking to me.

'What?' I ask.

He gives me a funny look, then volunteers that Madeline is buying one of my watercolors. 'She wants you to come to tea.'

'Tea? Do people really do that?' I ask.

He chuckles. 'In Charleston they do.' He hands me a business card. 'This is her address. Tomorrow. Three o'clock. She wants you to help her decide where to hang it.' The watercolor, I assume. I reluctantly take the card. I don't need any more friends, and I don't especially like tea, although the need for more cash flow is a good motivator.

I glance over at the laptop, forcing myself look away again. It only took one second and the craving is back. I didn't even do anything but a simple search. It takes so little.

'If you go and be nice, she'll buy more.' Randy winks, misunderstanding my hesitation.

'OK, sure.' Even though I really am not sure at all.

'And dress nice,' he says as he starts out the door. He knows my predilection for shorts and T-shirts.

I make a face at him, and he chuckles. I follow him, but I can't help but look back one more time at the laptop.

I don't come into town too often, usually only to bring Randy my work or to go to one of these gallery soirees. The sun is setting as I walk along King Street, glancing in shop windows, until I come to Queen. If I go further, I'll end up on Meeting Street, which would lead me to the City Market and the throngs of tourists. I'm not in the mood for that tonight. I turn in at a local restaurant for a drink. The walls are brick, like many of the homes around here, and I sidle up to the bar and order a bourbon. I don't make eye contact with anyone except the bartender, who recognizes me from the few times I've been here and gives me a nod as he puts the glass on the bar in front of me.

As I sip my drink, I keep an eye on the door. It's habit from being on the run for so long, from being a target. But I must be out of practice because I'm so deep in thought, that picture of Zeke circling around in my head, that I don't even notice someone has slid into the seat next to me until my elbow is jostled.

'Excuse me.' Even though he's polite, he isn't looking at me when he says this; he's trying to get the bartender's attention. He is tall, with thick black hair that's cut too short on the sides. His suit jacket strains against broad shoulders and muscled arms. I study his profile, which is dominated by a hooked nose. Another woman might find his swarthiness attractive – sexy, even.

I turn back to my drink, shifting a bit in my seat so there won't be any more physical contact.

He notices and stares at me. 'I won't bite.' He is not smiling and definitely not flirting, despite the words. His gaze unsettles me, and I swallow the last of my bourbon, suddenly anxious to get out of here.

I can't explain how I feel, and I'm certain that I shouldn't show the fear that's now creeping up my spine, grabbing hold of me so hard that I'm not sure I can breathe. I have no idea who this man is. I have never seen him before. I tell myself that I'm spooked because of seeing Zeke's picture online, and as I perch on the edge of my barstool, ready to flee, the man turns to me.

'You're that artist. At the gallery tonight.'

His words surprise me, and I try to remember whether I saw him there. But there had been about an hour or so where there were a lot of people going in and out, so I can't be sure.

I reluctantly nod.

'I like your work,' he says.

I shift uncomfortably as I throw some bills down on the bar. I can't really explain what's bothering me about him, but my instincts tell me it's time to go.

'It was nice meeting you,' I say, even though I haven't actually 'met' him, and slide off the stool and rush out.

I glance behind me to make sure he's not following, and he's not. He's chatting up the bartender with no indication that he's even noticed I'm gone. I need to chase away the panic attack that's sitting at the edge of my chest.

I take a few deep breaths and my heart slows considerably. The air sticks to my skin and I think about Miami. The humidity and palm trees, though, are the only things that remind me of my hometown. This city has a soft gentility about it, a Southern charm that urges me to relax and not take life too seriously. None of which I can do.

I pull my cellphone out of the backpack and punch in a familiar number. I give the cab company an address about three blocks from here, and the walk calms me further. I don't have to wait too long before the car pulls up next to me; the driver leans toward the passenger seat, a question in his eyes. I nod and climb in, settling in for the ride home.

I shed my dress and heels and put on a pair of shorts and a T-shirt before heading outside with my phone. It's dark now; the clouds hang low in the sky over the water, and the crash of the surf soothes me. It's been all I can do not to scream with frustration, but this has been a daily exercise in self-restraint. Today, however, it's worse. Ever since I saw that picture online.

I hit the speed dial.

'What's wrong?' It didn't even ring. It's as though Spencer Cross was waiting for my call.

I met Spencer six months ago in Miami. He and Zeke go way back to their teenage days of hacking and brief prison terms. Zeke turned to law enforcement, but Spencer started a lucrative cybersecurity company that landed him on the pages of *Wired*, *Rolling Stone* and *GQ*, among others. It was only when he blew the whistle on the government by revealing that two refugees who turned terrorist weren't properly vetted that he ended up underground with Incognito, an offshoot of Anonymous.

I don't bother identifying myself, since he clearly knows who it is. 'He's in Paris. At least he was a few months ago. Don't tell me you didn't know that.'

'I didn't know that. He's been under the radar. I haven't seen him anywhere online. And I'm not in Paris.'

I almost ask him where *he* is, but he won't tell me any more than I'd tell him where I am, although I'd be surprised if he didn't know. He gave me the phone; I'm sure there's a GPS installed somewhere in it. Maybe it's because I want him to know where I am that I haven't bothered to try to find it and get rid of it. I am so tired of hiding.

'What's going on, Tina?' Worry laces his words.

I tell him what I saw – the news story, the picture of the man who put a skimmer on an ATM.

'Are you sure it's him?' I hear the familiar tapping on a keyboard; he's looking for it. Before I can answer, I hear him say softly, 'Oh, shit.'

A surge of jealousy rushes through me as I picture him at his keyboard. I gave it up, but he didn't. I give myself a mental shake. I'm being unreasonable. I'm offline because I choose to be. It's a self-imposed exile.

'What's he up to?' I ask, pushing aside my thoughts.

'Honestly, Tina, I have no idea.'

'He's FBI. Aren't they supposed to be *keeping* people from installing skimmers?'

He doesn't bother to answer because it's a stupid question. Zeke's been undercover before, and he's probably undercover now.

'Is there an updated story? Did they ever find him?'

'Who, the kid?'

'No. Zeke.'

A short pause, then, 'No one's come forward with any information.'

At least no one else has identified him. If he *is* undercover, he'll stay that way.

'How exactly did you find this story?' The question startles me, even though it isn't a surprise. It's a four-month-old story. I'm not going to be reading it in today's newspaper.

'I was doing a search on someone who has the same last name as the kid who's gone missing. I thought maybe she knew my father. She keeps saying I look familiar.' I wonder if Madeline isn't related somehow to Ryan Whittier.

The surname is unusual, and there *is* a Charleston connection.

Spencer interrupts my thoughts. 'You've been online? You've got a computer?' His tone is not accusatory, merely curious.

'No. I used someone else's. It was just for a few minutes. I haven't been online in months. And right after I saw the article, I stopped.' I don't tell him that was because Randy was there; if he hadn't been, who knows what else I would have done.

He knows, though, without me saying anything.

'Do you think she knows who you are?' He's asking about Madeline.

'I don't think so. Even if she *had* been one of my father's clients, it was a long time ago and I never met any of them.' Maybe it's my paranoia from being on the run so long that makes me suspicious of everyone. And maybe it was just a good excuse to get online for the first time in six months.

He's quiet for a second, then asks, 'Do you think you've been there too long?'

I see where he's going with this. I can't take the chance that *anyone* knows who I am. If it's not Madeline, it could be someone else – someone on the beach, someone who sees me on my bike. It could the next person who shows up at Randy's.

Tony DeMarco has not lifted the hit on me. I stole two million dollars from him more than fifteen years ago. He believes that I orchestrated a hit on *him* six months ago. To him, I am an extension of my father, who also stole from him – and had an affair with his wife. It doesn't matter that Tony's testimony is what put my father in prison, where he died a couple of years ago. It doesn't matter that I paid him back. It's personal for him, and he wants me dead.

Even if I'm not online, even if I stay under the radar, his people have resources. Tony DeMarco doesn't forget, no matter how old or sick he may be. And he is sick. Even if he dies, though, his daughter – my half-sister, Adriana – hates me, and there is no knowing how involved she is in his business.

Tony knows I'm an artist, that I would gravitate toward a gallery. Word could get back to him that the artist 'Tina Jones' has a similar style to Helen White on Cape Cod or Nicole

Jones on Block Island, and he might send someone after me. Sometimes I wish that the hit on him had been successful, because then I wouldn't have to keep looking over my shoulder. Like with that man at the bar tonight.

I hear Spencer tapping on the keyboard in the background. It's almost as though it's an extension of me; I close my eyes and I can see it.

Suddenly, he says, 'Forget you ever saw anything.' His tone is sharp, curt.

'What do you mean?'

'You never saw the story. You didn't see the picture.'

'But it's him.'

'You have to stay out of it. And, Tina? Maybe it really *is* time to move on.'

And then he hangs up.

THREE

I try calling him back, but he doesn't pick up. I don't even get voicemail. He found out something about Zeke, maybe what he's up to with that skimmer and the ATM, and despite his warning I am itching to find out what it is. But I don't have a computer; I don't even know where I could borrow one. Besides Randy, I have kept to myself, not wanting to get close to anyone. I think about the hotel on the beach, the big one, and consider that they might have a business center, somewhere a guest might be able to download a boarding pass or check on a flight. But I can't do what I need on a public computer. I wouldn't have the tools, and I can't download any software that would raise red flags.

I am ignoring Spencer's warning, because I can't forget – no, I don't *want* to forget – what I saw, although his advice to move on resonates. Perhaps I *have* been here too long. Ironic, really, that I'm thinking this way, since I spent fifteen years on Block Island without incident, and the only reason anyone found me was my own stupidity. Since then, though,

the longest I've been anywhere has been a year. I was only a
few months on Cape Cod, less time than I've been here.

I have no idea where Spencer is. He could still be in Miami,
where he left me at the airport with the cellphone, his number
queued in. He called me once, when I went back to Block
Island, to tell me Zeke had disappeared. It had been a risk to
go back. It wouldn't take long for Tony DeMarco's people
to track me down. I stayed one night and left in the morning,
promising I'd be back someday. I've believed that Zeke's
disappearance had everything to do with DeMarco, since he's
been chasing the man for years. Maybe, however, it didn't.
Maybe it just had to do with Zeke.

And the reason why he's putting skimmers on ATMs in
Paris.

Why was Spencer so abrupt? Why couldn't he tell me
anything? What could he possibly have discovered?

I am barefoot, and the sand is soft underneath my feet. My
eyes have adjusted to the dark, but the lights on the pier flash
bright, interrupting. I make my way back along the water's
edge, the cool water splashing over my feet.

By the time I get back to the condo, my mind is made
up. I can't stay away. I don't want to. I need a laptop.

I toss and turn all night, forcing myself to stay in bed and
allowing myself to get up when I see the clock turn to six-
thirty. I go out on my small balcony with a cup of coffee and
watch the surfers waiting for waves down below. I've toyed
with the idea of learning how to surf while I've been here,
but I've never gotten around to it. I eye the bicycle that I keep
in the entryway. I am a bundle of nervous energy and need to
get rid of it.

I change into my bike shorts, a T-shirt and sneakers. I tug
my helmet on and wheel the bicycle outside to the elevator.

Folly Beach is a small island with one main thoroughfare
lined with surf shops with boards and T-shirts in their windows.
Several rustic restaurants serve local she-crab soup and grits,
and the rooftop bars have views of spectacular sunsets. I haven't
been here long, but it hasn't been difficult to fall into this life.

I turn onto East Ashley Avenue and pump the pedals hard,

feeling it in my calves. I pass pastel-colored houses on stilts and pickup trucks and palm trees. The road is flanked by overgrowth between the houses, and suddenly it opens up to my right beyond the small wooden fence that runs alongside me. The ocean spreads out past the sandy beach. Beachfront houses obstruct my view, but these are tidier, more expensive. I concentrate on my route as I feel the sweat drip down my chest and back.

I reach the end of the road at the lighthouse preserve. I put on the brakes and stand, staring out over the water while straddling the bike. Another day I might leave the bike and take a long walk on the beach, but something holds me back today.

It's the same thought that has been playing over and over in my head since I got on the bike, the same thought that filled my head each time I pressed down on the pedals.

I take it more slowly going back, the streaks of light in the sky pushing against the soft clouds.

My hands shake as I drag the old backpack out of the closet. I have a lightweight dress that I can roll up and it won't get wrinkled, so I stuff it inside, along with a pair of strappy sandals. Randy said I'd need to dress for tea. I don't anticipate having time to come back before I have to meet with Madeline.

While I am comfortable being anti-social, I'll admit to a curiosity about how she lives, and I do appreciate that she likes my watercolors. If going to tea with her helps Randy in any way, then why not? I owe a lot to him, and this is one way I can pay him back. That, and I might as well experience 'tea' before I move on again. I also could ask her if she's got a relative named Ryan.

The backpack seems almost empty with just the dress and shoes. I consider packing it more completely. Maybe I shouldn't come back here. The more I think about it, though, there is no indication that there's an imminent threat against me. Spencer's suggestion that I move on was just that: a suggestion. But he's right that I may have been here too long. I feel bad about leaving; I'll miss it here. I'll miss Randy. But I've always known it was inevitable that I'd move on at some point.

I stick my hand inside the backpack and find the false bottom that I've created since I got here. I don't know why I hadn't done that long ago, to hide the cash that I need, but it's useful now. I slip bills underneath it, counting it in my head, hoping it will be enough and adding a little more to be on the safe side.

I take a shower and change into another pair of shorts – not bike shorts – and a tank top. My heart is pounding, and another cup of coffee doesn't ease the anxiety. But I don't know what to do with myself until the clock's hands tell me that it's time to go.

While I could take the bike into town, it's easier to call a cab, and one shows up about fifteen minutes after I call. I climb in and gaze out the window as we travel to the city. The salt marshes are bright green as far as the eye can see, until they disappear into the concrete.

I'm silly for having the cab drop me at the entrance to the Fort Sumter museum, as though I have to hide my real destination. The cabbie doesn't care, but I do, and maybe as I walk up Calhoun I can talk myself out of it.

But despite my own best efforts, I end up on at the store on King Street. The moment I push open the door, it is almost as though I have life breathed into me as I see the rows of laptops, desktops, tablets and smartphones. I wave off one of the sales guys; I don't need his help right now. I merely want to drink it all in. I've been away too long.

Spencer's voice is in my head, telling me to turn around, walk out before it's too late, before I go online and expose myself again. But I push him aside; I want this. I tell myself that there really is very little risk if I go online. I can use a VPN to divert my IP address; I will use passwords, screen names that I've never used before so they can't be traced to me. I know how to hide behind the code as much as I know how to hide out in the open, off the grid. I've had years of experience at it.

I find a laptop that seems to suit my needs. It's small and sleek and powerful. It weighs half of my old one, and I think about how the backpack will be lighter than in the past.

Cash is usually not the currency of choice here, where

customers hand over credit cards for such large purchases, but it's all I've got and, after a little bit of explaining to the incredulous store manager that I don't possess a credit card, we finally complete the purchase.

I slip my new laptop into my backpack, sling it over my shoulder and go back out onto the street. The sun has risen higher; more people are on the sidewalks. I make one more stop before going down to Meeting Street and to the City Market. I walk through the covered stalls, checking out the sweetgrass baskets and homemade jewelry and jars of jam. My watercolors might reach a larger customer base here, and while I don't want to take away any business from Randy, if I stay, maybe I could mass produce smaller works to generate a little more income. I shift the backpack; its weight reminds me of my real mission today and I push aside the idea.

Waterfront Park isn't too far, and I pass the giant pineapple fountain as I head toward the park benches beyond. I find a bench with no one nearby except a mother with two small children chasing each other on the grass.

For a moment, I stare out at the water. I can see the *USS Yorktown* in the distance, on the other side of the river. The air is still; children's voices carry across the park. I tug the laptop out of the pack and set it on my lap, the backpack at my feet.

I open the laptop. The first thing I do is take the masking tape I bought at the drug store out of my bag and tear off a small piece, placing it over the camera. I made the mistake of not doing that once before and regretted it. While I don't plan on being hacked and shadowed again, I can never be a hundred percent sure that it won't happen. Now that I've taken care of this, I finish the setup of the laptop, ignoring the Cloud since I don't want anything anywhere that might point at me. There are Wifi networks nearby, most of them locked. But I don't need any of them. I rummage around in my backpack and pull out the small hotspot router that creates my own wireless network. While I may not have had a laptop, in a moment of weakness I bought this at an electronics store, thinking that it may come in handy someday.

Today is someday.

FOUR

A sense of calm overtakes me as I download the VPN and the software that will allow me to go into the deep web and the chat rooms. This is my world, the world I am most comfortable in. I can lose myself in my painting, my watercolors, but it's not like this. This overtakes me; the laptop is an extension of myself.

Zeke understands. We met online when we were teenagers, learning from each other, falling for each other behind the code. Using his screen name Tracker, he helped me hack into a bank site to steal ten million dollars seventeen years ago; two million of that was Tony DeMarco's. I didn't know that Tracker was really Zeke Chapman, the FBI agent who followed me to Paris after the theft. Zeke told me he loved me, that he'd left his wife for me, but after a confrontation he got shot, and I left him for dead and vanished to Block Island. When we were in Miami six months ago, he let me know that his feelings for me were still even stronger than his loyalty to his job.

That's why I'm having such a hard time knowing he was in Paris. Knowing where he was, period. We went our separate ways because of the hit on me – he wanted me safe while he went after DeMarco, at least that's what he said – but I've been secretly hoping that he'd suddenly show up on my doorstep and we could disappear together. I've been alone a long time and I'm comfortable with myself, but my connection with Zeke is strong and Miami brought us together physically rather than merely virtually. For the first time in a very long time, I find myself daydreaming about having a real relationship with someone again. Seeing that picture online, however, makes me dubious that will happen anytime soon. Again, I think that sending me away alone might have more to do with his job than with me; if, in fact, the skimmer has to do with his job.

I admonish myself. It *must* have something to do with his job. It has to.

First things first, though. I need to make sure that Madeline Whittier was not one of my father's clients before I head to her house for tea. While I have mostly dismissed the idea, there is still a nagging feeling somewhere in the back of my head that she wouldn't say I looked familiar if there wasn't a reason. I had little time when I was on Randy's computer, but now I can do a more thorough search. I type in Madeline's name and my father's – Daniel Adler – to see if there's a connection between them.

Both names get hits, but I don't see any that links the two. For a second, I consider reading one of the old news stories about my father, but decide it's not a good idea to revisit the past. I know all about how he ripped off his celebrity and wealthy clients; I was inside his computer when I was a teenager. I discovered all his secrets.

Instead, I open one of the links that mentions Madeline Whittier. It's a local story in the Charleston newspaper about a fundraising event for Charleston College. It's dated a year ago with a photo of Madeline and her husband dancing beneath tiny white lights on the college lawn. Her gown is a glittering white; her hair piled up on top of her head with a tiara. Maybe she doesn't know me, she doesn't know my father, but I know her and her world. Although in mine, 'tea' is less tea and more cocktail hour. As I remember the way she was with the wine last night, maybe it is in hers, too.

I toggle back to the article with Zeke's picture and read it again, but there are no more clues to Zeke's whereabouts since the sighting than there were before. What was it that Spencer saw that made him warn me off? It can't have been here.

A child's scream startles me, and I look up from the screen to scan my surroundings. I spot the child and her friend frolicking in the water of the pineapple fountain, two mothers deep in conversation. I turn my attention back to the laptop.

The picture of Zeke mesmerizes me. After not knowing what he looked like for so long, his face is now embedded in my memory and I have no doubt at all that this is him, despite the lousy quality of the image and the funny angle. It still nags at me that he's putting skimmers on ATMs.

I find my way to the chat room, the one where I have met Tracker – Zeke – so many times. If he's undercover, he won't be here, but it still draws me in. I create a new screen name to sign in, a new password. No one will know me. Or so I keep telling myself.

The chat is crowded and, as I look closer, there is a certain buzz about a new television program about hackers. I smile to myself as I read the threads – how these hackers are insulted by the portrayals, how it's unrealistic and the hacks featured aren't even remotely possible.

I've only been gone six months, but it's as though I've moved into a new neighborhood and everyone is a stranger. There was a time when I knew almost everyone here, and Tracker was always around.

I want to ask if anyone's seen him, but it would raise too many red flags. Spencer comes around the chat room using the screen name Angel, and I don't want to deal with him and what he'd have to say if he discovers I'm asking about Tracker. Yet I am still tempted.

To keep myself from doing anything rash, I log off and make my way back to the search engine. My initial search had been on Madeline Whittier and the article had popped up, so I wonder what I'll find if I look for the missing Ryan Whittier. I type in his name, adding 'Charleston' after it. The story I've already seen is the first one that appears. But, oddly, there is nothing else. Is it because four months have passed? No, that can't be it. If a college student had gone missing in Paris, the media would be all over it.

I can't explain why I fixate on it, except that it's the only connection I've had to Zeke in six months. I really don't care about Ryan Whittier beyond that, but I read the article again, which was published in a Paris English-language newspaper, even though by now I have committed it to memory.

A college student from the United States has been missing for three days, and police have no leads in his disappearance.

Ryan Whittier, who attends Charleston College in South Carolina, was reported missing by the manager at the Hotel

Adele near the rue de Rivoli when staff noticed that Whittier had not returned to his room, but all of his belongings were still there, including his wallet and cellphone.

When checking his credit card records, police discovered Whittier last used his ATM card at a machine nearby. Just moments before, a man had placed a skimmer on the machine that would compromise any card inserted in it. Police are uncertain if this had anything to do with Whittier's disappearance, but they are searching for the man who installed the skimmer.

I have focused only on the photograph of Zeke, but now I study the image of Ryan Whittier that accompanies the story. He's a young man with a baby face who barely looks old enough to travel on his own to Europe. He has light brown hair, brown eyes and chubby cheeks. He is hardly distinctive, which makes it easy to overlook him. The article is as vague as he looks. It only says that Ryan went to Charleston College. It has no hometown for him, and there is no mention of parents. There is so little information about Ryan that it raises suspicion. It should be a bigger story, and yet it's not. Where *are* the parents? His family? Everyone knows that a college student – or any young person – missing anywhere in the world would be the subject of a frantic search. The French authorities should be desperate to make sure the young man is found; the family might be offering a reward for information.

But there's nothing here. Nothing at all.

Perhaps social media has some answers. But when I look for Ryan Whittier in all the usual places, he is nowhere to be found. It's rare for someone – especially a college student – not to have some sort of Internet footprint.

I find my way to the Charleston College website and put his name into the search bar. Nothing comes up with his name. This might not mean anything, except that he is also under the radar at the college. He may not be involved in athletics or be a top scholar.

On a whim, I pull out my cellphone and call the school's main number. I'm not very adept at social engineering, but this is easy. When I get the receptionist, I ask for the media relations department.

'This is Callie, how can I help you?' The voice is young. She could be a student worker.

'I'm with the *Paris News* in Paris, and I'm calling to find out about a student of yours, Ryan Whittier, who was reported missing here four months ago. We are following up on the story.' I have no idea if there is a newspaper called the Paris News, but it sounds good, and Callie doesn't pick up on it.

'Ryan Whittier? What year is he?'

'I'm not sure. We don't have much information, except he had an ID that indicated he went to school there.' This is another white lie. I have no idea if they found a college ID; in fact, I don't know exactly how they even knew he went to this college or where the photograph came from.

'Hold on.'

I am on hold long enough that I am ready to hang up when I hear: 'Who is this?' This is no longer Callie; now I'm talking to a man.

'I'm with the *Paris News*. I'm calling about a student of yours, Ryan Whittier, who went missing here four months ago.'

He's quiet for a second, then says, 'I don't know what sort of game you're playing, miss, but we don't have a student here by that name. We never did.'

And then he hangs up.

FIVE

I am more confused than ever. Who is the young man in the photograph? Is anyone missing at all? Except, perhaps, the man who was putting the skimmer on the ATM? But *he* is most likely missing by choice.

It occurs to me that this might possibly be fake news, that 'Ryan Whittier' doesn't actually exist at all, and the story may have been planted to either incriminate or locate Zeke.

I look back up at the water again, my fingers lightly tapping the keys without typing anything. A nervous habit, one from my past. Ryan Whittier still nags at me, but I didn't buy a laptop to find out about *him*. I bought it to try to find Zeke.

As if it agrees, my stomach growls, and I look at the time. I've been here too long. I pack up the laptop and head out of the park. The number of tourists has increased in the last couple of hours, and I wade my way through them, along the sidewalk on Meeting Street. The familiar weight of the laptop inside the backpack settles against my side.

As I'm crossing Queen, a white Cadillac slows down. It has tinted windows, so I can't see the driver. I can't tell whether the car wants to turn or slide into the parking spot just ahead and is waiting for me to pass. When I finally reach the other side of the road, the car inches along beside me. I begin to move a little faster, my heart thudding inside my chest, but then the car speeds away, skidding slightly on the pavement. I stop walking and watch it until it turns a few blocks down.

I immediately regret not packing everything. While the car was probably just a tourist who wasn't sure where he was going, my paranoia has ratcheted up to a level that I'm uncomfortable with.

I make sure the white Cadillac is nowhere to be seen as I head up Broad Street toward Gaulart & Maliclet, where I can get a ham and cheese baguette and a glass of wine. It's a smallish enough restaurant that I should be able to have some privacy.

I push the door open and walk into the chilly air conditioning that causes goose bumps to rise on my arms. I ask the waitress if I can be seated in the back, facing the door. She escorts me around the corner and to a more private table, from which I can see anyone coming in. I order my lunch and, while I wait, gaze at the French posters on the walls. This place *could* be in France, in Paris. My thoughts stray back to Zeke and what he was doing there. I reach over and pull the laptop and the hotspot router out of the backpack.

My sandwich and glass of wine are set down in front of me, and I absently take a bite and a quick drink. Zeke put that skimmer on an ATM on the rue de Rivoli. A familiar map program lets me 'walk' down the street with an actual street view.

I manipulate the direction and 'look around' the block. I feel a sudden longing for my adopted city, the city I spent so much time in when I was a child with my grandmother, and where I fled when the FBI – Zeke – was after me after the bank job. And where he finally found me hiding on a houseboat on the Seine.

I am about to change direction yet again when something catches my eye. The Hotel Adele.

If it were here, in the United States, it would be called a boutique hotel, but in Paris it's like hundreds of others peppered around the city. Ryan Whittier had been staying at the Hotel Adele, according to the article online. Seeing it here shows me that this bit of news wasn't fake. I 'walk' to the corner at rue de Rivoli, and I spot an ATM. Is this the one? There's no real way of knowing, but it's close to the hotel.

I tell myself that none of it means anything. The article dates back four months. Zeke was there then, but it's possible he's long gone, vanished into thin air once again.

Still, I can't help myself. I put the hotel name into the search engine and pull up its website. It has an automated reservation system, which, to my advantage, seems to be several years old and outdated. The hotel is a small one and it's not geared toward very wealthy guests, so they probably don't feel that the system is a security risk. I'm happy to discover that the system isn't connected to a larger hotel network, otherwise it would have made what I'm about to do a lot more difficult.

I need to be able to become an administrator. I scan the code, looking for a way in, and suddenly it's there.

It's too easy.

There's a back door. Someone left it wide open for me.

I sit back a second and stare at the screen as a chill runs down my back. Something's not right here. Someone was here before me.

And then I wonder: what if it was Zeke? What if he'd manipulated the code, inserted the back door?

I take a deep breath. I'm reading into things. I want to believe that I'm chasing Zeke, but it's possible that's very far from the truth. There's no reason to think that there is any link between Zeke and this hotel. The hotel system is antiquated; it would have been easy to break in even without the back door.

So why is it there?

I can't shake the feeling of foreboding that's come over me. It's almost as though I'm violating someone else's property. This back door is here for someone else, not me. Again, I think about how this hotel isn't part of a big chain. I toggle back to the maps page and take another look at it. Nothing about the hotel makes it stand out in the area; it looks like any of the buildings that flank it. It is a typical Parisian building, with a large, ornate door and windows on each floor. The only thing that identifies it as a hotel is the sign next to the door.

I can't resist. I slip in through the back door and scan the lines of code. It's the most basic code I've seen in ages, which I chalk up to the fact that it's an old system. No one has updated it in a long time. The back door may have been there for years, undetected, because no one is checking on the site. No one is concerned about network security.

If I can do what I'm here to do, then they might want to reconsider that.

Because I am able to slip inside as an administrator and soon I have access to every reservation Hotel Adele has booked. I don't care about all of them, though, as I scroll through the names of the male guests four months ago, then check the months previous and afterward. There are no names that stand out.

Except one: Ryan Whittier.

That's not a surprise, if the article is real. I begin to doubt my suspicion about it being fake news even though I can't explain any of this.

And then I do find something that I'm not expecting at all.

The credit card that Ryan Whittier used to pay for his hotel room is not in his name. The name on it is Spencer Cross.

SIX

Instinctively, I glance down at the backpack, where the cellphone is tucked in the front pocket, as though Spencer Cross is physically in there. I'm trying to wrap my head around this.

Spencer is a fugitive. So I rather doubt that he has an active credit card.

But then I have another thought: is this the reason he warned me off? Told me to forget I ever saw anything? Does he know?

It didn't seem as though he knew anything when I called him, but something came up during our conversation, and maybe this was it. Maybe he knew his credit card was being used by someone, but what if he didn't know by whom – at least not until I called him and alerted him to the story? That could explain the abrupt end to our conversation.

Or maybe it's not *this* Spencer Cross. Maybe it's another Spencer Cross. There have to be dozens of Spencer Crosses in the world, if not more.

No. It has to be the same one. While my curiosity about Ryan Whittier was piqued only because he used the ATM with Zeke's skimmer, now I'm more suspicious about what might have been going on in Paris four months ago.

I check the hotel records again. Nothing has changed. The reservations were made online in Ryan Whittier's name, but charged to the credit card issued to Spencer Cross. Since I don't have a credit card, I've never made reservations this way. It seems easy enough.

Maybe I can get more information about this card and its owner. While I don't have the name of the bank that the card was issued on, I do have all the other information at my fingertips. There are websites that can tell me which bank issued the card just by inputting the first six numbers on it, which is the bank identification number. You don't have to have any special skills to do this. I call up one of the webpages, type in the number and wait for the result.

When it pops up on the screen, I make my way to the bank website. Online banking makes it easy to hack without actually hacking – especially if the person who holds the card hasn't signed up online for access to the account. Spencer Cross is one of those people. He has not set up a log-in or password. I need an email account, so I quickly create one on a free site, then go back to the bank. I input the credit card number, create a log-in and password, and the bank sends me a link to my email.

Granted, most people have done this, and it's pure luck that Spencer Cross hasn't. I glance at the backpack, thinking about the cellphone. I have more questions than answers. I certainly can't ask Zeke what's going on, but I do have a direct line to Spencer. Maybe there's a logical explanation. I reach down and fumble in the front pocket of the backpack until I'm holding the phone. I only hesitate a second before hitting the speed-dial number.

It rings and rings, but Spencer never picks up, just like when I tried to call him back before. He's avoiding me. Or at least avoiding my questions. I picture him sitting in front of a bank of computers somewhere, curtains shrouding the windows, as he smokes his weed and listens to the phone ring.

My anger and frustration rise as I think about him – and Zeke. What if they're into something together? If I hadn't stumbled upon that picture, I'd have no idea about any of it, but I did and I do.

Maybe the answer as to why is under my fingertips.

I look back at the screen and Spencer's account.

I've had no idea where Spencer is these past months, but the charges on this card show that whoever's been using it has been everywhere. Besides the Hotel Adele, he's also racked up bills at hotels in Vienna, Berlin, Lisbon and Barcelona. The only charges I see are for hotels, though, which is odd. None for food or transportation. What's even odder is that the charge for each hotel is only for one night. The nights in the hotels are also not consecutive, with days in between unac-counted for. The charges only go back four months, to when the card was used at the Hotel Adele. Before that, there's nothing. No statements, no charges.

It strikes me that if the mysterious Ryan Whittier has been using this card, he's been using it ever since he vanished. The last charge is a hotel in London. Whoever used the card stayed there two nights ago.

Even though Ryan Whittier is not a college student from Charleston, that card can't travel by itself.

The thought makes me take pause. If someone is using this card to make reservations online, he doesn't actually have to be traveling anywhere. He could merely be online – and in one place. That could explain why there are no transportation or food charges, because 'Ryan Whittier' lives in the Internet and could be using Spencer Cross's credit card to create what looks like a false trail.

The credit card. I toggle back to the article. I reread it again, the claim that Ryan Whittier last used *his* card at the ATM – not a credit card with someone else's name on it – and that he's been reported as missing. If he had a card, why not use that at the hotel? Why use Spencer Cross's?

I click on 'my info' in the dropdown menu. The email address I've created is recorded, along with the name Spencer Cross, but everything else is blank. There is no address or phone number.

I go back to the account information, noting now that payments have been made. Since there was no online account set up, I can only assume that the payments weren't made through this site, but from another one. I doubt that someone's writing checks, but I can't rule it out completely.

No matter how much I try to get inside, I can't crack this. The payment source eludes me, and I am concentrating so closely that I barely notice the waitress has put my check on the table next to the empty wine glass. I blink a few times, focusing on it, but my head is elsewhere.

The more I try to work all this out, the more I don't understand.

I go back to the idea that Spencer Cross – *my* Spencer Cross – does not have a credit card because he wouldn't. It would be too much of a minefield for someone who's in hiding. Just as I wouldn't have a credit card in my real name.

But as much as I circle around this, *someone* has been using a credit card with Spencer's name on it.

Footsteps come up behind me, startling me. I look up to see the waitress hovering. A glance at my watch tells me I've been here almost two hours. I pull out some cash and leave a very generous tip, apologizing as I reluctantly close the laptop and stuff it in the backpack, slinging it over my shoulder and making my way back out into the heat.

I don't have much time before I have to meet with Madeline and I have to get dressed, but I missed my chance to change in the restroom at the restaurant. It's probably not a good idea to go back and ask to use it.

Randy's gallery isn't too far, and I have to go that way anyway, so I head up Broad toward King Street.

I notice the car out of the corner of my eye as I'm waiting at the corner to cross. It's come up from behind and pulls into a parking spot, idling next to the curb. It's a white Cadillac, and its windows are tinted. Is it the same one I saw earlier? I wish I'd taken note of the license plate number, but I hadn't. I can't see the plate from this angle, either, to find out whether it's from South Carolina or somewhere else. It could be a rental; rental cars no longer advertise their status. If I had the plate number, I could get into the DMV to find out whom it's registered to.

My imagination begins to spin out of control. What if it's one of Tony DeMarco's men? What if he's watching me like this, lying in wait until I'm no longer out in public so he can execute the hit on me?

The crossing sign changes and, as I walk, I force myself not to walk faster or look back. I don't want him to know that I've noticed him. I have to figure out how I'm going to handle this. How I'm going to get out of town without him noticing.

When I reach the other side of the street, the car has turned, and I let out the breath that I've been holding.

I don't know how much longer I can live like this.

SEVEN

R andy is picking at a salad at his desk in the back office of the gallery when I arrive. He looks up and grins. 'I didn't expect you,' he says. 'I thought you were having tea with Madeline.'

'In about half an hour,' I say. I hold up the backpack. 'I need to change first. Late lunch?' I ask, indicating the salad.

Randy sighs. 'I got hung up hanging some new work.' He pauses, then adds, 'Madeline's considering another one of your watercolors. She said I should give you a show of your own.' He's nodding, as though he agrees with her, expecting me to share in his enthusiasm.

I muster up a smile. 'That would be great,' I lie.

'Maybe in the fall. What do you think?'

'Sounds great,' I say.

Randy frowns. He's finally noticed that I'm not completely paying attention. I am still too distracted by the Cadillac. 'Are you OK, Tina?'

'I have to get ready,' I say.

Randy glances at the clock on the wall and nods. 'You shouldn't be late. She hates that.'

I don't have to do this. I'm going to leave town anyway. Madeline Whittier will never see me again. The watercolors she buys will be the last. I'll have to change it up, though, in the next place. I can't keep doing watercolors. Maybe I can start with acrylics. They dry faster than oils. Or maybe pen and ink. Maybe I'll go up to Maine for the summer. I could really go to Portland. I picture it being a more bustling Block Island, with rocky beaches and spectacular sunsets. I might be able to get comfortable there.

Who am I kidding?

I excuse myself and head into the lavatory next to the office. I shimmy out of my shorts and tank top and slip the dress over my head. It's a sleeveless shift with a blue and white pattern, made from a soft cotton with a little stretch that hugs my curves. I take off my sneakers and slip on the sandals that have a small heel. My clothes go into the pack, on top of the sneakers. There's a full-length mirror on the back of the door, and I assess my appearance from different angles. The dress is nice enough, but it makes me look my age, and I'm not sure I'm ready for that. I'm over forty, although not by much, but it's still a bit of a surprise when I look in the mirror and see the crow's feet that have nestled in the corners of my eyes and the gray in my hair. The salt and pepper curls didn't bother me when I was living on Block Island, but I've found myself wondering what Zeke sees when he looks at me. I'm certainly not the young woman he was in love with all those years ago. The biking has given me a leaner look, though, and I'm in better shape than I was back then, which is a bit of a consolation.

I run my hands under the faucet and comb my fingers through my hair, which I've cut shorter again while I've been here. I adjust my glasses and pick up the backpack, which doesn't go with the dress but I don't have a choice, so I'll have to own it. It's all about attitude.

The woman who walks out of the restroom is a different one than the woman who walked in. I like that other woman – she is more like Nicole Jones, who I was when I was on Block Island – and I am uncertain about this one. But fortunately I only have to play this role intermittently, even though the idea of having tea with anyone terrifies me.

Randy grins approvingly when I emerge.

'Perfect,' he says. 'Now you have to charm the hell out of her.'

I give him a small smile, as though I'm agreeing with him. Escape again crosses my mind. Wherever I go next, I shouldn't make friends. It's too hard to leave them, and I hate knowing that I've disappointed anyone. When I had to leave Steve on Block Island six months ago after my long absence, it was as though I was leaving him again for the first time – for both of us. Maybe the better rule is to never go back.

The thought of that makes me so sad.

I force a bright smile for Randy. 'Is there anything else I need to know about her?'

'Besides the fact that she thinks you're an amazing artist?'
He grins. 'Not at all. That's the only thing.'

I tend to doubt that. I shift the backpack over my shoulder
and start for the door.

'Oh, but there might be one thing.'

I stop and pivot, waiting for Randy, whose expression has
grown dark. I immediately get a bad feeling.

'Madeline likes you, Tina. But it doesn't take much to get
on her bad side. Be friendly, smile a lot, let her talk. If she likes
you, you're golden. But if she doesn't, then you're done in
Charleston.'

I study his face and see that he's serious. Since I'll soon be
gone anyway, his warning doesn't resonate, but I humor him.
I put my hand on his forearm and give him a smile. 'Don't
worry, Randy. I'll be on my best behavior.'

I see it then, in his face. It's not so much about me but his
relationship with Madeline that could be on the line, depending
on how this goes. I don't want to be the cause of a rift between
him and Madeline. Not to mention that I owe him.

'You're going to be late,' he teases, glancing at the clock.

I can use this to my advantage, as I've been a little concerned
about seeing that Cadillac again. 'I need to call a cab.'

Randy gives me a curious look, then nods. 'It's not that far,
but it's hot out and you really should be on time. An Uber is
faster.' He knows I don't have the app on my phone, so he
uses his.

'Thanks,' I say, squeezing his arm. I really am going to
miss him, and I feel terrible about not telling him that this
will be the last he'll see of me.

When we see the Uber car pull up out front, I start to leave,
but he says, 'Oh, wait.' Randy pulls open the side desk drawer
and takes out an envelope. 'I forgot to give this to you last
night.' He hands it to me. 'This is from the watercolor Madeline
bought, but I also sold a couple of others, so you've got a
little windfall this week.'

The envelope is thick, and I can't help but think it's good
to replace the money I've spent on the laptop. I unzip the
backpack and shove the envelope inside, then zip it back up
again. 'Thanks, Randy.' This time, I take another step toward

him and lean in, giving him a kiss on the cheek. 'It's nice to know you're always looking out for me.'

And then I really do go.

Meeting Street, down where Madeline Whittier lives, is lined with elegant homes that reflect this charming Southern city. Madeline Whittier's house is painted an eggshell white, the ceiling of the long side porch a robin's egg blue, common throughout the city. I've been told that this is so bees and hornets think it's the sky and won't build nests.

I climb out of the car, glancing around, but the Cadillac is nowhere to be seen. I don't approach the porch door that faces the street, as it's merely to protect the family's privacy, and instead climb the steps to the main door, which is ornately carved. As I ring the bell to the right of it, I try to devise a way to get out of here sooner rather than later without getting on Madeline's bad side.

The door swings open, startling me out of my thoughts. There's a girl on the other side. She's maybe sixteen, with thick dark hair and red cheeks.

'Miss Jones?' she asks before I can say anything.

I nod, and she indicates I should come in, so I do so. The foyer stretches into a long hallway with a gigantic mirror at the far end and long tables covered with antique vases on either side. I look up to see a chandelier overhead that reminds me of the one in the foyer of the house I grew up in. Instead of being a comfort, though, it feels ominous somehow. I can't explain it, but something is off here. Maybe Randy's warning has spooked me a little too much.

'Tina, dear.'

I turn to see Madeline Whittier come out of virtually nowhere. She's wearing a long white tunic and flowing, black silk pants. Her feet are clad in small red Chinese slippers. Her silver hair is piled high on her head; diamond earrings dangle from her earlobes.

I am definitely underdressed, but I don't know that I can be blamed for that. Being invited for tea is not something that happens in my world. Madeline doesn't seem to notice that I'm uncomfortable. She is suddenly next to me, her hands on my arms, pulling me close so she can kiss me on each cheek, European style.

'My dear. You look lovely.'

She's lying, but I forgive her because she's such a natural at it.

'Come in, come in.' She takes my hand and pulls me alongside her. We go into a side room that's full of plush sofas and armchairs and teak coffee tables, but we don't stop here. She leads me through French doors onto the porch that's surrounded by ornately carved railings. Gleaming silver utensils and a china tea set decorated with small blue flowers sit on a table covered by a crisp white cloth.

She indicates I should sit across from her, and I look out over the meticulously manicured gardens that are bright with flowers I don't recognize. 'Isn't this the most delightful porch,' she declares as she pours tea into my cup.

Her hand is steady and when my cup is full, she pours herself one. I am out of my element, despite the fact that I, too, grew up with money. My family's money wasn't old money, like Madeline's, but new money – stolen money. Vulgar, Madeline would probably call it.

The girl moves swiftly toward us, holding a silver platter. She puts it on the table. Small, dainty finger sandwiches sit on white paper doilies. Madeline moves her head slightly, indicating I should take one. I take two, placing them on my plate. They look too delicate to actually eat, and when I pick one up and put it in my mouth, the bread melts immediately like cotton candy, the crunch of the cucumber reminding me that I still have to work for my food.

'Delicious,' I say, taking a sip of the tea, which is too hot and scalds my tongue.

I consider the best way to segue into the question about Ryan Whittier, but while I'm thinking about it, Madeline says casually, 'I have friends in Portland.'

I try not to show that unnerves me and take another sip of tea.

'They've never heard of you.'

'It's a big place,' I say, surprised that my tone is steady.

'Not so big.' Madeline smiles at me, but again, it doesn't

reach her eyes. 'And you'd think someone with your *talent* would not go unnoticed. Those beautiful watercolors.'

I remember that she'd mentioned how she loved Seattle more than Portland, so I assume she's talking about the one in Oregon. I can tell her that she's made a mistake, that I'm really from Maine. But it might raise red flags with her, since I didn't say anything last night. It's also possible that she's already checked me out in both cities. She seems the type who'd be thorough in her inquiries. I wait for more but she doesn't elaborate, just drinks her tea and watches me.

'Randy said you might be interested in another watercolor,' I say.

'Possibly,' she says, 'but probably not. Under the circumstances.'

Butterflies begin to flutter in my belly.

'How long do you think you can keep it up?' she's asking.

I put the cup down carefully. 'How long what?' I ask.

She stares at me, straight in my eyes. 'Did you really think I wouldn't notice? That I wouldn't know who you were?'

It's then that I know, but I don't have time to respond before she keeps going.

'Your father took millions from me. And so did you.'

EIGHT

I can't breathe. She knows who I am. She knows what I did. How can I explain that I didn't know whom I was stealing from, that I only had account numbers? It was a job, a dare, almost, to see if I could do it. I didn't stop to think that there were actual people on the other side of those accounts.

I am making excuses.

My father, on the other hand, *did* know his victims. He befriended them; they knew exactly who was stealing from them and he took as much as he could from under their noses before he got caught. Was Madeline Whittier one of the victims who testified at his trial? How much did he steal from her?

Had she fallen in love with him, like most of his women clients had? My father was a handsome man, with chiseled features and a wide, warm smile that made anyone on the receiving end of it feel as though she was the most important person in the room. That's how he seduced Tony DeMarco's wife.

Madeline Whittier leans across the table, her hands set on the edge of it, her diamonds glittering in the glare of the sun that's settled across the tea set. Her expression is hard, her eyes flashing with anger. 'I heard a lot of things about you. That you were in hiding. I hoped you were gone for good. And then you show up at Randy's. What have you taken from him?' Her voice is low and hard.

I can't justify what I did any more than my father could justify his actions. I can't defend it. Looking at her, I don't think she wants me to. What she wants is my blood. She wants me to pay.

I shake my head in response to her question. It will do no good to talk to her, to explain what I've done with my life since I stole her money. Technically, I didn't really steal it since Zeke intervened and managed to restore most of it, but she knows that I tried. That, for a little while, I had access to her account and moved her money somewhere she might never find it.

I stand, reach down and pick up my backpack, surprised that I am as calm as I am, that my hands are not shaking.

'I'm sorry,' I say, and begin to walk away.

But she's fast. She's managed to get between me and the French doors, her arms outstretched so I can't get past.

'You're *sorry*?' she spits at me. 'You certainly will be sorry. You're not going anywhere. You can't run and hide this time.'

I spot the young girl who answered the door just outside the room we'd come through to get to the porch. She is wringing her hands in front of her, shifting back and forth on her feet, her eyes trained in the direction of the front door.

Someone is coming. Someone is coming for me. Madeline does not mean for me to escape.

My memory flashes on that white Cadillac with the tinted windows that was behind me on the street. Maybe my paranoia was not so misplaced, but it's possible that it's not only Tony

DeMarco who wants me dead. It certainly seems as though
Madeline Whittier might, too. Maybe they've joined forces. I
wouldn't put it past her to reach out to Tony, to tell him where
I am. He is old and sick, but his power and vengeance still
has a long reach. It's too bad that the FBI couldn't make any
charges against him stick. Zeke and I found a deep web child
pornography site that we traced back to him but by the time
we could do anything about it, the money trail we'd found
had vanished. Still, even if he'd been convicted, it wouldn't
have stopped him.

Right now I need to stop thinking about him and figure
out how I'm going to get out of here before anyone shows up
to give Madeline her revenge.

Madeline is elderly; her long, spindly arms are no match
for me. Yet something in me hesitates. I don't want to hurt
her physically when I have already done so much damage in
so many other ways. But maybe I don't have to hurt her, and
maybe I don't have to go back out the way I came in. Maybe
I shouldn't.

The long porch runs the length of the house. There's a door
that leads out to the front, but it's not a room, per se. It's
merely a porch with a railing – and it's not so far a jump to
the gardens below. One problem, though. It might be difficult
to leap over a railing while wearing a dress and sandals. But
perhaps not so difficult just to run the length of the porch and
take my chances with what's at the other end. It's worth trying.

I pivot and, as I do so, I sling the backpack over both
shoulders, securing it against my back. Before Madeline knows
what's happening, I'm running, my sandals clacking against
the wood floor. I'm glad that they don't have high heels, which
makes it much easier.

I hear some sort of commotion behind me, but I can't stop,
can't hesitate. I'm at the end of the porch now; there are steps
that lead down into yet another garden. I stumble a little as
my foot misses the stone path and settles into the soft dirt,
but I manage to regain my footing and leap from stone to
stone. The path leads around to the back, disappearing behind
a tall green hedge. I circle around, following it, the hedge now
between me and whoever is after me.

I glance around once but I don't see anyone behind me because I'm shrouded, and when I turn back I hit an iron gate, bouncing off it and struggling to catch my breath. I run alongside the gate, my hands and eyes searching for a way out. Just when I think that I'll never find it, it's there. I reach for the clasp and flip it up, pushing the gate open and into the yard of the house behind Madeline's. I slam it shut behind me, hoping that it will slow down whoever is after me. I see a man out of the corner of my eye, but I don't stop.

The neighbor's yard is not nearly as long as Madeline's, and within seconds I'm at a long driveway. The pavement is hard underneath my sandals, but I can't get distracted and slow down. I'm soon on the sidewalk, and I turn left, toward town. If I'd gone in the other direction, I would have dead-ended at the waterfront park and I'd be even more exposed.

I look around for a hiding place, but it's too residential here. I have to head for a busier street, maybe one with a lot of restaurants and bars. My head is spinning with ideas; I'm more than aware that my breaths are raspy as I pull in more air. Running is far different than riding a bike, and I'm using muscles and energy I'm not used to. I'm also not wearing my sneakers, which have settled against my back in the pack. Blisters are forming on my toes and heels from the sandals that I've only worn a couple of times.

I focus on these things to keep from thinking about who might be after me. Did Madeline call the police? I'm technically not a fugitive anymore, so the police wouldn't be able to hold me on anything. The statute of limitations ran out years ago on the bank job. But it's more likely as I first suspected: she may very well be in contact with Tony DeMarco. If it's his people who are after me and find me, no one else ever will.

I'm running in the direction of Randy's gallery, but of course Madeline will have told them about that, so I can't go there. I also don't want to involve Randy; he doesn't deserve the trouble and I don't have time to explain.

Cars are passing me; motorists are taking notice of me. I'm on Meeting Street and there is a hotel up ahead, one with an awning and a valet parking sign. I hear heavy breathing behind me. Whoever is after me is catching up, despite my head start off the porch. I can't afford to get caught, but I'm slowing down with exhaustion, despite the adrenaline that's pumping through me.

And then I see it again, the white Cadillac. It's coming toward me on the road. Maybe it's not the same car, but my imagination is going wild. I fully expect to be gunned down right here, in the streets of Charleston, and Tony DeMarco will be able to die in peace knowing he finally got the justice he's thought he's due. I should have stayed in the gardens, going from yard to yard, staying more hidden.

Before I know what's happening, the Cadillac screeches up to the sidewalk next to me, up over the curve. I stop short and slam into the hood of the car. The impact knocks the wind out of me and I step back, struggling for breath as the driver's window rolls down an inch. I wait to see the barrel of a gun, but instead I only hear a firm command: 'Get in. Now.'

NINE

I hesitate only a second, because another car is careening toward me and I spot the man following me on foot, since he is quickly gaining ground on me. If I hadn't recognized the voice from inside the car, I wouldn't have pulled the back door open and scrambled inside, but I do. The car shoots back into the road even before my door is closed, and the movement throws me across the seat.

'Careful!' I say.

Spencer Cross turns slightly to look at me and then looks back at the road. 'Seat belt.'

I look out of the back window and see the other car getting closer. I don't want to stay in the back seat, so I shrug off the backpack, climb quickly over the center console and settle myself in the front passenger seat, finally pulling the seat belt across me.

'What are you doing here?' I ask.

He shakes his head as he grips the steering wheel, his eyes darting from the rearview to the side-view mirror and back again. I keep an eye on the car behind us in my own side-view mirror. It doesn't seem to be gaining too much ground as Spencer's foot is heavy on the accelerator. His mouth is set in a grim line as he maneuvers the side roads, zigzagging as though he actually knows where he's going.

He *must* know, because we take a quick turn into a driveway. A garage door in front of us is rising. I twist around in my seat to check out where the other car is, but I don't see it. Within seconds, we are inside the garage, the door closing, and Spencer is unlatching his seat belt.

'Come on,' he says, not waiting for me as he climbs out of the car. I reach behind for my backpack. By now he's already going through a door, and I scurry to follow him. I pause just for a second in the doorway to see if I can hear the car outside.

'We're OK,' Spencer says from somewhere within the house, and I step inside, closing the door behind me. I'm not so sure about the 'OK' part, but right now I feel like I'm in an alternate reality after what I've just experienced.

The kitchen could be something out of a magazine, with bright white cabinets and gleaming stainless-steel appliances. It's what I would have imagined Madeline Whittier's kitchen looks like. I go over to the window and peer outside. I don't see any cars idling; there are no cars on the street at all.

'Where did they go?' I ask.

Spencer shrugs as he takes a pitcher out of the refrigerator. 'Sweet tea?' he asks, holding it up. He's acting a little too nonchalantly, while my heart pounds inside my chest and I feel as though I can't breathe.

'I think I'd like something a little stronger,' I manage to say.

He gives me a grin and seems to magically produce a bottle of bourbon.

'That's more like it,' I say as he pours a short one and hands it to me.

I take a drink and savor the heat in my throat, taking the moment to really *see* Spencer. He's cut his hair since the last time I saw him; the long ponytail has been replaced by a much shorter look, and he's actually clean-shaven. His eyes are clear, not glassy, which surprises me, but it's possible he might not have been able to drive like that if he were stoned, so I'm grateful for his sobriety. It's going to be short-lived, though, since he now lights up a joint.

He offers it to me, but I shake my head, indicating my glass. No peer pressure, because Spencer merely nods and takes a drag.

'Are you sure that we're OK here?' I ask, still a little uncertain as to where 'here' actually is.

He nods. 'No worries.'

But I *am* worried. He showed up out of nowhere and rescued me. But Madeline or Tony DeMarco or both could be lurking outside, ready to make good on that hit. A closer look at Spencer indicates that he really isn't as worried – or worried at all. I peer outside again but the street is quiet; there are no cars passing by, no one walking on the sidewalk. I take a deep breath and face Spencer when I'm almost certain that we might be safe.

'What are you doing here?' I ask. Now that my heart has stopped pounding quite so hard, my curiosity has come back. It's no coincidence that he is in Charleston.

'Thought you might need a little company,' he says simply. 'Come on.' He leads me out of the kitchen and into the living room. I expect to see half-a-dozen computer screens, a setup similar to what he had in his house in Coral Gables. But I don't. The room is crowded with antiques. It's more like a store than a living space. I spot a sofa in one corner and a chair in another, but the antique oddities like the large Chinese vases that stand as tall as I do, a table covered with five tea sets, two – no, three – cigar Indians, a wooden baby's crib and more are overwhelming. There is barely room to move.

'Ridiculous, isn't it?' Spencer says. 'But after a while, you get used to it.'

'Who lives here?'

'I do.'

'I mean, who owns this house? All *this*?'

He looks me straight in the eye, and I can see he's not quite stoned – not yet, anyway. 'I do.' He shrugs. 'I mean, it's from before. You know, when I had my company.'

'You're serious.'

'I never really lived here, though, and if anyone checks, it's owned by a holding company. My name's not associated with it anywhere,' he says, almost apologetically. 'I bought houses everywhere. I've gotten rid of most of them, but this one, well, you can see why it might be a little harder to sell. I had a little bit of a hoarder problem.'

Understatement. I don't even want to move. I worry that I'll break something. It wouldn't be too difficult because it's a bit stifling.

'Where did you get all this stuff?' I ask.

He shrugs. 'Here and there. I did a little bit of traveling and bought things. I had them shipped here.'

'Nowhere else?'

He takes a long hit off his joint. 'Somehow this house became the repository. And then I stopped coming here because it reminded me that I should stop buying shit. But I didn't stop. Not until, well, you know.'

'Why don't you have a garage sale or something?'

'The idea of that is a little overwhelming.'

'You know there are people who would do it for you.'

Spencer rolls his eyes. 'Yeah, I know.' He pauses. 'I haven't been here in a long time, but when I found out you were in Charleston, I figured I should keep an eye out, and since I had a place to stay and all . . .' His voice trails off. 'You're not really surprised to see me.'

I shake my head. 'I figured you had a GPS in the phone.'

'Why didn't you disable it?'

I'm quiet for a second as I take another drink of bourbon. 'Maybe I wanted to be found,' I say softly.

He studies my face. He knows what I'm thinking. 'Just not by me,' he finally says.

I don't want to talk about it. 'Who was that after me?' I ask, eager to change the subject. 'And don't pretend that you don't know. You showed up in that white car for a reason.' And then I remember. 'You've been following me. How long?'

'Not long. Just today. I got in this morning.'

I am about to ask 'from where,' but before I can, he heads down the hall toward an elaborate wooden stairway. I note the

ornate crystal chandelier and the oil paintings on the walls as
I scurry up behind him. One of the paintings makes me stop,
though. It's an ocean scene, with a small white ferry amid an
angry purple sea. I take a deep breath.
   'That's mine,' I say.
   'That's right.'
   I look up to see Spencer on the landing above me. 'How . . .'
   'I bought it at that gallery. You know, on Block Island. From
your friend. Veronica.'
   A million questions rush through my head. 'When?' I ask.
   A sheepish expression crosses his face.
   'How long have you been following me?' I ask.
   'You shouldn't have gone there.'
   'When you called me to tell me about Zeke, how he was
gone, were you on the island then?'
   He doesn't need to answer me; I can see it in his face.
   'I can't believe that you've been following me.'
   'Zeke wanted me to watch out for you,' he says quickly.
   'Why didn't *he* watch out for me? Why you?'
   'He had business.'
   'What kind of business?'
   Spencer shakes his head. 'Come on, Tina.' He disappears
around the corner, and I don't have a choice. If I want answers,
I have to follow him.
   It's up here that I find what I'd been expecting. Five computer
screens are set up in a semicircle on tables; a chair on wheels
sits in the middle. As in his house in Coral Gables, the windows
are covered with dark fabric to keep the daylight out. I'm
taking it all in as he sits in the chair with a keyboard in his
lap. Suddenly, the screens all spring to life.
   'Take a look,' he instructs, and I step forward, although I
don't need to.
   It's on the screen. What he warned me about. I could never
have found it myself. Because somehow he's managed to hack
into the street security camera system in Paris on the rue de
Rivoli, where the ATM machine is. The one mentioned in the
story that had Zeke's picture.
   I peer more closely, unable to believe it. The image is grainy,
but there's no mistaking what's happening.

Zeke's not wearing the hoodie anymore. In fact, he doesn't look at all like the image in the story about Ryan Whittier. He looks more like himself, in a button-down shirt and jeans. He's clean-shaven; his hair is shorter than the last time I saw him. He looks good, I can tell that much even from the poor quality of the video, and a rush of emotion hits me.

But it's replaced by curiosity as I see what unfolds on the screen. A long black car – is it a limo? – pulls up and the door opens. Zeke leans down, his hand on the door, but before he gets in, he stands and looks straight up into the camera. Almost as though he knows we're watching.

And then he gets into the car, the door closes and the car pulls away.

'What's happening?' I mutter to myself.

Spencer replays the video in slow motion and suddenly stops it as he jabs at the screen with his finger. 'See?'

The license plate. I still don't get it, though.

'I ran a search.' Spencer hesitates a second, and then he surprises me. 'The car. It's owned by Tony DeMarco.'

TEN

There has to be some mistake. Zeke was undercover with Tony's operation a couple of years ago. He hasn't been with him in a while. And anyway, in Miami six months ago, Zeke revealed himself as FBI. There's no way he could be working for Tony now.

Could he?

'I don't understand,' I say.

Spencer sighs. 'The FBI's involved in a carding forum. It might be why Zeke's putting skimmers on ATMs.'

Carding forums are sites online where people can buy and sell credit card information. One of the ways to get that information is through skimmers.

'How do you know this?'

One of Spencer's eyebrows rises. 'Come on, Tina.'

Right. He's with Incognito. He's got eyes everywhere. Even, it seems, at the FBI.

'But this video makes it look more like he's working for Tony DeMarco and not the FBI,' I say, shrugging him off.

'Or maybe he's working for both of them.'

'A double agent?'

'Undercover, Tina.' He rolls his eyes at me, like I should know better. I suppose I should. 'DeMarco's had his hand in this sort of thing for a few years now. This is what Zeke was doing with him two years ago, but he couldn't make it stick.'

Just like the kiddie porn site. Zeke never told me what his undercover assignment had been with Tony DeMarco, but this makes sense. He's a hacker, so the FBI should know how to use him and his skills. 'But all that stuff in Miami six months ago . . .' I can't wrap my head around this, '. . . Tony knows that Zeke's FBI, so how can he be undercover with him?'

Before he can answer, the chat room pops up on yet another screen. I recognize it, but it's not current.

'These are the archives of the chats. Tracker reached out. He invited a few people to the forum,' Spencer explains.

That's how it works. You can't just join a carding forum. You have to be invited. Someone has to vouch for you. And then it hits me. '*Tracker* reached out?'

Spencer nods. So he's right. Zeke is on the inside. *Really* inside. Tony DeMarco has been involved in a lot of illegal activity for a very long time but he's dying of cancer. While it might seem logical for him to hang it all up at this juncture, maybe it's not in his nature to do that. Maybe he just *can't*.

But then there's Zeke. I don't understand how he could again get involved in any aspect of what Tony DeMarco is into. I say as much to Spencer, adding, 'Tony didn't just want to kill *me*, he wanted Tracker – Zeke – dead, too.' Suddenly, the reality of what I've just said hits me, and I'm filled with fear for Zeke.

Spencer rolls his eyes at me. 'Tina, we've been over this before. He's FBI. It's his *job*.'

I know that, but it doesn't mean I can't be afraid for him.

'What does this have to do with Ryan Whittier, though? Who *is* Ryan Whittier? He's not really a college student.' I regret not having time to ask Madeline about him. I tell Spencer about my phone conversation with the media relations guy at Charleston College. 'They said there's never been a student there by that name. He has no Internet footprint. If it weren't for the hotel reservation, I'd think he doesn't exist.'

'What hotel reservation?'

I explain about the Hotel Adele.

'Maybe it doesn't have anything to do with him,' Spencer says. 'Maybe it's just a coincidence.'

I shake my head. 'No. It's definitely more than that. Ryan Whittier used a credit card with your name on it. He used it to pay for the hotel room. If it were just a coincidence, how do you explain that?'

'What are you talking about? *My* name?'

I tell him what I found online and how I got inside the reservation system and the credit card site. 'So you didn't know about this?'

'How could I? It's not my credit card. I don't have one in my name anymore.'

'But you did have one, right?'

'Of course. But it's been a long time, and the last one I did have was through my company. So it can't be the same account number. Can it?' He pauses. 'We both know something's going on with credit cards, so it's got to be connected to that.'

'But since it's *your* name, then is it possible that someone's connected you to Zeke, or Tracker? I mean, it's too coincidental that the name on the card is Spencer Cross. And what if it *is* your old account number? Someone could have hacked it and it's out there now.'

He doesn't say anything as he mulls this over, realizing that I'm right. Finally, he says, 'If this Ryan Whittier is using a card with my name on it, we probably should figure out just who the hell he is.' He pauses, then adds, 'Maybe I should reach out.'

I don't have to ask to whom. He's going to see if anyone in Incognito knows anything. If anyone does, it would be them.

The sound of a doorbell jars us out of our thoughts.

'Are you expecting anyone?' I ask softly.

Spencer shakes his head. 'No one.' He jumps up and goes over to the window, pulling aside the curtain. 'Shit.'

I'm on his heels, and I lean over his shoulder to peer outside. A police car sits in front of the house, a couple of patrol officers pacing on the front porch.

'What do they want?' I mutter.

'Beats the hell out of me.'

'Have you ever had any contact with local law enforcement?'

'Not even when I was legit.' Spencer's eyes are wide, and it has nothing to do with the weed he's smoked.

'You should answer the door,' I say when one of the officers rings the bell again and the sound of it echoes throughout the house.

'And I thought I was the only one who was high.' He lets the curtain fall. 'They'll go away.'

'What if they don't?' I begin to imagine scenarios. 'What if Madeline has told them about me – the police, I mean? What if she told them I stole millions from her? That I ran away from her when she confronted me?' I am vaguely aware that my voice has risen, and Spencer slaps a hand over my mouth.

'Ssh,' he hisses in my ear. 'We can't let them know we're here. They'll go away, and then we'll leave.'

'Where will we go?' I whisper through his hand.

He pulls it away and stares me straight in the eye. 'Maybe we should go to Paris. Find out what's going on with Tracker. And if we leave, disappear, maybe they' – he cocks his head in the direction of the window – 'will give up on finding us for the time being.'

I don't have much hope that they'll stop looking, since people have been looking for me for seventeen years, and the idea of going back to Paris frightens and exhilarates me at the same time. But he's right. If we leave, if we escape, put thousands of miles between us, our survival is more guaranteed than if we stay here.

'I've already got documents for us,' Spencer says. 'Tracker told me to do that when he left, just in case.'

Just in case. Zeke anticipated that we might have to make a quick getaway. I shake the thought away. There is no way he could have known that I'd come across Madeline Whittier, since he didn't know where I was going to end up when we said goodbye. But he did know that Tony DeMarco and his people weren't going to stop looking for me.

The doorbell again pierces the silence. We look at each other and I can't help myself. I pull aside the curtain slightly. I feel Spencer's breath on the back of my neck as we watch the scene unfold outside.

It's no longer just the two officers. I count four police cars, their lights flashing. Officers are lining up in front of the house, guns drawn.

My body begins to shake. 'What's going on?'

Spencer is no longer behind me. He's shutting down his computers, pulling wires out of the machines.

'Hard drives?' I ask, ready to help.

He's already two steps ahead of me. He hands me a screwdriver. Within minutes, we've managed to take all five hard drives out of the computers, and that's when I see it: the degausser. It's small enough to be hidden behind the door on a tabletop. Spencer slips one of the hard drives into the front slot. When it pops out of the back, it's been demagnetized and erased. A degausser isn't something that just anyone would have hanging around, but it makes sense for Spencer to have one. It's really the only way to completely erase a hard drive quickly and completely.

It only takes a few seconds for each drive, and we leave the degausser and the empty drives in the middle of the floor. Spencer grabs two laptops and shoves them into a messenger bag. He picks up my backpack and thrusts it at me. 'Come on.'

'You've got backup, right?'

He grins. 'Don't underestimate me.'

I really don't. 'How are we going to get out of here?' I ask.

'There's a way,' he says, 'but you have to trust me.'

I have no choice.

ELEVEN

We hear shouting and banging on the front door, but neither of us pays attention. We're not going out that way – or even through the back door, as it turns out. Spencer hits a button on the wall and a door slides open. A hidden elevator. It's small, but we can both fit if we stand sideways. I hold my backpack over my head. The elevator door shuts, and we are plunged into complete darkness. It jerks slowly downward, until it stops suddenly and the door opens. I almost expect to be in a basement, then realize that a basement in a city that floods on a regular basis is probably not a good idea. Instead, we're in a pantry, from the looks of it. Shelves full of dry goods and cereal, large, clear jars that contain rice, sugar and flour line the walls. The scents of several different spices mix in the air.

I don't have time to figure out exactly what those spices are, because Spencer is on the move. A backpack is shoved under the bottom shelf, and he picks it up and shrugs it onto his shoulders. It looks as though he may have anticipated a quick getaway, whether with me or not.

He doesn't check to see if I'm following – I am – and we move quickly around the door and to another one that looks like it hasn't been opened since the Civil War. Spencer gives it a rough shove with his shoulder, and it squeals open. We both look up and behind us, but we don't hear anything at all. This concerns me, and from Spencer's expression, it concerns him, too.

The car is on the other side of the house in the garage, but Spencer clearly does have an escape plan. We wend our way through a small garden, and soon we're on the other side of a hedge that's not unlike the one at Madeline's house. But here, instead of a wrought-iron fence is a small tool shed. The door is secured with a combination lock, but Spencer quickly opens it and we step inside into more darkness.

He's handing me something round and smooth. 'Put it on,' he instructs.

It's a helmet. But not a bike helmet. A motorcycle helmet. As my eyes adjust to the darkness, I see Spencer putting the laptops into a saddlebag on one side of the bike and his backpack in another on the other side. 'You can keep your pack on your back,' he says.

I don't have much of a choice.

The closest I've been to riding a motorcycle in the recent past has been a moped on Block Island, and that was two years ago. I can't wear the dress, though, it just wouldn't work, and I've got shorts in my backpack. I pull them out, along with a tank top. 'Turn around,' I say. Spencer might be stoned but he's not that stoned, so he does as I say. I shimmy out of my dress, quickly changing and shoving the dress into the pack. I want to change out of the sandals and into the sneakers, but I feel like it would take too much time.

'All set,' I say as I slip the helmet over my head and secure the strap under my chin. I feel top-heavy. It's going to take a little getting used to.

Spencer swings the door open further and climbs onto the bike. I get on behind him, tightening my pack against my back. The motorcycle feels clumsy between my legs, and it's humming underneath us. Within only a few seconds, we shoot out onto the lawn – the tool shed was clearly only for the landscaper – and I lean forward and wrap my arms more securely around Spencer's waist.

I have no idea where the police might be or whether they've figured out what we're up to, but we don't bother to wait around to see. Soon we're speeding up the street behind Spencer's house, heading who knows where. I doubt we're going to the beach to get the rest of my things. I think longingly of a change of clothes other than the dress, but I'm glad that Randy paid me before I left the gallery. The money is secure under the false bottom in the backpack, and hopefully I can make it go pretty far. I'm sure Spencer's managed to bring his own cache along. I'm not sure how long it will keep us afloat, especially if we do end up heading to Paris like Spencer suggested.

While I'm ruminating on what I've got on hand, we're winding our way around traffic. We've gotten on the highway, and I am acutely aware of my bare legs and practically bare feet. Yet the longer I'm on the bike, the more comfortable I feel and my body sways with its movements. Spencer is driving safely under the circumstances, despite the weed. But he doesn't seem impaired. Not that I have much of a choice if he is.

We're getting off the highway, and I tighten my grip on Spencer's waist. I almost let go, though, with surprise, when I see where we're heading.

The outlet mall.

We've done this before. Shopped together. But this time, it is definitely more practical than it was before.

Spencer parks the motorcycle between a large pickup truck and an SUV. We climb off, and I tug off the helmet. He's one step ahead of me and has taken his backpack and laptops out of the saddlebags. 'We need luggage. Real luggage.' He cocks his head at my backpack. 'That thing looks like it's about a hundred years old.'

I don't tell him that I bought it in Montreal, that it's traveled so many miles with me that it feels like an old friend.

'And some clothes. We have to look normal.' Spencer is walking away, and I jog a little to catch up. I haven't been normal in a long time, so I wonder what it will feel like.

I am a bit curious about how we're going to load our new carry-on luggage onto the motorcycle once we've finished shopping, but I don't get a chance to ask before the Uber car drives up and Spencer holds the door open for me. I anticipate a short ride to the airport, but instead we head to a neighborhood I haven't visited before.

'Train,' Spencer says simply, seemingly unconcerned that we are abandoning the motorcycle.

We haven't spoken much since we arrived at the mall. I've tried to ask Spencer what the plan is, but he merely shrugged me off and told me to go find some clothes suitable for the city. So I bought some jeans and tops, a new pair of canvas

sneakers that look a lot better than my running shoes, and
some necessary underwear.

'Train?'

Spencer nods. 'They'll be looking for us at the airport.'

'*They* won't look for us at the train station?'

'We can get on without being scrutinized as much as if we
flew.'

He's got a point. 'So where are we heading?'

'New York. We can catch a flight out of there. Lots of
people. Lots of flights.'

Makes sense. 'How long's the train ride?'

He shrugs. 'I don't know. Twelve hours?'

I think about my morning on the bike at the beach, the
wide, empty spaces. I don't relish the idea of being stuck
inside a moving train for so long. My claustrophobia is usually
not quite so physical.

The train station in North Charleston has a red brick and
green panel facade. We carry our bags inside, and Spencer
leaves me in the corner while he goes to buy the tickets. I'm
not used to someone else taking charge; I've been on my own
and having to figure out how I'm going to survive for so long
that it feels odd. Spencer and Zeke have been pulling all the
strings ever since we left Miami. As I stand here, I realize that
I haven't actually been alone for the past six months, even
when I thought I was. Spencer wasn't just a cellphone call
away; he was actually closer than I thought. And Zeke made
sure that we would have the means to get away if we needed
to. Was it a coincidence that I ended up in Charleston, where
Spencer owns a house? As I think back, he may have mentioned
the city to me as a possible destination. Maybe the power of
suggestion had been strong enough that I found my way here
subconsciously.

'Come on.' Spencer walks over to me, hands me a ticket
and grabs the handle of one of the wheeled carry-on bags.
He's got a new leather backpack over one shoulder, but I still
carry my old, tattered one. He thought I should get a fancy
tote bag, one that a woman of my age might use to take to
work on a public commute, or a new leather backpack to match

his, but I nixed both ideas. I can't give up my backpack. It's
traveled too far with me and I'm not about to give it up that
easily. I pointed out how I can still conceal the cash I've got,
which did impress him. I didn't mention that I want – I need
– to have control over something.

The train is waiting for us, and we hand our tickets to the
attendant. We are directed down a couple of cars, and when
we arrive where we're supposed to, we encounter another
attendant and again show our tickets. He points to the
left, and we make our way down an aisle. This is not what I
expect, and when Spencer stops and pushes a door open, I am
surprised. It's a small compartment with two seats, a long steel
counter with a sink facing them.

'The seat pulls out to a bed,' he says. But then adds quickly,
'There's a bunk that pulls out over it, so there are two beds.
I thought about two compartments, but it might be better if
we share.'

'It's OK,' I say, although I'm not sure I mean it. I could
use a little time by myself to sort everything out, and the space
is very tight. I pull on a door and see an enclosed toilet and
shower.

There is space for our bags, but it's good we only have
the two carry-ons. I suppose there's a place somewhere
on the train if someone has a larger bag.

'There's someone who comes and pulls the beds out at
night,' Spencer's explaining. 'All our meals are included, too.'
He raises his eyebrows and gives me a grin. 'It's not a bad
way to travel.' He plops down on the seat and pulls one of
the laptops out of his backpack.

I yank the blue accordion curtains closed over the door's
window so no one can see inside before I sit next to him,
curious. 'What are you doing?' I ask.

He's already in the deep web, using his own wireless hotspot
router. He looks up at me and grins. 'Let's get ourselves an
invite to a carding forum.'

TWELVE

'We don't have anything to sell,' I try, but I admit I'm intrigued by the idea. Immediately, I tell myself I should walk away. I loved all those years on Block Island, under the radar, living my quiet existence, meeting Steve on Friday nights for burgers and onion rings, hiking Rodman's Hollow, taking in the Mohegan Bluffs on a brisk, autumn day. I need that kind of life again. I was happy. Content.

Spencer doesn't have a clue what I'm thinking, because he doesn't know what it's like to live without a computer. Even after he got caught, he went underground and stayed online.

I thought about it every single day.

'We don't need something to sell,' Spencer's saying. 'We could say we want to buy a dump.'

By 'dump,' he means credit card information. Names, addresses, Social Security numbers, bank account numbers, phone numbers, security codes, answers to security questions, everything associated with the card.

'Do you know how this works?'

'We can't do anything until we get an invite,' he says. 'We have to find Tracker.'

I freeze at the sound of his name. Spencer notices and smiles but doesn't say anything.

'So where do we find this carding forum connection?' I ask.

'Do you not pay attention in the chat rooms?'

I remind him that I haven't been on a computer for six months, that I have only had my laptop since this morning. He gives me a look that tells me he doesn't quite believe me. It's not worth arguing.

'Are people actually talking about being in a carding forum in the chat rooms?' I ask. 'Wouldn't that be something you might not want to advertise?'

He rolls his eyes at me. 'And you call yourself a hacker.'

I don't have a chance to respond because he's rummaging around in his pocket and produces a joint.

'I don't think you're allowed to smoke in here,' I tell him.

He hasn't considered that. He jumps up, shoving the laptop onto the cushion next to him. 'I'll be right back.' And he disappears out the door, shutting it behind him.

I'm finally alone, although only because Spencer's addiction is worse than my own. I eye the laptop, which is still powered up and hooked up to the wireless hotspot router. As I reach for it, I feel the train jerk underneath me, and it starts to move slowly on the track. I vaguely wonder exactly where Spencer's disappeared to, where he thinks he'll be able to smoke.

I pull the laptop onto my lap and hit one of the keys to get it out of sleep mode. Spencer has rigged it so I need to use a password to get in. I don't have time to try to figure out how his mind works. I take my laptop out of my bag and push his aside. Within moments, I'm online and inside the chat room.

I don't expect to see Tracker here. I don't expect to see anything about a carding forum. I'm here with another new screen name; I'm going to have to make a list at some point to remind myself who I've been so I don't begin to repeat myself.

I lurk a little, but there really isn't anything of interest, proving that Spencer's pronouncement that carding forum discussions are out in the open might not be quite the truth. Again, I wonder where Spencer is. I would have thought he'd be back by now. How long does it take to get stoned, anyway?

When I turn back to the screen, what I see makes me stop breathing for a second.

'*Le soleil brille aujourd'hui*,' I read. *The sun is shining today*. It's the French phrase that Tracker and I devised in order to identify ourselves to each other. But Tracker hasn't posted it. Instead, it's someone called d4rkn!te.

I hesitate. Other people have found out about our phrases and have used them to trick me into downloading a remote access Trojan. I don't know for sure that this is Zeke – Tracker – or someone else connected to Tony DeMarco who wants me to make another mistake so he can find me.

The message isn't directed to anyone in particular. It's just there, in the thread of public messages, taunting me. Daring me to engage.

My hands are literally shaking. I desperately want to find out if this is Zeke, but I can't take that chance.

I contemplate the screen name: d4rkn!te. *Dark night*. It's not very creative, since nights *are* dark. Nothing about it gives me any clue as to his identity.

A knock at the door startles me. I hesitate, but pull the curtain aside to see that it's the attendant. I open the door. To his credit, he doesn't step inside, just stands on the doorjamb. He's an older man with gray hair and smile lines around his eyes.

'I'm Harry; I'll be your attendant. Can I show you how things work?'

For a moment, I'm confused, and then I realize he wants to show me around the tight space that Spencer and I will be habituating for the next twelve hours or more. I glance over at the laptop. 'I think I've got it.' I say.

'The bed can be tricky,' he says, but he finally senses that I am not paying complete attention to him. 'I can come back in a little bit.'

'Yes, that would be great. Thanks,' I say.

The smile fades for a second, and he gives me a look I can't read, but then, 'Perhaps I can come back when you're at dinner.'

'Yes, thank you.' I am too distracted, and he finally steps to the side. I close the door, wondering again where Spencer is. I stand, staring at the laptop that's still open. The screen is dark as it's gone to sleep. But in my head, I can still see the French words that are emblazoned in the thread.

If I respond, d4rkn!te will give me a link – I'm sure of it – to a private chat. That's how it works.

I take a step toward it, but the door swings open behind me and I catch my breath. I expect it to be Harry, coming back because he forgot to tell me something about the bed or something else about the compartment, but it's Spencer. He stumbles in, a goofy smile on his face. 'Sorry I was so long,' he says, collapsing on the seat. He spots the open laptop. 'Find anything?'

I nod, sit and hit a key to bring the screen back to life. The message is still there, but there are even more below it now so it takes a moment to find it. I turn the screen toward Spencer. He frowns. After a moment, he says, 'Maybe you should respond.'

'Do you think it's Zeke?'

Again, he hesitates. 'Not sure,' he says.

'If it isn't him and I respond, who's to say there isn't a remote access Trojan in the link?'

'You can create a link for him. You don't have to follow his.'

He's got a point.

'And we can turn the tables.'

We can try to trace d4rkn!te, rather than the other way around. I get it now. But I'm still leery. If Zeke is undercover, then he's really *undercover*. He wouldn't come out like this on a public chat; he'd find another way to contact me. This can't possibly be him. I say as much to Spencer.

He nods. 'Yeah, maybe. But aren't you just a little bit curious about this dude? I mean, he's *trying* to lure you out. Everyone else is looking at that French shit and saying, what's up with that? But this guy knows that if you're there, you'll see it, too, and maybe he'll—' He stops and frowns, like he's just this moment realizing what he's saying.

A joint is dangling from the corner of his mouth, but it's not lit. He notices me noticing. 'It's how I work.'

I ignore that, and say, 'So, you think that this is some sort of trap?'

Spencer shakes his head. 'I have no clue what this dude is up to. But he's got a message for you. Let's find out what it is.' He grabs his own laptop. 'But if you're nervous about using your laptop, we can use mine. My encryption might be a little more intense than yours.' He's got a point, since I haven't done much to safeguard my laptop since I bought it this morning. Although I would argue that I haven't had the time.

Spencer logs in with his password and within moments is in the chat room. D4rkn!te's message is now on both our screens. He pushes the laptop toward me. 'Do your thing.'

Despite my hesitation, I admit that I am curious. So I type: *'Non, le ciel est nuageux.'* *No, it's cloudy.* I don't send it immediately, though. 'I need a link.'

'You need a link with a remote access Trojan,' Spencer corrects me. He takes the laptop now and inserts a URL into my message, but not before I see him embed the code for the RAT in it. And then he hits send before making his way into the chat room where we wait for d4rkn!te to find us.

We stare at the screen for a few minutes. He begins to sway a little, the joint bobbing up and down in the corner of his mouth. He's trying to take a drag, but it's not lit, and he gets frustrated and pulls it out of his mouth and tosses it on the small table. I am about to tell him that maybe he should take another walk when we see d4rkn!te come into the private chat room.

But instead of saying something, we see an image appear on the screen.

'What's this?' Spencer leans closer to see the image better, but I don't have to.

It's a photograph of me.

Boarding this train.

THIRTEEN

'He's here,' I whisper. 'Whoever it is, he's on this train.' I don't know who *he* is. Is he someone sent by Tony DeMarco or is he someone Madeline Whittier sicced on me at her house? Could those two people be the same person?

Spencer's shaking his head as though he doesn't believe what he's seeing. 'No, that's not right.'

'What isn't right?' I ask. 'That he's uploaded a photo of me getting on the train? *This* train. No, you're right. That isn't right at all, and we have to get off. Now.' But as I say it, I realize that he probably knows which compartment we're in. He's probably lying in wait outside, maybe even right outside our door.

Remembering how Spencer left me alone sends a chill down my spine. He could have gotten to me then. He could've pushed his way inside and . . . What about Harry, the attendant? Is he really the attendant? I opened the door for him. But if Harry were d4rkn!te, he might not have left. He had his chance, so maybe he's really the attendant. That means, however, that d4rkn!te is still here somewhere. Which means I can't stay. I have to get out of here.

'What's the next stop?' I demand.

Spencer's shaking his head. Maybe he's more stoned than I thought, because he seems to be having a very hard time with this. From the time that he picked me up in the Cadillac, he had been in total control. He was more like the Spencer Cross he used to be, when he really *was* in control. Now, though, he's merely the stoned hacker I met in Miami with the dark fabric over the windows, paranoid that the feds would discover his hiding place.

I take a few deep breaths, trying to calm myself down, sorting it out again in my head. If it is someone associated with Tony DeMarco, why would he post something in the chat room rather than just breaking in here and killing me? Tony wouldn't play those kinds of games, and I doubt a professional hitman would, either. Not that I know much about professional hitmen.

More likely, this may be someone associated with Madeline Whittier. She knows I'm in the city, and she knows that I'm a hacker. She had a lot of lead time to set everything up before I arrived for tea this afternoon.

'Have you ever seen d4rkn!te in the chat room?' I ask Spencer, who's still puzzling over the picture on the screen.

I half expect him to say no, that d4rkn!te is a stranger, but he looks me straight in the eye and says, 'Yes.' That's all he says, though, before going back to the screen.

This is why he was so hesitant when I showed him the message. I tug on his arm and push the laptop away. He reluctantly meets my eyes again.

'Who is it, Spencer? Do you know?'

He shrugs. 'I'm not sure, but I think he's got something to do with Tracker – I mean, Zeke.'

'Something to do with him in what way?' I ask carefully. Spencer reaches for the laptop, but I stick my hand out and cover his. 'No. Answer me.'

'Well, he knows about your French phrases.'

'So did the shadow that was in my computer last year.'

He shrugs. 'He's been around the chat. He's actually the one I was going to reach out to for the invite to the carding forum if Tracker wasn't around.' He pauses and frowns, as though he's thinking out what he's going to say. It's not going to help to push him. Finally: 'I think he and Tracker set up the forum.'

I'm trying to wrap my head around this. 'But Zeke is FBI.'

'And he's undercover,' Spencer reminds me. 'I don't think d4rkn!te is a fed.'

'Why don't you think he's a fed? I mean, if Zeke can be plausible as Tracker, then why can't d4rkn!te? And anyway, he's posting a picture of me getting on the train, telling me that he's physically here. Not just hiding behind a screen name somewhere. Why would he do that?'

'He doesn't have to actually be here, you know.'

I think about the implication of what he's saying, and he's right. D4rkn!te could have an accomplice. Someone who sent him the picture. Or if there are cameras at the train station, the image could be extracted from those. Any hacker might be able to get into the system to pull the video. I'd rather the latter, because with the former, someone is here. Watching me. But either way, whoever it is knows my location.

This is worse than when I discovered the shadow in my laptop in Quebec. The shadow didn't know exactly where I was.

Spencer is quiet, his feet tapping against the floor. He's fidgety. He's got a theory, and he is uncertain how to tell me. 'When Zeke left, he was in touch. I didn't know where he was but we chatted online. I haven't heard from him in four months, though.'

I begin to do the math in my head, counting backward to when we left Miami. He sees me working it out and waits for me. 'That article I found online,' I say slowly. 'That was four months ago.'

'And the video I found, where he's getting into the car owned by Tony DeMarco, was the same day,' Spencer finishes. 'I haven't heard from him since.'

'So you were in touch. Before he vanished.' There are so many questions pinballing around in my head. 'What were you in touch about?'

He rolls his eyes at me. I get it.

'Me. You were in touch about me.'

'He told me to keep an eye on you.'

'But you didn't talk about anything else?'

'It's not like he could talk to me about his work.'

'Why not? He didn't ask you for any help with what he was doing? I mean, he knows what you can do. Who your connections might be.'

Spencer shrugs. 'No. We've got a code.'

I resist the urge to laugh. 'A *code*?'

'He stays out of my business and I stay out of his.'

'Except when it comes to me.'

He eyes me for a second. 'Yeah. That's right. He worries about you.'

The way he says it makes me take pause. 'He worries he won't find me again,' I say softly. 'That's what it's all about.'

His silence confirms it.

'He's the one who left this time,' I point out. 'Not me.' I let that sit between us a few seconds, then add, 'You weren't worried, though? I mean, that you hadn't heard from him?'

'I knew he was undercover. But I was starting to get concerned. And then when you called about the article . . .' His voice trails off, but I can see there's something else.

'What?'

'Whatever Tracker's working on, I think he's in trouble.' Spencer is visibly uncomfortable now. 'The DeMarco thing, getting into the car. You're right. DeMarco knows who he is, and the fact that he hasn't been in touch . . .' His voice trails off as he glances toward the window, where the landscape is passing us by.

His words underscore my worry and knowing he's got the same concerns makes it worse. Despite being FBI, Zeke's not infallible, as much as we might want to think he is. We're not just going to Paris on a whim to escape the police here. We're going because Spencer thinks Zeke needs our help, although I'm not quite sure how we're going to do that. We also don't know for sure that he's still in Paris, but we have to start somewhere.

Spencer interrupts my thoughts. 'You need to get off the train. But no one can know. No one can know where you are.'

No one knew where I was until today. Is it a coincidence that today is the day Madeline Whittier confronted me with my past?

In the last seventeen years, I have been so very good at hiding, but it's always some small thing that manages to reveal me.

'So how are we going to get off a moving train without anyone noticing?' I ask.

'Who said we were going to get off a moving train? We're not in a fucking movie, Tina. We have to wait for the train to stop.' He rolls his eyes at me and picks up the joint, putting it back between his lips. 'We need a plan.'

The two carry-ons sit at the edge of the seat, the backpacks next to them. So much for looking like regular travelers. I have to do something, so I open the carry-ons and begin pulling clothes and toiletries out of them. In short order, I've got the backpacks organized and ready for whatever happens next. Spencer watches me with wide eyes.

I merely shrug.

I don't tell him that packing has helped me to calm down a little, although I am still uncertain how we're going to get off the train without my stalker seeing us. Especially since the train may be stopping in some very backwater towns. It might be best to get off in a larger city so we can disappear more easily.

'What's the next city that we stop in?' I ask, but Spencer is already a step ahead.

'Raleigh.'

I peer over his shoulder to see the list of stations. I wish we could manage to stay on until Washington, D.C., because it seems that might be a better place to disappear. I'm not sure Raleigh is big enough. But it's bigger than some of the other places listed on the website.

Suddenly, a thought strikes me. 'How did he know I would be online?'

Spencer frowns. I haven't made myself completely clear. 'How would he know that I'd be online? That I'd be in the chat room to get his message? I mean, I haven't been online in months. I haven't had a computer until today.'

FOURTEEN

My heart pounds inside my chest, and I feel dizzy. I put my hand on the small table to steady myself or I might fall over. I have no idea who d4rkn!te is, but he seems to be closer than we thought. Was he in the park when I was there earlier? Was he in the restaurant when I had lunch? Maybe he really *has* been stalking me. Maybe it's even gone on longer than just today. And then I have another thought.

'If he knows about me, then he knows that you're with me,' I say.

Spencer's head swings up, fear in his eyes. He can't be discovered any more than I can, but for different reasons. There's no hit on him, but the feds would love to know where he is. But then something crosses his expression, and he frowns. He hesitates a couple of seconds before speaking, asking, 'How do we know that the message was for you?'

I'm confused. 'It's the French phrases.' It's pretty clear to me, but maybe the weed has addled his brain a little.

'No, I mean, yeah, he knows the French phrases, but what if he was trying to lure Tracker in?'

It takes a moment, but I finally see what he's saying. 'So he was trying to make Tracker think that he's *me*?'

Spencer shakes his head. 'Tracker knows d4rkn!te, and he knows it's not you. But think about this: maybe d4rkn!te doesn't know you're online. He doesn't know anything except that you're on the train. But what if he wants Tracker to know that he knows. That he knows where you are.'

A shiver shimmies up my spine. This is not reassuring.

I don't like the implications of what he's saying. 'You think that this might not be someone who's after me because of *me*, but because of Zeke. Someone who is trying to threaten him through me.' My throat feels dry.

Spencer wisely says nothing and looks back at the screen again. I pick up my backpack. Its weight feels comfortable. Maybe I should be concerned about that, but I'm not. I'm relieved that I didn't cave to Spencer's suggestion that I get a new one. The leather might have been heavier. Deep down, I must have known that we couldn't travel like normal people, that something would happen that would mean I'd have to run again.

'You can get off at one of the sidings,' Spencer says, his voice piercing the silence.

I have no idea what he's talking about. 'What's that?'

'A siding. We left half an hour later than we were scheduled to.' He says this like it's supposed to mean something. 'That's a good thing.'

'Good for what?'

He sighs as though I should already know. 'The train will veer off on to a small siding when a freight train needs to get past. We'll stop, and the freight train, which has a tighter schedule than we do, will go by us. It'll be incredibly loud.'

I know what he's saying now. We can get off the train while the freight train passes and no one will be the wiser. Maybe. 'What about an alarm on the door? Don't they have them wired?'

Spencer looks me straight in the eye. 'Probably. You don't have much of a choice.'

He's right. We have to take our chances. But then I hear what he's actually said. He said 'you.' Not 'we.' He's actually been saying that all along. He sees that I've finally noticed.

'I'm not sure both of us can get off without being noticed,' he says.

I roll my eyes. 'It doesn't matter how many of us get off, they'll know we did. And you can't stay here. If the stalker knows I'm here, he probably knows you're here, too, and you can't risk getting caught, either.'

'True, but he won't kill me.'

'Are you so sure about that? And anyway, if it really *is* someone who was trying to get Tracker's attention and not mine, then there's a whole different agenda than we think. And since we don't know what that agenda is, we have to figure the worst.' I don't want to think about the worst, but ideas careen through my head: I'll be kidnapped, held for ransom until whoever it is gets whatever he wants from Zeke, and then they'll possibly kill me. My imagination is far too active. But, no, I don't want to go alone, and I don't want to leave him here to face whoever's watching me – and possibly the feds. 'You have to come with me. Zeke wouldn't like it if you let me go by myself.'

'Zeke sent you away by yourself. He knows you can take care of yourself.' His words resonate, but I can see that I've made him nervous. That he's thinking about what will happen to him if *he's* caught. Spencer's like me: he has a very strong survival instinct.

'But he had you keeping an eye on me,' I say, bringing home my argument. 'You have to come with me. It's the only way.' As if to prove it to him, I hold up his backpack, which I have also packed. 'When does this siding thing happen?'

He makes a face at me, but I can tell that he's resigned himself to come with me. It wasn't as difficult as I thought it might be. 'I have to check freight train schedules on this route.' His fingers move on the keyboard. I double-check his backpack. There has to be enough room for his *two* laptops. I tuck cash into each pack, enough so if we're separated we'll both be able to pay for a room and some food for a couple of days. A thought strikes me: if we went onto the carding forum, we could use a stolen credit card to pay for things. I shake the thought aside, since my criminal activity is why I'm here in the first place.

Our pending escape has put the carding forum on hold, too, for the time being. Again, I think about Zeke and how he might be in trouble. But Spencer and I have to get out of this predicament first, and I can only hope that we'll be successful. I'm a little dubious, looking out of the window into the darkness.

Spencer clears his throat. 'Looks like we're probably going

into a siding in about twenty minutes,' he announces. 'There's a door at the end of the aisle. We just have to make it down there.'

Without anyone noticing.

I have an idea. 'The attendant. I think his name was Harry. He said he'd come back to show us how to set up for the night. Maybe we could get him in here, distract him?'

Spencer looks dubious but nods. 'It's worth a try, but shouldn't we be here with him?'

I shrug. 'Maybe not. Maybe we get him in here and tell him we'll be back in a few minutes when it's done, and we take off.'

He looks a little less dubious. 'OK, it might work.' But then he frowns. 'What about the backpacks?'

They're stuffed to capacity, and the laptops aren't even inside yet. If we're carrying them, they'll be conspicuous. Granted, the moment the door opens, there will probably be some sort of alarm, but with any luck we can disappear into the night before what's happened registers with anyone. I glance out the window and can barely make out the outlines of the pine trees. This might be one of the stupidest things I've ever done, but it's better than being kidnapped or dead.

I worry a little bit about Spencer. While I am in very good shape, he doesn't look quite so up to this physically. Maybe I'm wrong. I hope I'm wrong.

He's still doing something on the laptop. I wonder if it's because I've been away from it that I'm not right there beside him. It's probably more that I'm focused on how we're going to get off the train, away from my stalker.

'Maybe you should log off for now,' I tell him.

'We might not have the Internet for a while,' he says, but doesn't elaborate, so I squeeze into the seat next to him to check out what he's up to.

He's in the source code of a site, but I can't figure out which one.

'Is that the chat room?' I ask.

He shakes his head. 'Can't find it.' He still doesn't elaborate.

It's then that I see he doesn't have to, because I know where he is. The remote access Trojan that he installed in the URL for the private chat has gotten him inside d4rkn!te's computer and he's trying to find the IP address so we can pinpoint d4rkn!te's location.

FIFTEEN

'Is he on the train?' I ask, peering more closely at the screen.

Spencer shakes his head. 'I'm not sure. It's tricky to capture IP addresses on a moving train. It might be possible when we stop, though.'

I think about that for a second. When we stop is when we need to get off the train. We won't have much time, and waiting even a few minutes is too risky. I'm trying to work the time out in my head, but Spencer's too engrossed to care.

'Look at that,' he whispers, as if to himself, as if he's the only one here.

Maybe he is. I've been where he is, when I've been so wrapped up in what's happening on the screen that I'm not aware of anything else.

Like the fact that the train is slowing down.

I tug on his arm. 'Spence, we have to go.'

He shrugs me off, but I grab his forearm. 'Now,' I say firmly. 'But look at this.'

I can't help myself, even though I'm already reaching for my backpack. He's watching d4rkn!te navigate a carding forum. Spencer gives me a look that says *I told you so*, but I'm distracted again. The train really is slowing down. 'We don't have time for this,' I tell him. 'We can do this later.'

'But—'

'We've still got the RAT, so we can find him later.' I reach over and close the cover on the laptop. For a second, I think he's going to fight me, but he finally gives in and shoves the laptop into the backpack I've put next to him. I've already put the other laptop inside. 'Come on,' I say, shrugging my pack over my back. It's too late to call Harry, tell him to set up the bed. We have to do this now; I have to get off this train. Even if d4rkn!te isn't on board, he could have someone waiting when we get off in New York.

I pull the curtain aside slightly to check out the aisle outside. I don't see anyone, but it doesn't mean he's not out there. I'm aware that my hands are shaking, and I put my palms against the wall. Spencer comes up behind me.

'Ready?' he whispers.

I'm not. Not ready. I don't want to do this. Everything within me is screaming against it, but the survivor in me turns the doorknob and pulls.

There's no one in the aisle. The train jerks, and I lose my footing, falling back into Spencer, whose hands are around my waist, steadying me. 'We need to wait a moment.' It's barely a whisper; I can feel his breath on my ear. I don't know how long I can stand like this, waiting.

And then I hear it: the freight train.

'We have to wait until it's closer.'

Spencer's words swirl around in my head, and I'm terrified that someone is going to show up and see us here hovering in the doorway, our backpacks slung over our shoulders, poised to run. But by some miracle, there is no one here. No one, at least, that I can see.

The freight train is nearing; it sounds like a tornado rushing toward us. The noise fills my ears until I'm convinced I've gone deaf. It mesmerizes me until Spencer pushes me, grabs my arm and pulls me down the aisle. We run to the door between the cars, and he yanks it open. A rush of cold air slaps me in the face; the freight train is even louder.

Someone is coming toward us in the car ahead. He's tall, his shoulders broad, his head bald. He is not an attendant; he is wearing jeans and a tight T-shirt under a suit jacket. My brain takes a snapshot of his face, but the only thing I can see is a scar across his cheek. I don't know if he's the one after me, but I can't stick around to find out.

Spencer and I turn at the same time. We reach for the door.

Neither of us expects it to be as difficult as it is to open it, but my fear gives me strength and suddenly the door slides open. I expect to hear an alarm, but all I can hear is that freight train. Looking outside is like looking into a black fishbowl.

I don't wait. I leap into the darkness. It's a lot further down than I anticipate, my ankles roll and I'm on my knees, spinning away from the train, the backpack breaking my fall. I glance up to see Spencer in the doorway, and then he's gone.

I wait a second, assess that I've not broken or sprained anything, and scramble to my feet, my eyes adjusting to the dark. Spencer's beside me, but then he's not; he's running, and I'm running, too, with only a glance back at the train, where I see the large, bald man staring out as the train begins to move again.

The ground is soft beneath my sneakers; the noise from the train fades. I weave between the trunks of the pine trees. Spencer's somewhere here, too; I can hear him breathing, or maybe it's me. Maybe it's the sound of my own breath in my ears. My heart pounds within my chest, and I regret never jogging. Twice today I've literally been on the run. Maybe I'll give up the bike for better running shoes.

'Tina!' I hear him hiss somewhere near me. The train is long gone, or at least it feels as though it should be. 'Tina!'

I follow his voice until I find him doubled over near a tree, gasping for breath. 'You OK?' I ask. My voice sounds odd in my ears, and I'm afraid I'm talking too loudly, that someone will hear.

'No.'

His honesty doesn't completely surprise me.

'I think I'm going to die.'

'Don't be ridiculous. We have to keep moving. We can't stay here.' Adrenaline has pushed me beyond my own exhaustion, but I'm afraid that the longer we linger, the less I will be able to keep going.

'Give me a minute.'

I glance back at the train. We're closer than we should be. It's moving now, faster, away from us. I don't see that anyone's followed us, but it would be easy to be shrouded by the darkness and I don't want to get overconfident that we've escaped. I've made that mistake before.

I reach out and grab Spencer's sleeve. 'We've got to go,' I say firmly.

He straightens up, shifts his pack on his back and, without another word, we head deeper into the forest.

We keep moving for about ten, maybe fifteen minutes. The only light is from the moon streaming through the branches of the trees overhead. I don't really want to stop, because I don't know what's out here with us. The ground is soft beneath my feet, but I can't tell if it's wetlands or a bed of pine needles.

'Tina,' Spencer hisses from somewhere behind me, and I pause, pivoting.

His watch is emanating a soft glow on his wrist. His face is a medley of shadows; his grin sinister because of it. 'GPS,' he says, and I realize that the watch is more than a watch – it's a small computer, and Spencer's got the wireless hotspot router in his hand. He raises the other one and points to our right. 'There's a town over there.'

As much as I like the idea of a town, a place to possibly get something to eat, a place to stay the night, I also don't like the idea of it. 'It's too close,' I say, remembering my trek through Vermont into Canada just a couple of years ago. I didn't dare stay in any towns. I had camping gear and a tent, which I would pay good money to have right about now.

'You're not the only one who's had to do this.' Spencer is reminding me that he's been on the run, too, and the way he says it makes me more curious about what he's actually done to stay hidden. I open my mouth to ask just as I hear a snap and the match illuminates our small space as he lights the joint that hangs from his lips. In a second, he blows out the flame and we're swathed again in darkness, with only the scent of weed between us.

I forget about my curiosity. I am really regretting arguing that he needed to come with me. We don't have the time to linger, to wait for him to get high before he can continue.

'Go ahead,' he says, a disembodied voice, the glow from the tip of the joint bobbing up and down as he takes another drag. 'You want to leave. We should probably separate anyway. They'll be looking for two of us.'

He's right, but my emotions are bouncing back and forth so much that I feel almost nauseous. I want to be alone, but at the same time, I don't. I begin to doubt my own instincts. Should we head for the town?

'There's another town that's a little bit further away,' Spencer says. 'What do you say—'

He stops talking, and instead of silence, I hear it.

Twigs cracking underfoot.

Someone's coming.

SIXTEEN

Instinct takes over, and I don't wait for Spencer. I turn and begin to run again, aware that every time my feet hit the ground, whoever is behind me can hear where I'm heading. We should never have stopped; we should have kept going. This is why Spencer and I have to part ways, not only because they're looking for two of us together. Spencer's a liability for me.

I push the thoughts away; they're distracting me. I don't even know if Spencer's following me. I can't stop to check.

Is it my stalker? D4rkn!te? Is he the one who's in the woods behind me? Am I going to escape this time? There have been so many times that I've doubted my own survival skills, but I've managed to get by on pure luck. The kindness of strangers. Zeke.

He's not pulling the strings this time, though. This is all me.

The adrenaline is pumping through my body, forcing me to keep moving. But I don't anticipate what happens next – whatever it is that lies in my path – because my foot catches against something, and soon I am tumbling forward, the backpack's weight not helping my balance. I have the thought that I shouldn't put my hands out to catch my fall, so I don't. Instead, I land on my shoulder, and before I can stop myself, I roll, slamming my cheek into the ground, knocking my glasses askew and scraping against something sharp. I force myself to keep rolling onto my back so I am now staring up at the sky, which is bright with the full moon. The wind has been knocked out of me, and I struggle to take a breath as I settle my glasses back on my nose. They seem intact, despite the impact.

The ground beneath me vibrates slightly as they come closer: Spencer and the unknown person. I take a deep breath, roll back around and jump up, my feet taking purchase against an invisible starting block. I plunge forward. I barely feel the backpack slapping against my body as I pump my arms and push past the stitch in my side, the ache in my legs.

I hear a cracking sound that I can't identify at first, but the second one jogs my memory. Someone's shooting at me.

I've become accustomed to the dark now, and I weave among the trees. There are lights in the distance, possibly houses on the edge of the town Spencer was talking about. I don't have time to bypass them. I want the light. I want a town. While I'll be more out in the open, whoever's shooting at me might not want to make it that public.

I need to make it there alive.

I have no idea where Spencer is. I've abandoned him. While my body seems to be moving on its own, my thoughts begin to focus. Has Spencer been shot? Is he bleeding somewhere behind me? I can't risk stopping to find out, as much as I'd like to. And I don't think my body will let me now. I am on autopilot; this is purely survival of the fittest.

I come up to the backs of some houses along what looks like a very suburban neighborhood. Street lamps create pools of light in the road. A lone car makes its way down the street. For the first time since I fell, I hesitate. I almost fall over again, but manage to get my balance. Another car comes down the street and pulls into a driveway. The garage door opens, and the car disappears inside.

I finally look behind me. I don't see Spencer – or anyone else, for that matter. Real worry creeps into my thoughts. Maybe he really did get shot. Maybe he's out there somewhere, needing my help.

I reach around and shrug off one strap of the backpack,

unzipping the front pocket. My fingers find the cellphone. I stop myself before calling 9-1-1. I can't call. If Spencer's out there, even if he's bleeding on the ground, the police mustn't find him. I'm not technically a fugitive, but he most definitely is.

I hear rustling. My whole body stiffens, and then I begin to run again, toward the street, toward the houses.

'Tina!'

I think I've imagined it, but there it is again: 'Tina!'

I pivot around, the pack slapping against me. Spencer's coming toward me, his breathing labored and loud. Relief floods through me to see him alive. He stops short when he reaches me and doubles over, trying to catch his breath.

'You OK?' I ask. 'I heard a noise. Like a shot.'

He straightens back up and holds up his arm. He's clutching something in his hand and I see it. The gun.

'Where did you get that?' I ask.

'Never leave home without it.'

He'd had a gun when I was in Miami last fall, but I had no idea he'd brought it with him. I hadn't seen it when I unpacked his carry-on and packed his backpack. 'Where was it?'

'You're not the only one who has secret hiding places.'

I realize I'm fixating on the gun itself, forgetting about the shots I heard. 'Did you kill someone?'

He shrugs, waves the gun around a little. 'I don't think so. I just scared him off. I couldn't run anymore.' He pauses. 'Not everyone is in good shape like you.' He says it like it's a bad thing.

I try to focus. 'Did you recognize him? Was it the guy from the train?'

Spencer shakes his head. 'I only saw his shadow. No way could I recognize him in a lineup. Anyway, he kept coming toward me, like he thought the gun was a toy or something. I fired it to scare him. It worked. He ran.' He's still waving the gun around, and I take a step back, afraid that it's going to go off again and I'll be in the crosshairs. He notices and chuckles. 'I know what I'm doing.'

I'm not so sure. 'So where is he now?' I scan the darkness, worried that the mysterious stalker is going to surprise us because he's not done with us yet, despite Spencer's threat to shoot him.

'I don't know. He took off,' Spencer says. He reaches around and sticks the gun in his backpack. 'Let's go.'

I'm not going to argue. I don't think we're totally out of the woods yet, and I won't feel safe until we're far away from this place. But where, exactly, are we?

We're approaching the houses from behind. Lights are on inside; we can see people moving around. We're trespassing, and I'm not sure our presence would be welcome.

A dark shadow looms ahead of us, and the closer we get, I can make out its shape. It's one of those large wooden play-scapes, with a slide and swings and even something that looks like a fort.

'It's larger than that train compartment,' I mutter to myself, but notice now that Spencer is looking behind us. He grabs my hand and pulls me along. 'What's up?' I ask, turning to see what's got his attention.

Just as I do so, a bright light flashes and it's as bright as day.

SEVENTEEN

It's a motion sensor light, and we have walked right into its path. Problem is, we are exposed, but we can't see beyond the immediate area.

'Who's out there?'

The voice startles me, and all my muscles freeze. Spencer's expression must mirror my own, the fear etched in his eyes, his clenched jaw. For all our efforts, we are still discovered.

I don't see beyond the shotgun that appears out of nowhere, pointing in our direction.

'I said, who are you?' He steps into the light then, the large man behind his gun. He's wearing pajama pants and a plain white T-shirt.

'We were hiking,' I hear myself say. 'We got lost. We didn't mean to trespass.'

The gun remains leveled at my chest, and then it swings slightly so it's aimed at Spencer. 'Hikers?' He's dubious, as I would be, too, but we have to make it look good.

I'm glad again that I didn't give into Spencer's plea that I abandon my tattered backpack, and it's dark enough that his might not look quite so new. Our jeans and T-shirts and sneakers aren't exactly hiker couture, not to mention how sweaty we are from running. I'm also covered in dirt from my tumble, and Spencer doesn't look much better.

'We got lost,' I repeat.

Spencer does speak then. 'We wouldn't be here if it weren't for her.' He pulls away and stares at me. 'It's your fault.' The edge in his tone is unmistakable, and I'm thrown for a second, until I see him give me a wink. I stand up a little straighter, now aware of what he's up to.

'It is *not* my fault.' My tone matches his.

Out of the corner of my eye, I see the gun barrel lower slightly. This guy doesn't want to get caught in the middle of a couple's dispute, despite the fact that our story is completely ridiculous.

'I don't want to spend one more night with you.' Spencer's ratcheted up the game, and he pointedly stares at the man with the gun. 'Can you get me a cab? She can walk home.'

The gun barrel is now pointed at the ground. The man looks a little befuddled, clearly wanting to stay out of it. 'There aren't any cabs out here.'

'There must be an Uber,' Spencer says. 'Anything to get me away from her.'

'I don't know anything about Uber,' he says. 'But there's a place up by the highway where you could stay the night.'

'What about me?' I ask. 'You can't leave me here.'

Spencer shakes his head at me. 'Just watch me.'

A door squeaks, and a woman is peering outside. The man waves the shotgun in her direction. 'Go back inside. I'll be back.' He turns to Spencer. 'Come on.'

Spencer gives me a shrug as he follows the man around the

side of the house. I'm uncertain what to do. This was not my
plan. Do I have to walk to this 'place up by the highway'?
'Come on in, dear.' The voice comes from the door, which
opens a little further. I hear the roar of an engine and watch
as a pickup truck careens down the driveway and up the street.
He really did leave me here.
'It's OK now. You can come in.' The woman stands in the
doorway. She's wrapped in a plush pink bathrobe, her hair
mussed. 'He shouldn't have left you like that.'
No kidding. I follow her inside.
The house is warm and cozy, and she leads me into the
kitchen, which is old fashioned, with wooden cabinets and
laminate flooring that has seen better days. She indicates I
should sit at the table next to the wall. 'Tea?'
I nod. I have no idea how I'm going to get out of here.
'I'm Joan,' she tells me. Then adds, 'He'll take your man
to the bar for a drink.'
I am momentarily thrown by her referring to Spencer as
'my man' before taking in the rest of what she's saying. 'The
bar' isn't exactly Spencer's scene, and it might be interesting
to see how he does there.
'Why don't we have a cup of tea? Would you like to clean
up a little first?' Joan is bustling around the kitchen, filling a
kettle and setting out china teacups.
Where am I? It feels like an alternate universe.
I think again about the man Spencer scared away with
gunshots. Is he really gone, or did he see us in that spotlight?
Does he know that Spencer's gone off with someone? Does
he know I'm in this house?
'I think I will take you up on the offer to clean up,' I say.
Joan smiles kindly and, despite the shotgun, I am taken by
these strangers. 'Down the hall to your left.'
I scoop up my backpack and head for the bathroom. It's
small, with pale yellow tile on the walls and a black-and-white
checkered tiled floor. It's straight out of the fifties or sixties.
I drop the pack on the floor and, when I look in the mirror,
I'm horrified. There's a long red scrape across my cheek, just
below my glasses, and a bruise is starting to form within it. I
remember now that I landed on my face, but the adrenaline

rush was so strong. That's probably why it didn't faze me that much.

As I wash my face, I gently touch the wound and consider that this might be why Joan is being so kind. She probably thinks that Spencer did this to me.

I shed my dirty jeans and T-shirt, take clean ones out of my backpack and put them on. It feels good to wear clean clothes again.

I hear a buzzing inside the backpack, and I realize it's my cellphone. I dig it out, recognize the number and hold it to my ear. 'Hey.'

'Are you OK?' Spencer's voice is soft, as though he doesn't want anyone to hear.

'Yeah. I think she thinks you beat me.'

'Yeah, I know. He does, too. We're at some dive bar. He bought me a beer and told me that violence isn't the answer.'

I resist the urge to laugh. The idea of Spencer Cross being violent – despite the gun – is too funny. With all of the weed he smokes, he's probably the most mellow person I've ever met. Except when he's paranoid.

'How long will you be there?' I ask.

'I don't know. I'm in the men's room. I tried to get online but my router's out of juice. I wanted to see what d4rkn!te is up to.'

I stare at the backpack at my feet. 'Hold on.' I close the toilet seat and settle in, pulling the laptop out of the pack. I leave the water running, so Joan doesn't wonder why I'm in here so long. I boot the laptop up, and see that they've got an open network with no password protection. Maybe I can repay Joan for her kindness by securing her Internet connection.

While I don't have access to the remote access Trojan and d4rkn!te's computer, I can check out the chat room and see if he's here. A scan of the threads of conversations tells me that he is nowhere to be found.

'He's not in the chat,' I whisper.

'Do a search. See if you can find out the last time he was there.' Spencer's voice is even more hushed. I wonder how long he'll be able to hide out in the men's room before Joan's husband discovers he's missing. Or how long I can hide out here before Joan starts knocking on the door.

I maneuver through the chat room and find a list of screen names. I spot the last one I used, but I don't see d4rkn!te's name here anywhere. Something's not right about that. He *was* here. Spencer and I both saw him, and he's the one who put out the message with the French phrase in it. He posted that photograph of me.

And then he erased his presence. There's no sign of him.

I am so engrossed in what I'm doing that the knock on the door makes me jump.

'Are you all right in there, dear?'

I realize I never told her my name. 'Yes,' I say. My voice sounds too loud, and it bounces off the walls in the small room. 'I'll be right out.'

'Tea's ready when you are. Take your time.'

Despite her assurance that I can sequester myself in here as long as I'd like, that's not realistic. She will, at some point, demand that I emerge. And it's probably best to do it before it gets to that point. So I should get this done quickly. As I have already looked for d4rkn!te and not seen him, it shouldn't take much longer before I give up. I have only one more card up my sleeve.

I manage to get into the private chat log. I scan the screen names. Again, I don't see d4rkn!te.

But I do see a name I recognize.

Tracker.

EIGHTEEN

'Spencer,' I whisper. 'Are you still there?'

Silence on the other end tells me that he's long gone. I tuck the phone back in the front pocket of the backpack while still staring at the screen, unbelieving. Zeke's been here and, from looking at the time stamp, he was here only an hour ago.

An hour ago.

I am able to get into the archive of the chat, and when I see what transpired here, my hands begin to shake. There is no conversation; there are merely photographs. I see the familiar one of me boarding the train, but there are others. Me riding my bike at Folly Beach, coming out of Randy's gallery, sitting at the bar having a drink.

My heart is pounding, and the blood pulses through my ears. The photographs were posted by d4rkn!te, who seems to have a bird's-eye view of my life, even though I've taken so many pains to stay hidden.

The thought of that is enough to give me a panic attack.

I force the fear down as I concentrate on what's transpired. D4rkn!te lured Tracker to the private chat with the French phrase, just as he lured me earlier. Since they're no longer here, I don't have much hope of tracing IP addresses for locations, although they both have most likely used Tor and VPNs so I might not have had any luck anyway.

Another knock on the door startles me. That's right. Joan.

I shut the laptop cover and quickly shove it into the backpack. I turn off the water and flush the toilet, the pack over my arm as I open the door. Joan's expression is curious and I don't blame her, but I try to pretend that nothing's wrong.

'I'm sorry I took so long,' I say, touching my face where I've got the bruise.

Joan gives me a kind smile, and I am really sorry for the ruse. 'Do you want me to run a load of laundry for you?' she asks.

'No, you've done too much already.' I hesitate a second before adding, 'I'm Nicole.'

She doesn't ask for a last name, just says, 'Come on.'

I follow her to the kitchen, where she's set the teacups and some sort of baked loaf on the table. She cuts me a slice. 'Banana bread,' she explains.

I haven't had anything to eat in hours, and I take three slices. As I chew, I glance toward the window. Whoever followed us is out there somewhere. I may be safer here than anywhere else right now. Whoever he is might not risk trying to get to me.

Spencer is still out there, though, with Joan's husband. But he's got a shotgun, and it seemed like he knew how to use it, so Spencer's probably safe, too.

'Does he do that often?' Joan is asking.

I force myself to focus. She means does Spencer hit me. I shake my head. 'No. Never before.' I hate that I lie, but it seems the safest thing to do.

She gives me a sidelong look as though she doesn't quite believe me. 'Where were you two heading?'

I shrug. I still don't really know where we are. 'We followed the train tracks,' I say.

She looks at my tattered bag and then stares at my bruise a little too long. 'You don't have anywhere to go, do you?' she asks softly.

All of the stress of the last twenty-four hours finally hits me and I realize that I actually *don't* have anywhere to go. Tears begin to slip down my cheeks before I can stop them. I put my hands over my face as I try to regain some composure, but the more I do, the more I cry.

Joan reaches over and puts her hand on my forearm. I take a few deep breaths and finally the tears diminish.

'It's OK. You can stay the night here,' she says.

My glasses are a little fogged and tear-stained. I take them off and clean them with the edge of my shirt as I ponder the situation. It might be best to stay, although the stalker could be watching the house, so leaving tomorrow in the light of day may be risky. But if we left now, the darkness could be to his advantage and not to mine. It's a tough call.

The door swings open, and Spencer and Joan's husband come into the kitchen. Spencer gives me a curious look as he spots the teacups and crumb-filled plate in front of me.

Joan pushes her chair away from the table, tugs on her husband's arm and says, 'We'll go make up the spare room.' Her husband looks from Spencer to me, then back to Spencer. He nods, as though they have an understanding, and then follows Joan out of the room.

Spencer slides into the chair that Joan's just vacated. 'Ron says we should stay the night.'

'She thinks we're homeless.'

'We are.' He says it so matter-of-factly. 'I think it's a good idea. We can slip out early, before they get up.'

'What if they're the type to get up at four a.m.?'

'We'll figure it out,' he says impatiently. 'Did you find anything online?'

I quickly tell him about Tracker and the photographs and d4rkn!te.

'It's like I said before. When you answered the French phrase, he thought you were Tracker using another screen name. He didn't know it was you.'

'But he knows where I am. He followed us off the train.'

'We don't know that it's the same person. It could have been someone on the train who saw us jump off and came after us because we weren't supposed to do that.'

I consider that for a second. He's right. We have no idea who he was. 'What if you actually shot him?'

'You mean hit him? With a bullet?'

'Yeah.'

'I doubt it. I was too stoned. I didn't really see him; there was no aiming involved.'

'But what if you inadvertently hit him?'

He looks as though this had never really crossed his mind. One of his eyebrows rises into his forehead. 'Does it matter what happened? Either way, we're OK for now.' He pauses. 'Except I could really use some weed.'

I don't have time to admonish him, because Joan and Ron have come back in. Spencer and I get up, and he slings his arm around me. I stiffen slightly, then remember that we have to keep up appearances and allow myself to relax a little.

'We really appreciate this,' I tell Joan as she leads us toward the spare room.

We have to walk through the living room, and I take note of the cozy plush furniture. A line of photographs adorn the mantle of the brick fireplace, and it's all I can do not to stop and stare.

There's a picture of Ron. Dressed in his policeman's uniform.

I can't tell if Spencer's noticed it, and I certainly can't say anything, so I keep following Joan.

The spare room is painted bright pink, with white frilly curtains hanging over the windows.

'It was our daughter's room, before she left home,' she explains. She gives my arm a quick squeeze and another smile before stepping out and closing the door behind her.

The bed is a double, with a multicolored quilt that looks homemade. As I'm surveying the room, Spencer plugs his laptop and router into an outlet. He sits on the floor with the laptop on his lap, and opens it. 'Show me what you found,' he instructs.

If he'd seen the photograph of Ron, he might not be so relaxed. I'm not quite sure how to break it to him. I slide down next to him.

'Ron's a cop,' I say.

He barely reacts. 'Yeah. I know. Tell me what you did.'

'Thanks for letting me know.'

He frowns at me. 'I thought you knew.'

'How was I supposed to know?'

'Maybe she said something to you?'

'Well, she didn't,' I say. 'How did you find out?'

'Let's just say that I'm a little more than familiar with the boys in blue,' Spencer says. 'And there was a whole sea of them in that bar. Not exactly the most comfortable situation.'

'And you thought that this was a good idea? Staying here?'

'Probably the safest place for us right now. Sort of like flying right after a massive plane crash.'

It's not the most comforting thought, but he does have a point. As long as we're here, we've got unofficial protection.

Spencer's moved on from our conversation and is back staring at the laptop screen. 'I found the conversation after getting into the private chat archive,' I explain, and watch as he follows my footsteps.

When the photographs pop up on the screen, it's almost as though I'm seeing them for the first time. This is different than when the shadow was inside my laptop. This is someone who's watching me on the outside, someone who's physically close enough to take my picture and not have me notice him.

Suddenly the screen goes black, and I know what's happened, what I've forgotten. Spencer had inserted a rat into d4rkn!te's computer. He's inside now, searching for d4rkn!te's IP address. I hold my breath when he finds it.

He's here.

NINETEEN

Instinctively, I look up at the window. I can't see anything outside; it's pitch black. The light's on, though, and whoever's out there might be able to see in. I jump up and flick the switch so we're swathed in darkness except for the light from the laptop screen. Spencer scoots closer to the bed and closes the cover slightly to keep it from illuminating too much of the room. I lean in so I can see better.

'He can't really be *here*, can he?' I whisper. According to the GPS map that Spencer's pulled up, we are in a small town in North Carolina.

He's shaking his head, frowning. He doesn't understand it, either. 'Maybe he's rerouted the RAT so it looks like it's here.'

'Which means he's found out about the RAT. And if he rerouted it, then he might have been able to pinpoint our location and he knows where we are.' I think about the man in the woods. I clutch at Spencer's arm. 'We have to get out of here.'

'We can't be that hasty,' he says, distracted by something on his screen. I lean closer so I can see what he's doing.

He's no longer hooked into the Internet through his wireless router. He's inside Joan and Ron's Wifi network. I see exactly what he's up to.

He's managed to hack into Ron's phone.

But he doesn't recognize the app until I point it out. 'That one,' I instruct. It's the one that remotely controls the house's security system, including those motion detector lights that surprised us earlier. Spencer opens the app and, with just a touch on the screen, the security system is disabled.

It's really not a good idea to have a Wifi home security system for just this reason, although, even with a wired system, it's possible to use a radio frequency to hack in. It's a little more difficult, but not by much.

Still, even with the system disabled, we can't exactly go out through the front door. 'What are we going to do?' I look around the room and see the window as a possible escape.

'You worry too much,' he says.

He doesn't know that worrying is my favorite hobby. I think again about d4rkn!te. 'What does he want?' I ask, more to myself than to Spencer.

'D4rkn!te's got something to do with the carding forum,' he says. 'He's got ties to Tracker through the forum. You're a link to Tracker.'

I still don't really get it. I've been in South Carolina for the last six months. Zeke seems to have been in Paris.

'Whoever it is, he's using these pictures as some sort of leverage against Tracker,' Spencer adds. 'It's the only explanation.'

'Then we need to find out why.'

'Later.' He rolls up the power cords and stuffs them in his backpack. 'Let's get out of here first.' He scrambles to his feet and goes over to the window. He unlocks it and pulls it up. Cool air rushes in, and I wonder why I didn't think to bring a sweater or a fleece, then push the irrational thought aside.

He unhooks the screen and holds it sideways so he can slide it inside the room, until there's nothing between us and the night. I shiver again, thinking about whoever was out there, whoever might *still* be out there.

'Maybe we should just stay here,' I suggest.

Spencer shakes his head. 'We don't know who d4rkn!te is. What his connections are. He *might* be a fed, too, and the feds are the cops. Ron's a cop. We're not. I don't think we can trust anyone.'

He's right. We push both backpacks out of the window and hear them land with a thud. I put my leg over the windowsill and climb out. The ground isn't too far down, and I roll, hitting one of the backpacks. I scramble out of the way just in time to see Spencer come out after me.

We run through the side yard. While we've disabled the security system through the app, it's still a relief that no lights

flash and no alarms go off. I don't know why I even questioned
that it would work, but considering everything that's gone on
in the last twenty-four hours, it wouldn't have been a surprise
if there had been a glitch.

We zigzag through back yards. I keep an eye on the woods
behind us, but soon it's in the distance, too, just like Ron and
Joan's house.

'Where are we going?' I ask.

Spencer seems to be on autopilot. He keeps checking his
fancy GPS watch. 'This way,' he says when we reach a
road. It's not a side road, either, but a main one with four
lanes.

'Are you sure about this?' It's the middle of the night, and
I haven't seen any cars, but you never know who might be
lurking. D4rkn!te is out there, somewhere, or at least someone
who's connected to him. We can't get too far on foot.

And then I see that we might not have to. A bus is coming
toward us. Spencer begins to wave his arms, and the bus slows.
It's a large bus, a touring one.

'What's going on?' I ask.

'Trust me.'

I don't like trusting anyone, but I don't have much choice,
and if I must trust anyone, it's him. Especially after today.

He gives me a grin and waves his wrist at me. 'You really
need to get one of these,' he says about the watch. 'Pretty
amazing thing. Bus schedules and routes are all online.'

The bus is stopping next to us and the door opens. The
driver gives us a dubious look.

'Our car broke down,' I say when Spencer seems suddenly
taken mute. 'Can we get a ride?'

The driver looks out of the front window and then back at
us. 'Where's your car?'

'We left it back there,' I say, waving my hand absently
for good measure but not elaborating on where 'back there'
actually is. 'We didn't realize it would be so far to a town.' I
pause a second. 'We can pay.'

The driver gives me a curious look. 'You're not too far out,'
he says. 'I can take you, but if you want to go further, you'll
need a ticket.'

I scramble up the steps. 'No problem,' I say. 'Thanks so much.'

The bus is not all that crowded, but I make my way to the back, shrug off my backpack and fall into a seat. Spencer settles in next to me. He leans over and whispers, 'We don't have to get off at the next stop.'

I don't understand.

'Get some sleep,' he instructs, leaning back and closing his eyes.

'What's going on?'

He smiles, his eyes still closed. 'He's not immune to a little payoff. Let's just say that. No one will bother us until we get to Washington. So get some sleep.'

I shift a little to get more comfortable, staring out the window into the darkness. Just as I begin to nod off, I hear him say softly, 'I really could use some weed right about now.'

'Sorry.'

'No need to be.'

I feel his hand wrap around mine. It's warm, and I give it a squeeze.

TWENTY

When I wake, my neck is stiff and my shoulders ache. I shift in my seat and realize my feet have gone to sleep. I sit up straight and wiggle my toes, the pins and needles feeling getting a little less so with each movement. The sun shines on my face, and I blink a few times and wonder just how awful the lavatory on the bus will be, then decide that it doesn't matter.

It's right about now that I notice Spencer is not next to me. I remember hearing his snores at some point, but I don't recall him getting up. I must have been in a very deep sleep.

I put my hands on the back of the seat in front of me and pull myself up, scanning the bus passengers. Everyone is in his or her seat; I don't see Spencer anywhere. Maybe he's in the toilet.

But the *vacant* light is lit above the door.

A look under the seat and then above on the rack tells me that his backpack is missing as well.

My backpack is still under the seat, but now I see something different about it. The front pocket is unzipped and something's sticking out of it. I lean down and stick my hand inside, bringing out a passport. The photograph is me; the name on it is Elizabeth McKnight. This must be the passport that Zeke had Spencer arrange for me, in case I needed to make a quick escape.

But where is Spencer?

The bus jolts as it moves along uneven pavement, and I make my way to the front, to the driver who took Spencer's cash so we could go all the way to Washington D.C. without being bothered.

'Do you know where my friend went?' I ask him.

He glances back at me, and then back at the road. 'He got off.'

'Where?'

'Baltimore. I have to ask you to get back into your seat. We'll be coming up on D.C. shortly.'

'But did he say anything? I didn't know he was going to get off there.'

The driver's expression changes a little. 'Maybe you're better off without him,' he says. 'You can get a fresh start.' He pauses a second, and then, 'You really need to get back to your seat.'

I head back, but before sitting, I go into the lavatory. I stare in the mirror and see that the bruise on my cheek has spread and it's an ugly, angry purple. I suppose I don't blame Joan and Ron and now this bus driver for suspecting that Spencer did this to me. I might think the same thing if I were them.

When I get back to my seat, I pull the backpack onto Spencer's seat next to me. He left me the passport. Maybe that's not the only thing he's left behind. I rummage through the pack, taking out the cellphone. I hit the button and see that it needs powering up. I find the cord and plug it into the outlet that's in the armrest. The screen shines bright, and for a second I think that Spencer might have left me a message, but a search indicates nothing out of the ordinary.

I take my wireless hotspot router out, and then pull the laptop from its sleeve.

A piece of paper flutters out after it. It's folded in half, so I open it and something drops out. I lean over and pick it up. It's a credit card. In the name of Elizabeth McKnight. I read the sloppy scrawl: *Sorry, but we need to separate. I'll meet you in Paris in two days. Hotel Adele.*

I don't expect the rush of anger that floods through me. He left me here. Left. Me. Here. With someone following me. With someone stalking me, taking photographs of me.

I take a few deep breaths to try to calm down. It doesn't do any good to be angry, even though it's completely warranted, in my opinion. Instead, I focus on the credit card. I turn it over in my hands. It looks legitimate, but it can't possibly be. Elizabeth McKnight doesn't exist.

Spencer didn't do this while I slept. This was already set up. Even if he'd been able to get into a carding forum, there is no way he could have gotten a physical credit card made up and sent to him on the bus. No, he had this as well as the passport when I met up with him in Charleston. This plan had been already underway.

It was Zeke. He did this. It's like Spencer said. He arranged all of this before he vanished. He knew I might have to escape again. But did he know exactly why? Did he know someone would stalk me, send him photos of me, proving that he knows exactly where I am? Or was it just a good guess that something would happen that would necessitate documents like this? It's not as though I haven't needed them before. Zeke, as Tracker, helped me get out of the country as Amelie Renaud after the bank job.

Why exactly did Spencer leave me here? After all we've been through, now he decides that we have to separate? Does he know something I don't?

I fiddle with the phone, noticing something else. It's not just the passport and the credit card. I've got an app that's got all my flight information loaded into it. My flight to Paris out of D.C. is tonight at nine. A closer look tells me that I've got an Uber app and account as well.

Spencer and Zeke really did cover all the bases, didn't they?

For a second, I consider not going. I've been on my own for so long and this feels like I'm being controlled.

I could get off the bus in Washington and make my way somewhere else: New York, California . . . somewhere no one would find me. I'll leave my laptop and live off the grid. I have proven that I can make a living, that I can survive.

As tempting as it might be, I shake off the thought. If I do that, I will have to hide forever. And I will never see Zeke again.

So I guess I have to go to Paris.

I get to Union Station and hunt down the subway. It will take me to the airport. Sure, I could call an Uber, thanks to Spencer's thoughtfulness, but I'd rather hide in plain sight on public transportation. I've got a few hours before my flight, but I'd rather just get there and wait. Somehow it feels safer, although I am constantly on alert, watching my fellow subway passengers warily. Every time I see a phone pointed in my direction, I am anxious that there will be another photograph posted online and sent to Tracker – to Zeke – showing that I am merely an arm's length away.

At the airport, I check in at the airline's desk, my passport verifying my identity. I easily pass through security. I notice people giving me sidelong glances, but I think it's more the bruise on my face, because when I meet their eyes they quickly look away. No one says anything to me, no one questions. I am Elizabeth McKnight, another pseudonym in a long line of them. As I sit at the airport bar nursing a cognac, I feel nostalgic for all of those other identities and regret having to take yet another one.

When my plane boards, I discover that Elizabeth McKnight is able to afford first class. Spencer does seem to think of everything. Even though I'm still angry with him, I am surprised that I miss him. I miss his company. I'm distracted by the backpack and think about the laptop inside it. For the next several hours, I won't be able to go online. I'm completely disconnected.

I settle back in my seat and feel the plane begin to move beneath me.

TWENTY-ONE

I haven't been to Paris in seventeen years. When I was a child, my parents would send me to France every summer to spend time with my grandmother. She was a glamorous woman, with her short hair a la Audrey Hepburn in *Roman Holiday* and her bright red lipstick. She was tall and slender and had a graceful way of moving that I tried desperately to emulate but couldn't master. She never wore slacks, preferring dresses that accentuated her figure. We would always spend the first month in Paris; her apartment was in the Marais, in a building that was two hundred years old, with a courtyard and a balcony with a view of the rooftops surrounding us. She let me drink wine with dinner and taught me about art at the Louvre, the Musée d'Orsay and the Pompidou. We never went to the top of the Eiffel Tower because she thought it was too touristy and gauche. I loved her desperately, because she loved me back, and I was never quite sure that my parents even noticed me. She died when I was thirteen, a heart attack probably due to the number of cigarettes she'd smoked through the years. I felt her loss so palpably.

It's not a coincidence that I disappeared online the first summer I wasn't in Paris.

I step out of the metro station and drink in the scent of the city, and it's so familiar that I almost expect to see her standing by her black Rolls-Royce, smiling, waiting for me. The ache that rushes through me as I realize I'll never see her again is as new as when I was thirteen.

It's a relief, actually, that these are the memories that come to mind and not the ones from the last time I was here, when I was with Ian Cartwright.

It is morning, and the city is still awakening. I spot a café with outside tables and slide into a chair, my backpack tucked securely between my legs. I order a café au lait and a croissant and watch the Parisians stroll by. I have two days here

– no, make that one, because of the traveling time – before I'll see Spencer. I'm not sure when exactly he'll arrive or what time we're supposed to meet. He merely said at the Hotel Adele.

I take the cellphone out of the backpack and wonder if it holds any more secrets. It did have his number in it, but when I call now, it goes to a recording that tells me the number is no longer in service. I look in the notes and in the contacts, but there is no sign of any current information for Spencer.

I'm certain, though, that he does know where *I* am. I never did disable the GPS tracking that he'd installed. I could do that now, but I choose to drink my coffee and nibble at the croissant. I'm not even tempted at the moment to take out the laptop.

I am not exactly sure that I have a reservation at the Hotel Adele, but when I push the door open, approach the desk and give my name, I am greeted with a warm smile and handed a key card. There is no sign that the desk clerk is even remotely curious about my bruise, which is typically Parisian. I resist the urge to ask about Ryan Whittier; I don't know how I could explain my interest in him or how I even know about him. And in thinking about it, since he doesn't seem to actually exist, they might think I'm a little bit crazy. That hotel reservation could be as fake as he is, come to think of it. The back door in the reservation system was there for a reason. What if it was to create a fake reservation, especially since it was 'paid for' with a fake credit card?

I squeeze into the small elevator that holds only one person and ride up to the third floor. When I push the door open to my room, I am again assailed by thoughts of how much I've missed Paris. French doors open to a small balcony with some potted geraniums and a wrought-iron table and chair. I leave the doors open to hear the street sounds below.

I take a shower to wash the traveling away, and as I look at myself in the mirror, I put my fingers to the bruise gently, then adjust my glasses. My hair lies in wet ringlets against my head, and I rub a towel against it, the curls springing up. I don't have any clean clothes, so I again put on the ones I changed into at Joan and Ron's house. I'm sorry now I didn't take Joan up on her offer to wash for me.

I sit cross-legged on the bed and take the laptop out of the backpack. Time to get to work.

Being here has made me realize that I have to go back to the beginning, because this is where it all started. I can't concentrate on my stalker, the photographs of me. I have to go back further than that, to four months ago when Zeke was putting the skimmer on the ATM, when he got into Tony DeMarco's car. If I can find out what happened then, maybe I can find Zeke – and put an end to everything.

I wish I had Spencer's computer and the RAT, so I could get inside d4rkn!te's computer, but I don't. I have to use my own wits and skills. I know where to find d4rkn!te, and I need to find out about his carding forum and whether there are any clues to where Zeke might be. While it would be best to hang out in the chat room for a while and get to know d4rkn!te, I have to find a way to earn his trust immediately.

But I'm getting ahead of myself. If I can get into his forum, if he actually invites me, I will need bitcoin. Even if I don't buy a dump, I'll have to register and possibly pay a fee. The easiest way to get bitcoin is to set up a wallet through an app on my phone and then buy them. The credit card that Spencer left for me is going to come in handy more than I thought.

The Wifi connection here is spotty, so I take my wireless router out of my backpack. I'm going to have to power it – and the laptop – up, and there's one thing no one thought of: a power adapter.

I don't feel like going out again, but if I'm going to get anything done, I will need to find an electronics store. The BHV, or le Bazar de l'Hôtel de Ville, is a huge department store that's only a few metro stops away and will likely have what I need. I can get the metro at Concorde.

I don't want to leave my laptop in the room, but the back-pack is a little heavy. I unpack my clothes and toiletries, which makes it a little lighter. I've still got cash, and I exchanged some at the airport for euros. I don't have a debit card, so an ATM isn't an option. I need to make the cash last. I can use the credit card, I suppose, although I'm a little skittish about it, worried that when I use it, some cashier will be tipped off that it's fake. I wonder who's going to pay off that credit card bill. When I get the laptop powered up properly and I can get online, I'll check out the bank information, like I did with the one 'Spencer Cross' used here at the hotel. Granted, I'll probably hit a wall on this card, too, but it's worth trying.

This reminds me of something else. I use some data on my phone and call up the article about Ryan Whittier. I save his photograph, and I also have a picture of Zeke. Once downstairs in the lobby, I approach the desk. The clerk, a young woman in her twenties, smiles at me. Her brown hair is pulled back in a tousled ponytail and she wears no makeup. In the States, she might look sloppy, but with the scarf around her neck and the blue suit that hugs her figure perfectly, she is the ultimate in chic. I regret having to leave the new clothes on the train back in South Carolina, since my jeans, T-shirts and sneakers will mark me as an American, even though I'm speaking French.

'Excuse me,' I say, happy that my year in Quebec kept my language skills intact, despite the difference between Québécois and Parisian French. I hold up my phone with the photograph of Ryan Whittier on it. 'Do you recognize this man?'

The woman squints at the screen, then looks back up at me, a quizzical look on her face. 'Are you the police?'

It's a logical question, and one I did not anticipate because I'm shooting from the hip. I think quickly to give a convincing answer and decide on the truth. Or at least the truth as it's known on the Internet.

'No. He's a friend and he went missing here in Paris four months ago. He stayed here, so I thought maybe you might have seen him.' The only untruth here is that he was a friend, although it is merely a little white lie.

She shakes her head. 'No, I don't think so.'

It's not an unequivocal 'no,' which is interesting. I decide to press further.

'Were you working here then?' I ask, more than aware that I'm prying, that the French are not nearly as direct as Americans.

'Yes.'

'But you don't remember seeing him?'

Her eyes dart around the lobby, as though she is looking for someone. I can't pinpoint why, but I begin to get a bad feeling about this. And not because she doesn't remember him and is becoming suspicious of my questions.

'I am sorry, I don't remember him,' she says carefully, her tone guarded.

It's possible she's telling the truth. I'm sure a lot of people have stayed here in the last months, although probably not as many as would be here during high season. But something in her tone tells me that he might not be as much a stranger as she'd like me to think.

I've got some time, so I'm not going to push her on it. At least not now. I remember the photograph of Zeke, and I pull it up on my phone. 'Have you ever seen *this* man?'

She has resumed looking at her computer, and I hold it out so she can't pretend she doesn't see it. Her eyes meet mine. 'No, I'm sorry. Is there anything else I can do for you today?' Her words are polite, but I sense something beneath them, in her tone. And when I glance down at her hands on her keyboard, I see that they are shaking. She's scared.

TWENTY-TWO

Something has happened here at the Hotel Adele. I can't tell if she recognizes Ryan Whittier or Zeke or both, but I don't think I'm going to get anything out of her.

Instead of pressing the issue, I merely ask her if she can recommend a restaurant for lunch, and she directs me to one a few blocks away. 'No tourists,' she assures me, her expression clearly communicating that she's relieved I've stopped my questioning.

I smile, attempting to reassure her, then thank her even though she was lying about the tourists. This neighborhood is all about tourists. I head out, although when I get to rue de Rivoli, I get distracted when I realize where I am. The ATM is just to my left, the one that Zeke compromised with the skimmer. I find myself standing in front of it. I reach out and touch it, my fingers circling the area where you'd insert your card. Instinctively, I tighten my grip around the card reader and give it a yank, but it doesn't move. There's no skimmer on this machine. If there were, it would have been placed over the card reader. I peer closely and don't see any telltale glue.

I stand back when I notice an older man who thinks I'm using the machine. He begins to go to the machine's twin right next to it, but I haven't checked that one and I don't want him to use it if it's got a skimmer on it. I move in front of it and wave my hand to indicate that he should use the one I've already inspected. He hesitates, but since I'm now in his way, he doesn't have any choice but to use the other machine. I don't have an ATM card, and he might wonder why I'm here if I am not getting cash, so I make a show of rummaging around in my backpack as though I'm searching for my wallet.

The older man takes his money and scurries past me without making eye contact. He probably thinks that I'm going to steal his ATM pin code. I wouldn't have to stand behind him to get that. As it is, the camera just over his head probably captured every keystroke.

As soon as he's gone, I grab the card reader and twist.

The skimmer comes off easily in my hand. I turn it over to see the small motherboard and wires. If someone puts his card into it, it will read the magnetic strip and copy it. I run my fingers across the keypad and pause for a second. It doesn't feel quite right. It most likely is an overlay, one that will log the number entered and presses the real key underneath. It will definitely capture the pin number.

I'm a little surprised that the skimmer is on this machine, especially since Zeke was caught in the act of installing one here four months ago. Maybe he – or someone else – decided that the authorities might not check these machines again since they'd already discovered they were compromised.

I tuck the skimmer into my backpack. It will be harder for the hacker if he only has to rely on the keypad overlay.

I am trying to picture Zeke here, trying to understand exactly what he was doing. As a hacker, I find it odd that he would be putting skimmers on machines at all. He'd be behind the scenes.

My thoughts wander to Tony DeMarco. He's had his hands in a lot of different illegal activities through the years: kiddie porn sites on the dark net being only one of them. Why wouldn't he be tempted by the possibility of gleaning information from hundreds, thousands, of credit cards?

Spencer said Zeke was undercover with Tony DeMarco two years ago and working these carding forums. But again it strikes me that Tony knows he's FBI after Miami. Why would Zeke risk getting involved with him again?

I can't shake the feeling that Zeke's in trouble, that he's not quite as undercover as he was the last time.

My head hurts, although it's probably more that I'm tired from everything that's gone on in the last couple of days, the fact that I spent the night on an airplane and didn't get much sleep.

I cross the street, so completely engrossed in my own thoughts that I almost miss the metro entrance. I blink a few times and mentally slap myself. I go down the stairs and head to the kiosk where I buy a five-day metro pass. I don't know how long I'll be here, but a five-day pass seems reasonable. I find my way to the metro line that ends at Chateau de Vincennes, although I won't be going nearly that far. I'm only going a couple of stops to the Hotel de Ville.

The train pulls up, and the doors open. I step inside and find a seat that's facing the open doors. They begin to close, and that's when I see him.

Zeke. Outside on the platform.

TWENTY-THREE

I stand just as the train starts to move, and I lose my footing, falling back into the seat. I have looked away only for a second, and when I look back, all I see is darkness. I cross the car to the window, straining to see the platform we've left behind, but we're going too fast and are deep in the tunnel.

Could it really have been him? Or is it merely my exhaustion playing with my imagination? I've been thinking about him almost constantly since I arrived; it wouldn't be a surprise if I'd conjured him only because I want desperately to find him, to know that he's OK.

I close my eyes, and again I can see him standing outside the train. But now I begin to doubt; my eyes must have been playing tricks on me. The man on the platform was too thin, his hair a shade lighter. No, it wasn't him. It can't have been him.

I recall how I'd seen him in a casino in upstate New York after thinking he'd been long dead. I thought I'd seen a ghost.

The train rumbles beneath me as it speeds along the tracks. I am momentarily discombobulated. Why have I come here? Even though Madeline Whittier discovered me, I could have disappeared somewhere else; I could have continued my life as I knew it.

Except that the moment I saw Zeke's picture online, I wanted to find him. I have missed him, but I'd had no idea just how much until then. To be honest, it wasn't just about finding him. It was about the skimmer and what he might be doing here in Paris. It intrigued me and, after another long Internet absence, I craved the thrill that I get when I hack.

I had to do it again. And if it meant I could be reunited with Zeke, all the better.

But as I sit here, I am suddenly overwhelmed by sadness, by a premonition that I might never actually see him again. He might truly be that ghost I thought I saw not so long ago.

The train stops, and we are at the Louvre. I can't stay, trapped in this car, so I step out onto the platform and make my way above ground again, where the sun beats down on the pavement and I might have more hope.

I came out today with a mission to find a plug adapter and then go back to hotel where I could begin my online search for d4rkn!te and Tracker, but the glass pyramid of the Louvre beckons. It's been so long since I've been here; it's like a magnet drawing me toward it.

It's here that I saw the *Mona Lisa* for the first time with my grandmother. The painting is small, much smaller than I'd expected from the photographs in the books. Her face holds secrets; her smile teases, but she'll never tell. When I saw her, I understood her. I lived with secrets, too.

I wander the cobblestoned courtyard outside the museum, holding my backpack close to my side. I want to go in, get distracted, pretend for a little while that I'm just another tourist.

But I'm not.

I turn and go back down into the metro station. I need a plug adapter. Maybe two. I focus on that; it will keep me occupied.

I come back to the hotel from the department store with more than I expected. I have four plug adapters – something tells me Spencer will have forgotten about this tiny necessity, just like I did – as well as another pair of jeans and four tops. I also bought a couple of fashion scarves. Walking around the store reminded me that women in this city look chic without even trying, and even though they will most likely pinpoint me as an American right away, I can at least try to fit in a little.

I've tossed one of the scarves around my neck, and when I push through the door of the hotel, the woman at the desk looks up and gives me a smile. I have no idea if it's the scarf or the fact that I'm not grilling her anymore, but either way, she doesn't seem to be holding our previous conversation against me. While I still have questions, it might be best to hold off for now. I return the smile as I go toward the elevator and my room.

My smile and mood fade as I settle in on my bed and open my laptop. I use the new adapter and plug it in so it will power up while I'm working.

When I log into the chat room, I scan the screen names. I admit that I'm looking specifically for Tracker, to find out whether he's been here again, but I don't see him anywhere. I push down my disappointment, telling myself that it was unrealistic to expect him to be here. Still, I check archives and the private chat rooms to make sure that I'm not missing him anywhere.

Still nothing, though.

But I do spot someone I recognize.

D4rkn!te. And to my surprise, he asks me to join him in a private chat.

TWENTY-FOUR

'm leery of any requests, especially since the shadow infiltrated my laptop, yet I'm curious what he wants to talk to me about. He can't possibly know who I am. Again, I've logged in with a screen name I've never used, so there's no way anyone could know who I am or who I've been before.

But this could be my chance. He might invite me into the carding forum. My hopes rise. Perhaps I can do this without Spencer's help. The thought of showing him up is appealing. Serves him right for abandoning me on the bus.

Before I can respond to d4rkn!te, however, he disappears.

I stare at the screen, uncertain what's going on. Is he playing games, or has he vanished because of something outside this world? Back in the day, when I was a teenager, there were times when I had to shut down unexpectedly because my father walked in the room or my mother demanded my attention. There could any number of reasons why d4rkn!te would do the same thing.

It bothers me, though. This is the same person who posted those images of me. Does he somehow know who I am behind the screen name? Is he doing this on purpose to unnerve me?

I shake aside the thoughts. There is no possible way he could know who I am. I am too paranoid. But the idea that he might nags at me.

I begin to wonder just who *he* might be.

He lured Tracker into a private chat and posted those photographs of me, so even if he doesn't know who I am online in the chat room, he does know Tina Adler – and he knows about my relationship with Tracker.

If he knows that much, then it's more than likely he knows

that Tracker is FBI Agent Zeke Chapman and he is even more dangerous than just someone who's running a carding forum. He may be linked to Tony DeMarco, who wants both Tracker and me dead. Using those pictures, d4rkn!te might have enough leverage for Zeke to come out into the open.

I wish that I had that remote access Trojan on this laptop rather than on Spencer's. I want to know what he's doing when he's not here. I remind myself that I don't need Spencer. That I have been hacking a long time without him and can do this on my own perfectly well.

My confidence rises as I devise a plan. Before I was distracted by the lack of a plug adapter, I was about to set up a bitcoin wallet in order to be prepared when I get into the carding forum. I push the laptop aside and take the cellphone out of the backpack.

Fortunately, bitcoin wallet apps seem to be free. I'm a little uncertain, though, about which one might be the best, so I spend a little bit of time reading reviews. I'm procrastinating. I finally choose one and download it, watching the little circle fill in on the screen. I'm watching the phone with one eye and the laptop with the other. My thoughts stray to d4rkn!te. He disappeared, but the more I think about it, he might not be gone.

It's not easy getting into the source code of the chat room; hackers have devised a lot of firewalls to keep someone from doing what I'm trying to do. But it's not impossible. And after a little poking around, I discover that I can access the php files, which will give me access to the databases. This isn't standard. In fact, it's as though someone *wanted* the site to be hacked. So while it's not impossible, for some reason, right now, it's incredibly easy.

First I navigate to the database that lists all the screen names, or user names. Whenever someone signs into the chat room, he or she has to pick a name, and the database will search to see if it's unique. If it isn't, then the person has to choose another one; if it is, then he's good to go. If someone hasn't been in the chat room for a while, his name's removed after a certain period of time passes. The screen names I used two years or even a year ago should be erased by now.

Except one isn't.

'Tiny' is still listed.

I stare at the name on the screen, a chill shimmying up my spine. Granted, someone else must have chosen it, but it's not very creative, not like the others. 'Tiny' was a throwback to the years before the Internet really exploded, before I knew better. It's the name that Tracker always knew me by. I haven't used 'Tiny' in seventeen years.

I check when Tiny was last in the chat room. This morning. I can't explain why I'm curious, except that something doesn't sit right with me, considering everything that's gone on in the last couple of days. I don't hold out much hope that I can find out Tiny's IP address, since everything's circumvented by Tor and VPNs, but when I get deeper into the code, I see it. This shouldn't be possible, but I make a copy and switch to an alternate screen where I can search for the location.

My curiosity and suspicion is justified.

The IP address is here. In Paris.

I tense up, then jump off the bed and cross the room, making sure that the door is locked. I turn and scan the room as though someone is going to jump out from the bathroom, from the balcony outside. This is just like when d4rkn!te was supposedly at the same address when Spencer and I were in North Carolina. No one would have known where we were, just as no one knows I'm here now except Spencer. I'm not using my real name; I'm not using a screen name I've ever used before. So how can the screen name I hid behind all those years still be active and originate from the city I'm in right this very moment?

It can't be a coincidence that 'Tiny' has an IP address in Paris.

I was hidden in Charleston until I met Madeline Whittier. But someone was watching me. Photographing me. I have not been as hidden as I thought. Maybe I'm not as shrouded online, either. It was easy to think that d4rkn!te had turned the tables on our remote access Trojan and traced us to our IP address, but I'm not using Spencer's laptop now. I don't have access to the RAT, and there is no way d4rkn!te could discover my true identity behind an obscure screen name.

Unless he followed me here as stealthily as he followed me around Charleston, around Folly Beach, and he's been watching me all along. He knows who I am, that I'm online, and he's trying to unnerve me by using the name 'Tiny.' He might not know that I'm already unnerved, having found the photographs. They were not meant for me.

They were not meant for me. They were meant for Zeke, for Tracker. What if using my screen name is meant for him, too? What if this is still more about him than about me?

I sit up straight and pull the laptop closer. Tracker was in the chat room earlier.

I go through the same steps I did to find Tiny, and there he is. But not where I expected, which is also here in Paris. Tracker is in New York City.

What if my trip here was in vain? What if Zeke really isn't here at all? I shake off the thought. IP addresses aren't always what they seem to be. The Tor software causes IP addresses to jump from one place to another so users can maintain their anonymity. So that their locations cannot be pinpointed.

And yet Zeke *was* in Paris. At least four months ago. Granted, he's had plenty of time to get back to the States – or anywhere else, for that matter. Maybe I should have stayed put and waited for him. He was in touch with Spencer, and Spencer knew how to reach me – and vice versa.

I shake the thoughts away. It's too late now. I can't go back in time, so I might as well see what I can find while I'm here.

Despite the fact that I've dismissed the accuracy of the IP addresses, I can't help myself. I look for d4rkn!te. He is not in Paris. According to the program, he is in Omaha. While this is most likely wrong, it gives me a false sense of security.

Even though I still want to find out more about the Tiny who has been visiting the chat room with my name, I'm realistic enough to know that I probably won't find much more about her – or him. And it might just be a coincidence that he shares my old screen name. I don't exactly have a monopoly on it. I try to focus on the reason why I came to the chat room in the first place: to get an invitation to the carding forum, where I hope to run into Tracker.

I wonder if I shouldn't devise a clue for him, so that if it really is him, he'll know that it's me on the other side of the screen. I can't use the French phrases; too many people seem to know about those and they've been used against us. The easiest way to get his attention is through another screen name, but I'm hard-pressed to think of one that will jog his memory and make him think of me – and one that won't make anyone else think twice, too.

It's at moments like these that I realize just how little time Zeke and I have actually spent together. Most lovers have pet names for each other, but we haven't even reached that point. I'm not sure, though, that's really who we are, anyway.

Suddenly, I think of something. He once directed me to a dark web site called The Waste Land, which was also the title of a poem. His knowledge impressed me. I wonder how versed he is in poetry.

I don't want to use 'The Waste Land', because there are too many people who are familiar with the dark web site, so I need a different poem. I can't make it too obvious, but Zeke does know my fondness for islands. I do a simple Internet search and find something that might pique his interest if he's lurking. My fingers hover over the keyboard as I read the first line: 'No man is an island.'

This by itself, though, might not give him enough of a clue that I might be behind the message. I log off the chat and sign back in, using a new screen name: TSEliot, the poet who wrote 'The Waste Land'.

It's a long shot, I know, and maybe it's a little too obtuse, but it's the only thing I can think of, so I type the first line from the John Donne poem in a public message, and wait.

TWENTY-FIVE

The sun is peeking through the window, casting shadows on the floor when I awake. I never even really went to bed, merely settled back on the pillows and closed my eyes, the exhaustion of travel overwhelming me. I glance at the clock and see that I've been asleep for more than twelve hours. I did not have dinner; I'm still wearing my jeans and T-shirt. The laptop is attached to the power cord. While I am anxious to know whether my ploy worked and Tracker has responded to me, I shove it aside and head into the bathroom. It's been hours, so a little more time isn't going to make any difference. I take a quick shower, brush my teeth, use my fingers to comb my hair. I peer into the mirror. Despite the bruise on my cheek, I look rested. I should.

My stomach growls, and I pad out into the main room wearing only a towel. The French windows are still open, and the cool morning air washes over me. The rooftops are a familiar sight, and I am at once content with my surroundings.

The bags that I brought back from the department store are untouched in the corner. I pull on a pair of jeans and slip a new top over my head. I also bought a pair of more stylish canvas shoes, so I can abandon the sneakers that are a bit worse for wear since the jump off the train and race through the woods. It isn't only my face that's bruised.

Since the laptop is fully powered up, as well as the wireless router, I unplug them and put them into the backpack, slinging it over my shoulder. I can be patient a little longer. I attribute this to the fact that I am not unaccustomed to living without a computer. Seventeen years ago, I would certainly not have had this type of self-control.

I toss one of the new scarves around my neck as I head out.

There is a different person behind the front desk now, a young man with a mop of dark hair that flops over his forehead and into his eyes. He wears a crisp white shirt and a suit jacket. I consider pulling out the photographs to ask him about them, but my stomach growls. It will have to wait until after I've eaten something.

The sidewalk is bustling; the cars and buses whiz past me on the street. I am famished, and I duck into the first café I see. There are tables and chairs out front, and I find an empty one that faces the sidewalk so I can watch people walk by. I am barely seated when the waiter comes out and offers me coffee. I order a café au lait and croissant. I may need two croissants. And two coffees. At least.

I take out the wireless router and set it up before I open the laptop. I don't trust anyone else's Wifi, and my router is password protected so no one can jump into my network. I find my way to the chat room just as my coffee and croissant arrive. I take a sip of coffee as I peruse the messages.

There has been a lot of activity since I fell asleep last night, but I don't need to weed through any of it. I am able to narrow down what I see by my own screen name. I spot the message I left, and I get a tingle when I see that someone has responded. I click on the message.

It's not Tracker. He wouldn't engage with me using that name, but still I'm disappointed. Instead, it's someone called Z3r0.

He's written something puzzling: *Every man is a piece of the continent.*

Wait a minute. I toggle screens and find the poem. This is the next line. I have either found Zeke or someone else who apparently knows the poem and is playing along with me. Who knows which. I'm uncertain what to write next, scanning the lines to see if there's anything that might continue this odd intrigue, but nothing jumps out at me. I don't understand it; I'm not one for poetry or literature or even sweet nothings. My idea of flirtation is sharing code, but you can't do that with just anyone.

It doesn't really matter anyway. Z3r0 has not been online for the last four hours. I was fast asleep when he continued the poetry recitation. But maybe it's worth continuing. I type in the next line.

If a clod be washed away by the sea, Europe is the less.

I see a woman at the next table with a small baguette covered in butter and strawberry jam and wish I'd ordered that instead. While I'm coveting her breakfast, I take another drink of my coffee and a big bite out of the croissant. The buttery, flaky pastry melts on my tongue, and I no longer regret my choice.

I feel myself relaxing as the hunger pangs are satiated, and

I'm no longer glued to the laptop screen. Paris is bustling, and the familiar smells and sounds comfort me. For the first time since I met Madeline Whittier, I am relaxed.

Until I look at the screen again.

All my muscles tense as I see that Z3r0 has materialized. He greets me with: *Any man's death diminishes me.*

I need to determine whether this is Zeke or merely someone with a poetry fetish. Before I can respond, another message pops up: *You like John Donne?*

I'm not a poetry reader, I write. That was Zeke's observation when he told me about The Waste Land site, and I can only hope that if this is Zeke, he'll remember the conversation and know that it's me behind the screen name.

He doesn't write another message, but a URL to a private chat room appears on the screen. I don't trust it. I don't trust *him*. It's too easy to get a remote access Trojan and insert it into the code, like Spencer did with d4rkn!te.

As I'm pondering the situation, drinking my coffee, Z3r0 adds: *What do you see?*

The words jar my memory. This is exactly the question Tracker would ask me when we first met, and even last year when we were hacking together again, he couldn't help but continue to be the mentor by asking me what I saw in the code. Is Z3r0 actually Tracker, or is this turn of phrase just a coincidence? I so desperately want it to be him. I want that connection again, even if it's online. That's all it was for years anyway.

I put my fingers on the keyboard, but I let them rest there, my head spinning. I left that message for him, and now I'm playing coy. No. I'm safeguarding myself. I'm protecting my identity, protecting my whereabouts.

Give me a URL.

He knows I'm hesitating. He knows I don't trust him. *He's* trusting *me*. He's trusting that I'm not going to put a remote access Trojan in the URL I give him. Does that prove he didn't put one in his message?

I don't want to test it. I send him a link, and even though for a moment I consider a RAT, I don't do it. Even if it's not Tracker – Zeke – there's something about Z3r0.

We both arrive in the private chat room at the same time. There are a million questions I want to ask, but I need to take it slow. I need to determine who Z3r0 is before I let my guard down. But he's one step ahead of me.

I'll never forget the first time I saw you on that chaise lounge at your father's house. Remember what we did the next day?

I catch my breath. FBI Agent Zeke Chapman first came to my house in Miami when I was twenty-five. I was outside by the pool when he arrived. I thought he was there about my father – since he'd been in prison, the FBI came around from time to time to keep an eye on things – but later I found out he was there about me. He knew I'd stolen the ten million from the bank, but I didn't know he knew. I also didn't know he was Tracker, who had helped me steal that money.

Both of us had been more than a little in love with the idea of each other ever since we met online when we were teenagers.

While this is enough for me, his question shows that I have to prove who I am. He suspects that it's me, but he needs to know definitively.

We went to the beach on your 1983 Goldwing, I type. He'd refurbished it himself.

Are you safe? he writes, making it clear that I've passed the test. But he's still wary and unwilling to identify himself or me any further. We don't know if anyone's spying on us. I've gotten into the private chat rooms unnoticed before; someone could be in here with us. Neither of us will take it for granted that we are alone.

Yes, I write back. *And you?*

I've been better.

Can I help? I ask.

This is the best thing you can do.

I take a deep breath, my coffee now cold, the rest of my croissant uneaten on the plate. *Let me be the judge of that,* I write.

There may be something you can do, come to think of it.

The waiter comes over and asks if I want another café au lait, and I nod. I nibble at the rest of my croissant, wondering what Zeke needs of me.

I don't have to wait long.

A link appears.

What's that? I ask.

It's an official invitation, is the response.

I assume it's not to Buckingham Palace.

No. It's to a carding forum.

TWENTY-SIX

Z eke doesn't know that I know about the ATM skimmer. That Spencer and I already figured out that he might be part of the carding forum.

What do you want me to do? I write.

You'll know once you get there.

It's very cryptic, but I admit to being intrigued. He doesn't have to know that Spencer and I were trying to figure out how to get such an invitation not so long ago, and here it is, falling right into my lap. The only thing I'm a little concerned about is the illegality of it. While the statute of limitations has run out on the bank job, if I commit another crime, it's possible it could come back to haunt me. Zeke is the one who told me what the repercussions could be, which means he might really be in trouble and somehow the carding forum is the only way he sees that I can help. He wouldn't put me in jeopardy otherwise.

Still, I can't figure out how a carding forum is going to help him. But it doesn't hurt to try. Spencer will be all over it, too.

I wonder when he's supposed to arrive today.

I've got to go. Zeke's words pull me out of my thoughts.

Where? I can't help but ask.

Just go to the link.

And then he's gone.

I stare at the screen, willing him to come back. I'm not ready to say goodbye. I make sure to bookmark the John Donne poem. I may end up using it again, since it was an effective way to identify myself.

I finish my second cup of café au lait. Between that, the hours of rest I finally got, and the adrenaline from my contact with Zeke, I'm ready for anything. But I remember Spencer again, how he's coming in today.

I've kept my phone tucked inside the front pocket of the backpack, but I fish it out and check the messages.

'Meet you at eleven at the hotel.' Spencer's voice sounds very far away, like he's talking inside a tunnel.

I glance at my watch and see that it's almost eleven now. The waiter has left the check on the table and I count out some euros and tuck them under my plate. As I'm packing up the backpack, a shadow looms over me. The sun is in my face, so I shield my eyes and look up at the silhouette of a man in front of me. I stop breathing for a second.

But then: 'Nice to see that you're enjoying yourself.'

Spencer drops down into the seat across from me, setting his own backpack next to mine. He's continuing with the clean-shaven look, and it even looks as though he's gotten another haircut. I sort of miss the ponytail. He wears a black T-shirt and a pair of jeans.

'You're looking very Parisian,' I say.

He gives me the once-over. 'Look who's talking.'

'OK, so I bought a couple of new things. We have to fit in, right?'

The waiter reappears, a question knit into his forehead. Spencer points to my cup. 'I'll have one of those,' he says.

'Do you want something to eat?' I ask.

'What's good?'

I tell the waiter in French to get us more café au lait – at this point I won't sleep again for days – and baguettes with jam and butter. He nods and moves away. Spencer is frowning.

'You really do know French.'

'What, you thought I only knew those two phrases Zeke and I used in the chat room? I spent summers here when I was a kid.'

'Yeah, I guess I knew that, but it's different seeing it. Hearing it. Hearing you speak.' He's a little all over the place, but

I chalk it up to the fact that's he's not stoned, and that's not his usual state.

I give a wave of my hand. 'Never mind that. I've got some news.' I proceed to tell him about the conversation I've just had with Zeke in the chat room. As I speak, his eyes grow wide and he leans forward, folding his hands together on the table.

'So did you check out the link?' he asks when I'm done.

'No. I was just getting ready to go meet you. I figured we could do it at the hotel.' I pause. 'I'm not really sure what he thinks we're going to find.'

The waiter comes back now, puts the coffee and bread on the table and discreetly moves away.

'I can't believe you let me order food and coffee and you're sitting on this the whole time,' Spencer says, but despite his protests, he puts jam and butter on one of the small baguettes. '*Now* I'm in Paris,' he says when he's devoured it in three bites. 'Why can't anyone else in the world make bread like this?'

It seems that both of us are distracted. It's probably the jet lag.

'Why did you leave me in Baltimore?' I ask.

He cocks his head to one side and narrows his eyes at me. 'Whoever was looking for us was looking for two people traveling together. I knew you'd be OK on your own, and I had a few things I had to take care of before I left the country.'

He doesn't elaborate, and I'm curious but I don't ask.

'Do you get a bill here?' he asks a little too loudly, finishing the last of the bread.

'Don't be an ugly American,' I hiss, tucking more euros in with the others I've already put under my plate. I stand and begin to walk away, not waiting for him. I hear his chair scrape against the pavement as he gets up and his heavy footsteps as he falls into step next to me.

'Now you're in a hurry?' he asks.

'I thought you wanted to check out that link Zeke gave me,' I say. All the coffee and the aforementioned jet lag have made me a little snappish. 'Sorry,' I add.

He shrugs. 'Guess a few minutes longer doesn't matter.'

Just before we reach the hotel, though, I stop short, and put my hand out to indicate he needs to stop, too.

'What?' he asks.

'Are we supposed to be together? I mean, are we supposed to let on that we know each other?'

Spencer's eyebrows rise and he nods. 'You've got a point, but I don't know that it matters. We traveled separately. Do you think you were followed?'

'Beats me.' I haven't noticed anyone following me, but I haven't been paying attention. I suddenly remember the man on the metro platform, the one who for a second reminded me of Zeke, and I shrug off the memory. That was my head playing tricks on me. 'If someone's following me, if someone's following you, they already know we're here,' I say.

'That's right. So I think it's OK we're staying at the same place.' He pauses a second. 'I've got my own reservation. My own room.'

That reminds me: 'If we're supposed to know each other, then maybe you should tell me what name you're traveling under. You already know I'm Elizabeth McKnight, but who are you?'

Spencer's mouth spreads into a wide grin, and he holds out his hand. I take it after a moment's hesitation. 'Maxwell Wellington. Max for short. Pleased to meet you.'

I can't help myself. 'That's not a great name, you know.'

'And you know this, how?'

'Because I've made it my business to come up with very ordinary, very forgettable aliases over the last several years. And "Maxwell Wellington," I say, using finger quotes, 'is going to draw attention to himself.'

'I don't think "Elizabeth McKnight" is very forgettable,' he mutters.

He's got a point. I'd asked Tracker to get documents for me using that name when I was planning to leave Block Island two years ago. I was supposed to pick them up in New York City's Chinatown but never got there. I wonder if Zeke's been sitting on them all this time.

We're standing in front of Hotel Adele. Spencer cranes his

neck and gazes at the ornate architecture. 'All these buildings look alike,' he says. 'I miss Miami.'

'And nothing there looks alike,' I say sarcastically, pushing the door open. 'Welcome to Paris, *Max*.'

I head up to my room while Spencer checks in. About fifteen minutes later, I hear a knock on the door. Spencer saunters in. He's shed the black T-shirt and is wearing one that tells me to get stoned and carry on. His hair is wet from a recent shower and sticking up on top of his head. He's wearing a grungier pair of jeans and a pair of red high-tops. Max is gone. Spencer is back.

I've got my laptop open on the bed.

He cocks his head at it. 'Did you click on the link?'

I shake my head. 'No, I waited for you.'

His eyebrows rise high in his forehead. 'That's a lot of self-restraint.'

I'm not about to tell him that I've been mentally paralyzed since I got back to my room. I've replayed my online conversation with Zeke over and over in my head as I've gazed out over the rooftops of Paris. I want more than anything to see him, to feel his arms around me. After all those years of a virtual relationship, I am now craving the physical one we'd only just discovered before we separated.

Spencer puts his own laptop on the bed before opening mine. The screen springs to life. I've already put the link into the search bar, but I haven't clicked on it. I reach over Spencer's shoulder and point at it.

'That doesn't look right,' I say.

He peers more closely at it. 'You say this is the link he gave you? To a carding forum?'

'I cut and pasted it straight out of the chat.'

He looks up at me. 'You know what that is, right?'

I do, but I wanted a second opinion and it seems I've gotten it.

It's a remote access Trojan.

TWENTY-SEVEN

'**A**re you sure that it was Zeke?' Spencer is asking.
I nod. 'Absolutely. It was him.'
'If we click on this link, he'll have access to your laptop.' Spencer doesn't have to tell me this.

I think about this for a few seconds, and an idea forms. 'Maybe that's the idea.'

'What are you talking about?'

'He said that if I click on the link, I'd understand. Maybe he wants to get into my laptop because he can communicate with me that way. He can use the message app and send me messages. Like the shadow did last year.' The more I think about it, the more I think this is exactly what Zeke had in mind. Spencer and I can get into the carding forum and we can be in touch with Zeke at the same time. Zeke and I were always in sync; it was like we could read each other's minds back when I was Tiny and he was Tracker. Why would this be any different?

Spencer's looking at me warily. 'Are you *sure* it was him?' he asks again. 'Because we don't want to let just anyone in here.'

He's starting to give me doubts. I'd been so sure just a moment ago, but maybe it's like that guy I saw on the metro platform. I thought it was Zeke, but when I looked a little more closely, I realized he wasn't.

But he knew about the chaise lounge. Would Zeke have told someone about that? I give a sidelong glance at Spencer. He might tell Spencer, but someone else? It reminds me yet again how Zeke and I have known each other forever, but we don't really *know* each other. I know more about my friend Steve on Block Island than I do about the man I love. There's something so wrong with that.

Which is why I have to believe this is Zeke. I have to go with my instincts, and everything inside me is telling me that it's him. I don't doubt for a moment that he's discovered the way into my life again is through a remote access Trojan. For some reason, he can't reveal himself to me in any other way.

'It's him,' I say decisively to Spencer. 'Let's do it.'

He holds up his hand. 'One thing first.'

I know what he's going to say. 'We need a bitcoin wallet. Because if we're going into a carding forum, we might need to pay a registration fee or maybe even buy something.' I'm feeling very uncomfortable. As much as I want to reconnect with Zeke, buying credit card information online is like stealing bank account numbers, and I've been there and done that.

But a bitcoin wallet isn't what Spencer was alluding to. Instead, he's making sure that there isn't anything in the laptop that we wouldn't want anyone to find. We also need to make sure that the IP address – our location – can't be discovered somewhere in the hardware. We need a firewall.

Spencer's already gotten out the portable router. In order to be protected, we have to hook into other networks; the router's firewall will protect us by making whoever's on the other side of the remote access Trojan think that we're somewhere we're not. While I don't know that I'd mind Zeke knowing where we are, we can't be sure that someone else isn't also on the other side of this RAT. Better safe than sorry.

When we're done setting it up, we check the software. We need Tor and the VPN, but everything else gets wiped clean.

'Wish I had that degausser now. I'd clear the hard drive,' he says, referring to the machine we used in Charleston to wipe his hard drives before we escaped.

Was that only a couple of days ago? It seems like it was forever.

Before I know it, Spencer's opened the link Zeke gave me. We both watch the laptop, as though Zeke is going to jump right out of it and shout 'boo!'

But nothing happens. Instead, we are at a sign-on page. We do have to register, and there is a fee. I shouldn't be surprised that Spencer's got a bitcoin wallet all set up. He sees me watching him closely.

'What?' he asks.

'Where do you get your money?'

Spencer grins. 'I made a shitload of money a long time ago, and I've got a very good financial adviser who knows what he's doing.'

I think about his house in Charleston. 'But it's not in your name, is it?'

'What do you think?'

Of course it's not. He's probably got everything protected by a company that can never be linked to him in any way. 'But you have access?'

The grin widens. 'There's no point in having it if I can't get my hands on it.'

I realize something now. 'You're not stoned.' I've never seen him completely sober.

'Not so easy getting my hand on weed here, but I've got a connection,' he says absently as he navigates the carding forum. He glances up at me. 'You want in?'

I shake my head. 'No. With my luck, I'll end up getting caught.'

'You never get caught,' he says. 'So I don't even know what you're talking about.'

I don't remind him that I was found on Block Island, which is why I ended up in Canada, where Zeke found me. Maybe I didn't get caught by the authorities, but I did get caught.

'We're in,' Spencer says, interrupting my thoughts. He scrolls through the exchanges, and I'm overwhelmed with the choices.

'What do we do now?' I ask.

'We look for d4rkn!te.'

He makes it sound so easy and, as I watch over his shoulder, it *is* easy. It's like the chat room, which is all too familiar and soon we are navigating the forum, taking note of the different screen names, but we don't see d4rkn!te anywhere.

I reach over and pull the laptop closer to me. 'There's got to be a way to get into the code, find out who's running this show.'

Spencer gives me an amused expression, and if he had one, he'd probably light a joint right about now. Instead, he merely lets me take over. The screen fills with code, and I scan the lines, looking for any clues, but nothing jumps out at me.

I look back at Spencer, who's leaning against the headboard behind me.

'I don't know—'

Spencer startles me by suddenly jerking forward, his eyes wide, his mouth a perfect 'O.'

A message has popped up.

You're not going to find anything that way.

We stare at each other, then back at the screen.

Who are you? I type.

Jesus, Tina.

My heart beats faster. It's Zeke. *Where are you?*

There are some things I can tell you, and some things I can't. Trust me. I'm OK. How are you? Is Spencer with you?

A million emotions are rushing around inside me, and I can't focus. Spencer notices and he types: *Dude.*

You taking care of her?

You know I am.

You stoned? Zeke asks.

Spencer's reputation precedes him. *Not today.*

Really?

Really.

Tina, you taking care of Spence?

I put my fingers on the keyboard. *Yeah. And he's really not stoned. Can you tell us what's going on?*

I need your help.

For a moment, I think that Zeke has left because there's a delay, but then he types: *I need you to put a skimmer on an ATM.*

TWENTY-EIGHT

A million thoughts circle around in my head and I'm not quite sure how to react – or what to say.

Spencer, however, isn't quite so tongue-tied. *Dude. That's more your thing, isn't it?*

What do you mean? is the reply.

We saw an article online about a missing kid that had a picture of you, Spencer types, *so we know about the skimmer and that the police were looking for you. Who is Ryan Whittier, anyway? We know he never went to Charleston College. Do you have anything to do with him going missing or was it just wrong time, wrong place?*

A few seconds go by. *What else do you know?*

He isn't answering our questions. Spencer isn't going to push him on it, though. *Someone's been taking pictures of Tina and blackmailing you with them. But we don't know why.*

You've been busy.

Who is d4rkn!te? Do you know? I ask.

I can't tell you anything right now. Can you trust me enough to help me?

I want to, I really do. But putting a skimmer on an ATM? Again, I'm worried about the criminal element of all this. I tell myself that Zeke's FBI, so maybe it's OK. Is it?

Spencer doesn't seem to be having the same inner turmoil that I am. He's already typing. *Tell us what we need to do.*

I put my hand over the keyboard. 'Are you sure about this?'

'Aren't you?' He is genuinely perplexed by my reaction, and I can't blame him. Until this moment, I have been willing to jump off a train and fly to Europe under an alias in order to track Zeke down, and now I'm waffling.

'I want to know more before we do this.'

'I don't think he's going to tell us any more. Something's going on. We have to help.'

The message appears on the screen: *It's OK, Tina. I wouldn't ask if it wasn't important.*

How does he do that? How does he know exactly what I'm thinking?

Spencer's responding to him. *I've got to step away for a few minutes.* He turns the laptop toward me. 'I'll be back in a few.' And he gets up and leaves the room, shutting the door quietly behind him.

I'm alone – with Zeke online. Like all those times so long ago. Every day for months – years, actually – we connected online in the chat rooms. We were almost like one person, each of us finishing the other's thoughts.

Tina?

I'm here, I type.

Take the tape off the camera.

I reach toward the screen and gently peel it off, exposing myself.

I miss you.

Me, too.

I'm sorry you had to leave the beach. I know how much you love the ocean.

You're not OK, are you? I want to see him, see his face. He won't be able to hide it from me if he really isn't OK. But before I can ask him to reveal himself, the words appear on the screen.

Remember where you shot me?

His question startles me. I don't like to remember that, how I accidentally shot him and thought I'd left him for dead. *Yes.*

Be there in an hour.

And suddenly the message box disappears.

He's vanished.

I sit for a few minutes, wondering what he's up to. He was still cryptic about locations. It's possible he's worried that someone's spying on him – on both of us. The news stories about me, about his alleged death in Paris, only mentioned the city. There were no details. Zeke and I are the only ones who would know where our meeting spot is. I think about that night so long ago. I was in Paris with Ian Cartwright, the man I hacked into the bank for, but Zeke showed up and wanted me to run away with him.

Now Ian Cartwright is dead, and I still have no idea exactly where Zeke is.

The door creaks open, and Spencer steps back inside, a questioning expression on his face.

'Everything good?' He notices the blank screen. 'What happened?'

I don't know if I'm supposed to tell him. I don't know if he's supposed to come with me or not. And then it dawns on me. 'He knows where we are. He must have traced us while we were online.' While we took a lot of precautions, I don't doubt that Tracker could get through the firewalls. Our IP address is still buried within the hardware, and someone as skilled as he is could unearth it. We should have known better, but I'm not sorry that he knows.

'Did he tell you that?'

I shake my head, still uncertain how much I should tell him. If Zeke has set it up so I'll see him, I don't want Spencer there. But someone's been following me, taking my picture, and even though I've traveled across the ocean, who knows who's watching?

'I have to go somewhere,' I say as I stick the tape back over the laptop's camera.

'Where?' His tone is guarded, suspicious. 'Are you meeting him?'

I sigh. 'I don't know. He told me I have to be somewhere. In an hour. But I don't know if he's going to be there.'

'Where?'

'Where I shot him.'

Spencer's lips quiver, like he wants to smile, but he manages to stop himself. 'That was on the houseboat.'

There *is* one other person who is privy to this information. I shouldn't be surprised, though, considering Spencer and Zeke's friendship. I nod.

'So he knows you're in Paris. That *we're* in Paris.'

I nod.

He gives a little chortle. 'He's too fucking good.' He's thinking, too, about how Zeke must have gotten through the firewalls. 'Did he tell you to bring me with you?'

'No.'

'I'm going with you anyway.'

I had a feeling he'd say that. I gather up the laptop and stuff it into the backpack, slinging it over my shoulder. 'OK,' I say flatly, as though he's putting me out, but the more I think about it, the more I'd rather that he tag along. Safety in numbers and all that.

The metro drops us at the Bir-Hakeim station. Spencer hasn't said anything; we've traveled in silence, both of us lost in our own thoughts. He's a little jittery, though. He must be going through weed withdrawal.

When we turn onto Quai Branley, the Eiffel Tower is in sight, but Spencer barely reacts. I wonder if he's been here before, but I'm too distracted right now to ask. Along Port du Suffren, the houseboats are lined up in a row along the side of the Seine. A chill runs through me as I remember the last time I was here: the sound of the shot ringing out, Zeke on the floor of the houseboat, blood trickling out from underneath him. I was about where Spencer and I are right now when I heard the second shot, the one I thought Ian had fired but it turns out it was Zeke. I didn't stop. I kept running through the dark; I was on a plane back to the States by morning.

I don't know if I can do this.

Spencer stares at me curiously. 'Are you OK?' he asks.

I shake my head. 'Too many memories. This wasn't a good idea.'

He puts his arm around me and slips something into my hand. It's a joint. 'I can't believe you. How?'

'The world is a small place.' He takes the joint and lights a match, taking a drag and then offering it to me. I hold my hand up, but he shakes his head. 'You need to relax, Tina. You're on edge.'

'I like it that way.'

He rolls his eyes, and takes another drag. 'Suit yourself.'

We reach the end of the fence so we can go down right next to the houseboats. The walkway is cobblestoned and it's uneven beneath my feet. I'm concentrating so much on where I'm stepping that I almost miss it. I stop short, and Spencer practically runs into me.

'Dude,' he says, stretching the word out into two syllables.

I cock my head at the houseboat, which I remember now is called a *péniche* in French. Most of these steel boats used to be freighters, built to navigate the rivers and canals. This one is painted chocolate brown with ivory awnings. It's got a terrace on the top with teak deck furniture and planters with colorful flowers. But that's not what's caught my eye. 'That's it.'

He frowns. 'That's what?'

'The boat.'

'Which boat?'

I'm going to have to get used to him stoned again. 'The one we were on that night.'

'That was a long time ago. You sure?'

I point to the brass plaque that's on the hull: '*Soleil*.' Sunshine. When Ian and I came to Paris after the bank job, we found this houseboat for rent and, because of the name, I couldn't resist. It reminded me of the French phrases Tracker and I had been using. Ian didn't know that, though. He didn't know about Tracker then. Tracker was my secret, and I didn't even know until last year that he and Zeke were the same person.

'Whatever he wanted us to find is here,' I say, walking up the short gangplank before Spencer can stop me. What if it's him? What if he's waiting on the boat for me? I so desperately want that.

And as I reach for the door, it suddenly swings open.

TWENTY-NINE

Instinctively, I take a step back, half expecting to see Zeke, but the woman who's opened the door has short white hair and is wearing a pair of neatly pressed jeans and a crisp white button-down blouse. She is hardly threatening as she smiles kindly and asks in French, 'Can I help you?'

I'm flustered. Zeke sent me here, but I still don't know why. I decide to be honest. 'I used to live here. A long time ago.'

Her expression changes and she studies my face. I shift uncomfortably. I'm not used to being stared at quite so intently by a stranger, although there is something about her eyes that seem oddly familiar. I'm also acutely aware of the bruise on my face. I don't know how to explain that, so I don't.

She finally says, 'I have been waiting for you. Come in.'

I'm not sure what I expected in coming here, but this woman is not it. Nor is the houseboat, which has clearly undergone a complete remodel sometime in the last seventeen years. This shouldn't surprise me, but it does. I take a step inside, noticing the sleek wood paneling, the plush red loveseat and chairs. Without seeing them, I know a bedroom and a bathroom are behind the floor-to-ceiling cabinet on the far side of the room. It's larger than I remember, and cozier.

Spencer is close on my heels. The woman frowns at him, her eyes skittering back to my face. She probably thinks he hit me, too, like Joan and Ron back in North Carolina. She looks as though she might say something, then thinks better of it and merely says, 'He told me there might be two of you.'

Her words pull me out of my memories. Zeke. Zeke *was* here.

'What else did he say?' I ask eagerly.

She shakes her head. But I need to know. I come further inside, my eyes straying to the spot where Zeke had lain, bleeding. I blink a couple of times, trying to unsee it, but I'm not successful. Instead, I focus on the woman, who has gone around a long wooden kitchen island and is reaching inside a cupboard. Spencer comes closer, as though the woman is going to pull a weapon out, but when she turns with only a large envelope in her hand, we both take a deep breath.

'Here,' she says, thrusting at us. 'Now you have to go.' The smile has disappeared, and she is much more agitated. Her eyes dart from window to window, as though expecting someone to be peering in at us.

I reach around and open the backpack, stuffing the envelope inside. Spencer and I start to head out, but suddenly she hisses, 'No. It's too late.'

A shadow crosses one of the windows.

'They can't see you,' she whispers.

Spencer and I share a glance. We both look around to see if there's an easy escape, but there's none. At least, none that we can see. My heart is pounding, and I can't breathe. The woman grabs my hand and pulls me around to a side door on the other side of the boat. Spencer scrambles after us.

She opens the door and points. I don't waste any time. Her fear is contagious, piggybacking on the panic I've felt ever since I saw those photographs of me online. I'm outside on a small platform, hugging the side of the boat, Spencer next to me. There's nowhere to go except in the water, and I can't do that. I've got the laptop and that envelope in my backpack, and I can't bring myself to submerge them or myself.

'Tina,' Spencer whispers, cocking his head. One more step to the left and we will no longer be hidden by the houseboat's living quarters – we will be completely exposed on the roof of the lower level.

It's at that moment that we hear the voices inside the houseboat – and if we can make it just a few feet, we will be only a short jump to the next boat that will provide more shelter for us. I give Spencer a nod and take a deep breath, swiftly sidestepping along the boat until I reach the end, until I don't have a choice but to jump. I pray that I'll make it.

I am momentarily airborne before my feet hit the deck. My ankle gives way, though, and I drop and roll, the backpack breaking my fall. I open my eyes – I didn't realize I'd closed them – to see Spencer's sneakers overhead. I put my arms over my head, but he clears the landing better than I did. Maybe I should have gotten stoned, after all.

I don't have time to catch my breath, because the voices are louder. I scramble to my feet. Spencer and I make our way along the edge of the houseboat, until we're again hugging the wall. I peer around the corner but, from this angle, I can't see anyone.

'We can't stay here,' I whisper.

Spencer's looking in the window of the boat. 'There's no one home,' he whispers back.

'How will we get in?'

He leans back slightly and surveys the side of the boat. 'Door,' he says simply and begins to make his way to it. I follow.

He tries the knob, but nothing happens. He reaches around into his back pocket and pulls out his wallet. With one hand against the side of the boat to keep himself balanced, he bows his head over the wallet and extracts a credit card with his teeth. If I weren't so nervous, I would be more curious about what he plans to do. But as it is, I just wish he'd get to it. We can't afford to be out here too much longer.

With the card still in his mouth, he puts the wallet back,

and then with one hand slides the card along the crack between the door and the doorjamb. He tilts the card toward the lock, and he jiggles it slightly. The card goes deeper into the crack. He then bends the card slightly the other way and the door pops open.

Spencer gives me a grin. 'After you,' he says softly, then shrugs. 'It's not exactly high-tech.'

I try not to show that I'm impressed. I move inside, stepping down into the living space of the houseboat. The windows along each side are covered with thick curtains, so it's fairly dark. This boat is smaller than the other, and it looks as though the kitchen level is below this one.

Spencer puts his finger to his lips to indicate we need to stay quiet. I am already moving through the room into the bedroom at the far end to see if there is another way of escaping. We can no longer hear the voices from the other boat. I'm dying to know what's happening, if whoever showed up has left or if they are still lurking around somewhere.

We crouch down by the bed, just in case anyone outside would be able to see our shadows inside despite the curtains. Spencer reaches around me, and I jerk back, but then realize he's reaching for the backpack. The envelope is sticking out of it.

Without speaking, I take it out and open it, peering inside. I turn it upside down and the skimmer slides out into my hand. But there's something else. A cellphone. Spencer frowns as he takes it, hitting the power button. It lights up, and it has all the standard apps. Nothing more.

I try to get inside Zeke's head. I understand the skimmer, since he wants us to install it, but the phone is a puzzle.

I don't have time to ponder it further, though, because we hear footsteps on the deck. My heart pounds, and I'm sure that whoever is out there can hear it, knows that we're here. Is it those men who showed up at the other houseboat?

I slip the skimmer back into the envelope, but Spencer's still holding the phone. The latch clicks, and someone's coming inside. Every muscle in my body is taut. I'm ready to run, but I have no idea where to go. I scan the room but there's no way out.

I hear the voices in the living area, and I shut everything out and focus on what they're saying. They're speaking some sort of Germanic language, so I have no idea what they're saying.

The voices come closer. Spencer scrambles to his feet, and he grabs my arm and pulls me up with him. We're standing like that, next to the bed, the backpack hanging from my hand, when three people come in. They are all middle-aged – one man and two women. They are frowning.

One of the women steps forward. She is wearing a white blouse, a black pencil skirt and black pumps. She's holding a folder filled with papers and has a Gucci bag slung over her shoulder.

'You were supposed to be out yesterday,' she chides in strongly accented English.

THIRTY

For a second, I'm confused, but then something dawns on me. She thinks we were renting this *péniche*. Relief rushes through me, and my heartbeat slows considerably.

'So sorry,' I say. 'We forgot something here.' I take Spencer's hand that's holding the cellphone and hold it up. 'We'll be going now.'

I begin to move past them, Spencer right behind me. We both try to look contrite as we continue through the living area and out of the door. I pause for a second, glancing around to see if anyone's lying in wait, but I see no one. The woman is coming after us; she's saying something about 'the agency,' her tone definitively angry. Spencer and I exchange a look and, without hesitating, we take off, running up Quai de la Seine in the opposite direction of the other boat.

We go under Pont de Bir-Hakeim and, up ahead, I see stairs that lead to the main road above. We make our way up, the muscles in my legs screaming now. We're not far from the Eiffel Tower. I point up at it.

'Is it really time to sightsee?' Spencer asks.

I roll my eyes at him. We've slowed now to a fast walk. We're on Port de Suffren, and our adrenaline pushes us so it doesn't take too long to get to the iconic tower. Hundreds of tourists are milling about, and we easily mix in with them.

'Do you think we were followed?' Spencer asks. His eyes dart around us, checking out our environs.

I shrug. 'I don't know.' I didn't notice anyone behind us, and no one stopped us, but that doesn't mean much. Someone had been taking pictures of me without my knowledge for who knows how long. I am clearly not all that aware of my surroundings.

Spencer's looking up, and I follow his gaze. I've never been here. My grandmother eschewed anything that was too touristy, except for the Louvre and the Musée d'Orsay, because she said they were part of my education. For the first time, I wonder how much of that 'education' contributed to my life as an artist. I've never thought about that before – how that may have influenced me. I needed a way to make money, and I discovered I had a talent for it. My Block Island seascapes and Cape Cod and Charleston watercolors were, in a way, reminiscent of what I'd seen as a child here in Paris.

I am so busy tossing this around in my head that I haven't noticed Spencer has disappeared. I circle around, trying to locate him. I finally spot him standing in line to get tickets. I sidle up next to him.

'What's going on?'

'I've never been up there,' he says.

I twist around and look up, the massive wrought-iron lattice tower looming overhead. 'Me, neither,' I admit. Tiny dots that are actually people are climbing the stairs. We are in the line for the elevator. I consider being up there, exposed to whoever is after us, trapped.

'Don't worry,' Spencer says as we move forward a little in the line. He doesn't seem worried at all. He actually looks relaxed. He leans closer and whispers in my ear: 'We're surrounded by people. This is probably the safest place to be right now.'

Maybe. I'm not completely sold, but I don't leave. The

number of people, however, while shrouding us, might also be a detriment. I pull my backpack around to my front and make sure all the compartments are closed. Pickpockets are a problem, and I certainly don't want them getting their hands on my forged documents or the envelope with Zeke's skimmer. Which reminds me . . .

'Is there any indication where we're supposed to install this skimmer? Did you see anything else in the envelope?'

Spencer shakes me off. 'Not now,' he hisses.

We wait in silence, until finally we reach the booth and pay for two tickets to the summit of the tower. We weave through the throngs of people and go to the next line, the one for the elevator. This one is almost as long, as the elevators are not very large. When we are finally ensconced, I watch the ground slip away beneath us, then look up as we ascend. I have a moment of déjà vu, but it might be more that I always wished my grandmother would take me here.

When we finally reach the first level, we get out. I spot a small snack bar, but before I can alert Spencer to the fact that I'm hungry, he's already heading out to check out the view. I reluctantly follow him, thinking that a cup of coffee might be a good idea. I blink against the sun, but then the view comes into focus.

It is spectacular. The city lies in grids below, the streets lined with the old buildings. Spencer begins to circle, and I lag a little behind, until we're staring down at the Jardins du Trocadéro.

Spencer's saying something, but it's windy and his words catch on the air and float away before I can hear. I step closer.

'What?'

'There's a message in the phone.'

I feel something in my hand; he's pressing the cellphone into my palm. I'm not quite sure why we couldn't do this while we were waiting, but I'll humor him.

He's right about the message, but it's not a conventional text. It's been written in the notes app: *rue Meslay and rue du Temple.*

I know that area. It's near the Place de la République. It's not far from where my grandmother lived, if my memory is correct. But it's been so long that I don't remember exactly what's at that corner. I do remember walking to the markets, and there are restaurants and shops within a few blocks on Temple.

'So we're supposed to trust him and put this skimmer on an ATM and see what happens?' I ask, making sure to keep my voice down, even though no one else is paying attention to anything except the view.

Spencer shrugs.

I only want to find Zeke. I don't want to get involved in whatever he's working on. Spencer's uncertain about this, too, I can tell.

'Should we do this?' I ask.

Spencer takes a deep breath and shrugs again. 'He wouldn't involve us if he didn't have to.'

He's right about that, but it means Zeke's got trust issues with the FBI, if he is, in fact, running the carding forum for them. 'The problem is, we don't know what's going on,' I say. 'I would be a lot more comfortable about this if we did.'

'You and me both.'

There's a tone in his voice that makes me take pause.

'What's bothering you?' I ask.

Spencer shakes his head and takes my elbow, steering me inside, near the snack bar. He stands so close that anyone looking might think that we are lovers.

'I think it's a setup.'

His words take me by surprise. 'He's setting us up?'

'No, that's not what I mean.' He hesitates as he considers what he's going to say. 'For some reason, he can't install that skimmer himself, which is why he wants us to do it.'

I get that, but there's something else.

'We put that skimmer on that ATM, and it's going to capture all the information on every card that's used to take out cash.'

I know where he's going with this now. 'You think that there's one particular person who's going to use his card and that's the information that Zeke's waiting for.'

Spencer nods. 'And whoever it is can't see Zeke. Which means he knows who Zeke is.'

'And he might know that Zeke is FBI.'

'Exactly.'

'Do you think it's d4rkn!te?'

Spencer shakes his head. 'Dude knows who you are. He's been sending pictures of you to Tracker. No, it can't be him. Tracker wouldn't put you in that situation.'

I try to piece this together. 'But what about that woman on the houseboat? He gave her the envelope. He could have easily asked *her* to install the skimmer. Why me?'

He's not paying attention, though, as he turns the cellphone over in his hand. 'Why the cellphone? Why not just the skimmer? He could have gotten us the location through the chat room.'

Spencer's right. 'Can I see it?' I hold out my hand, and he gives me the phone. There's no security code that keeps anyone from getting inside, which is odd, too. I scroll through the apps and, on a whim, decide to open them one by one.

And when I open the music app, it's suddenly clear.

I know exactly why Zeke chose me. Chose *us* to do this.

THIRTY-ONE

The music app doesn't contain any music. It's a banking program, with options to transfer funds from one place to another. It's sort of like a bitcoin wallet, but when I think of it in conjunction with the skimmer, it makes a lot of sense. Someone will put his debit card into the skimmer and it will automatically record all of the card information in this app. And from here, it's possible to transfer any and all of that information to a pre-determined designated location. Exactly where that is, I don't know right now, but between Spencer and me, it might not take long to figure it out.

'I think it's time to get going,' Spencer suggests. I don't point out that this little excursion was his idea, although the view from up here is something I'm glad I've experienced. Despite my love for my grandmother, I'm feeling a little resentful right now that she never brought me here, to share her city from such an impressive vantage point. Sometimes touristy things are well worth it.

We head toward the elevator, past the souvenir shop with the kitschy refrigerator magnets and replicas of the Eiffel Tower. As we descend, I begin to wonder if we shouldn't just head to the Marais, which is where Zeke wants us to go.

'We might as well,' I say, making my case to Spencer. He's more interested, though, in trying to figure out how the app works first. 'Maybe if we see it in action, it'll make more sense,' I argue.

'You know what that means, don't you?' he asks.

I do. It means we put a skimmer on an ATM and then we watch the card information flow into the app. Something nags at me, though, about this. 'How does this usually work?' I'm not sure why I'm asking Spencer, but it seems like something he'd know.

I'm right.

'Usually the information's stored in the computer in the skimmer, and then someone retrieves the skimmer with everything on it. But this setup is a little different. It looks like it might be set up with Bluetooth, which means the information can be downloaded wirelessly. I'd have to check out the skimmer a little more closely, but with the phone app, that makes sense.' Spencer runs a hand through his hair, and he frowns. 'I've never seen it set up with an app, though. The card information isn't going directly to a server. It has to be manually transmitted from the phone app, which makes the person wielding the phone pretty powerful. That person would make the decision whether to download the information or not.' He hesitates for a moment. 'It's possible Tracker wrote the software code himself, which means he's pretty valuable to whoever he's working for, whether it's the FBI or someone else.'

I let that hang between us for a few moments. 'Someone else' could easily be Tony DeMarco or one of his minions. I'm still trying to fit it all together: the ATM; Tony DeMarco's car; the article on the Internet about Ryan Whittier being missing and the search for the mysterious witness.

We may have traveled across the ocean to find Zeke, but we still have more questions than answers.

If he did develop this app, then Zeke is very likely setting someone up, because it's clear he can pick and choose which information gets passed along.

As we get out of the elevator, I indicate that we should walk toward the Champs du Mars, which spreads out beyond the Eiffel Tower. People are sitting on the lawn, strolling along the dirt paths that run parallel to each other, sitting on the benches. It's a beautiful spring day and everyone's enjoying it. Except, perhaps, us.

We walk along the path, ignoring the panhandlers who are trying to get our attention.

'That app indicates Zeke might be able to download the information and save it before sending it along to whoever he's working for,' I tell Spencer after I've sorted out my thoughts. 'If he sends it at all.'

'That's right.' Spencer taps his fingers against his thighs as we walk. 'I'm going to reach out. Now that we have maybe a little bit more information.'

'Do you think your "friends" might know something?' I ask, making air quotes with my fingers.

He rolls his eyes. 'My "friends"' – his air quotes are a bit more exaggerated than mine – 'probably most definitely know something.' He shoves his hands in his pockets. I'm not sure if it's to stop the tapping, but it was making *me* nervous, so I'm glad about it.

'Do you think you'll be giving him away if you start asking about this? I mean, if he's the only one with the app and someone knows him and knows about it, they might put two and two together and then he could be found out as FBI.'

He hasn't thought about that. I can tell by the way his expression changes. We both realize that we're caught between a rock and a hard place. We don't want to give Zeke away to anyone, but we need more information from the inside.

'What about d4rkn!te?' I ask. 'Do you think you can get some information about him out of your people? Maybe they've seen him around and know who he is. You said you saw him in the chat room, but you never interacted with him. Maybe some of your people have.'

'My *people*, as you call them, won't give up names. You should know that.'

I do, and I'm sorry I've asked. 'I'm feeling a little desperate. I want to know what's going on with Zeke. Make sure he's not in any trouble.'

'You and me both,' Spencer says curtly, but then he takes a deep breath. 'Sorry, Tina. I really need a toke. I can't think like this.' He reaches into his pocket, but I put my hand on his arm before he pulls out a joint in the middle of a public park.

'You can't do that here.'

He cocks his head at a group of teenagers hanging around a bench up ahead. 'Tell them that.'

I am about to say that they're not getting stoned but, as we get a little closer, I can smell it. 'You're an American,' I say. 'It's not the same thing.' I don't point out that he's a fugitive, that if he's caught he'll end up in prison for a very long time. I don't point it out because I don't have to.

He doesn't care. He lights up and takes a drag, a wide grin spreading across his face. I start to walk away; I'm not going to get caught. I've spent years successfully avoiding prison. I'm not about to spend my first days behind bars in Paris.

He catches up with me a few minutes later. I can smell it on him, which makes me paranoid. He has no such problem, though. The tenseness has melted away, and he's definitely more himself.

'You need to chill, Tina. Let's go see how this skimmer works with this phone,' he suggests.

THIRTY-TWO

It is not a straight shot to our destination. I lead Spencer back into the park and we walk down to Place Joffre, heading to the École Militaire metro station. We can get the 8 line in the Pointe du Lac direction to get to République. I check the map inside the station to make sure we're going the right way. We don't say anything to each other the entire journey. I am incredibly aware of the skimmer and the cellphone in the backpack. I have no idea what's going to happen when we get to our destination, but I am again taken by the fact that what we're about to do is illegal and I can't afford to get caught. Neither can Spencer. I glance over at him to see if he's having doubts, too, but he's got earbuds in his ears and his head is bobbing to whatever rhythm he's listening to. It's nice to know that he's relaxed, but I feel an unexpected surge of annoyance about it. After spending so much time alone, there has been way too much togetherness in the past days. I begin to wonder what would happen if Zeke and I actually had time to spend together. As far as I know, he's been alone, too. Would we drive each other crazy? Would we crave time alone, sabotaging any attempt to have a real relationship that's in person and not just online?

I'm still deep in thought when we finally reach République. The roundabout that circles the Place de la République with the statue of the symbol of the Republic, Marianne, is busy with traffic. I try to orient myself, but it's been too long. I was last here as a child and saw things from a much shorter point of view.

Spencer is looking at me expectantly. Again, the annoyance rises, but I push it back down. It's not his fault, since I *did* tell him that my grandmother lived in this neighborhood. I find myself staring down rue du Temple.

'This way,' I say, far more confidently than I actually feel. A wave of nostalgia overwhelms me as we cross the street, but it's quickly replaced by sadness because I can't remember exactly where my grandmother lived. Everything looks the same in all directions.

And yet suddenly it's there. At the corner of rue Meslay and rue du Temple. An ATM.

Spencer and I exchange a glance. The ATM is out in the open; people are walking by on the sidewalk. I look up and see the camera trained right on it. Zeke had been wearing a hoodie, at least. We don't even have hats. I suppose I could use my scarf to hide my face, but that could draw more attention than not.

'This might be a little harder than we thought,' I say, aware now that we're standing here, staring at the ATM, which in itself could create suspicion. I grab Spencer's arm and steer him to the intersection. A patisserie is across the street. 'Come on.'

The scent of bread causes my stomach to growl. My breakfast was a long time ago, and with everything that's gone on today, we haven't exactly had time for food. But now, I am having sensory overload and I want to buy and eat every pastry I see. Spencer seems to be experiencing the same thing, but it's probably more the weed with him.

We buy a couple of fruit tarts, a bag of croissants and a couple of café au laits, sipping and nibbling as we step back outside.

'Your French is really good,' Spencer says with his mouth full.

I'm not going to explain again to him why that is.

We eye the ATM across the street, but we haven't figured out how we're going to do this yet.

'Maybe we could pretend that we're getting money out and we can slip it on,' I suggest. It seems too simple somehow. Too easy. But then there's the problem of the camera that's trained right on the machine. In the movies, the bad guys use black spray paint on the camera lens, but we don't have spray paint, and anyway, it's too high up. Neither of us is that tall and a ladder would be suspicious.

Spencer's nodding. 'That could work, but what about the camera?' He's a few steps behind; it's probably because he's stoned. I'm surprised he can do what he does online, because coding does require a little bit of concentration. But if that's the state he's used to being in when he's hacking, then I suppose it doesn't matter.

'Maybe you can use your scarf,' he suggests. 'Wrap it around your head.'

It might be our only option. Spencer can't do this. Even if we were able to buy him a hoodie, like Zeke had, if his image is captured on camera, he will be recognizable. He was at one time on the covers of a lot of magazines because of his international cybersecurity company. Someone will know who he is. I, on the other hand, have not been in the public eye. The photographs of me before I disappeared are a mere shadow of what I look like. I was in my early twenties; faces change, and the glasses do help.

No. It has to be me. I explain this to Spencer, and he's nodding, although he does have a concern.

'You've never installed a skimmer, have you?' The way he asks this makes me suspicious that he knows exactly how to do it, but I don't want to know why or how. 'Where is it?'

I shake my head. I don't want to do this right here, on the sidewalk. We need a place to go. I spot a Monoprix up the block. I cock my head toward it. 'Come on.'

You can buy anything at a Monoprix: groceries, clothes, books, toiletries. Spencer follows me past the shampoos and conditioners, back to the escalator. We ride up to the level where clothes are on display. There aren't a lot of people here, so we maneuver between the racks toward the back, and I pretend to be very interested in a sweatshirt as I take the skimmer out of the backpack. 'Tell me what I have to do,' I whisper.

Spencer inspects the skimmer a little more closely than he had earlier, spending quite a few minutes checking out the tiny motherboard. Finally, he looks up at me. 'This is more sophisticated than I thought.' He points at something, and I lean over to get a better look.

'That's a cellular network chip,' I say.

Spencer nods. 'This can send a text to someone's phone with the information that's captured from the card that's swiped through the skimmer.'

It's all too clear now. 'And then the app transfers the message to a server somewhere.' I don't understand something, though. 'Why did he give us both? The skimmer and the phone? Why didn't he just keep the phone for himself?'

'Unless he's got it so it sends a text to his phone, too. Or maybe even his laptop. It could go anywhere. No one has to be close by; no one has to retrieve the skimmer for the information. It's fucking brilliant.'

But that still leaves me with the question: why did he even bother giving us the phone? He's not here to answer, so I shrug it aside.

Spencer holds out the skimmer and explains what I'm supposed to do.

'Won't it fall off?'

'It'll be snug. If someone yanks on it, it'll come off, but do you ever do that at an ATM?'

I remind him that I don't have a bank account and have never used an ATM. He rolls his eyes at me as he tucks the skimmer into my hand. The smallness of it strikes me. It fits neatly into my palm and I close my fingers around it comfortably.

'Time to go,' he says.

THIRTY-THREE

I buy a baseball cap in the Monoprix, lying to myself that the brim will disguise me. I wish I had sunglasses, and Spencer suggests it, but I have to wear my glasses. My eyesight has gotten that bad. I'll take my chances.

Spencer will wait for me in the Monoprix. I don't want him to watch me; I'm nervous enough. He reluctantly agrees. He'll hold my backpack and the phone.

I've got the skimmer in the front pocket of my jeans. I cross the street and approach the ATM. My eye is on the camera, and I make sure to keep my back to it, my head down. I'm not sure if anyone watching will be alerted to a middle-aged woman approaching the machine. My experience is that middle-aged women are invisible, which has served me well these last couple of years in hiding.

And then I have the sudden thought that maybe *Zeke* is watching.

I am momentarily distracted by that, but then shake it off. Whether he's watching or not, I've got a job to do, even if I don't quite know why. With my back to the camera, I block the machine as I slip the skimmer out of my pocket. I glance around once, but no one is paying any attention to me, and in one swift move I stick the skimmer over the card reader. It fits snugly, and Spencer is right. Only if someone really pulls on it will it come off.

I pretend that I am swiping a card and cover the keyboard, punching a few random numbers, then make a show of stuffing my imaginary card back in my pocket. Still with my back to the camera, I walk away, affecting a gait that may lead someone to think I've got some sort of problem with my hips. I wish I'd thought about that on my approach, but it's too late now.

It's a huge leap of faith for Zeke to ask us to do this, and I suppose we could have said no. But admittedly, the adrenaline that's rushing through me now is akin to the way I feel when I'm online and, even though I'm a little ashamed of it, I would do it all over again just for the rush.

Spencer is loitering outside the store, holding a plastic bag. He holds it up as I get closer. 'I got what we needed,' he says loudly, laying it on a little too thick, but the natives will just think he's a loud American and ignore him. When I am close enough, he adds in a whisper, 'Looks like it went OK.'

'We'll see.' My face feels flush and my heart's pounding.

'You're fine,' he says, giving me a wink. 'Maybe we should find another skimmer and do it again.' He knows how I'm feeling, and I'm too far gone to be embarrassed.

'I'm not sure about that,' I say so he doesn't get cocky.

I catch movement in the corner of my eye, and someone is at the ATM. I am aware that I've stopped breathing for a few seconds as I watch the transaction take place. I almost expect the skimmer to come off, for the woman to track down a police officer, but nothing happens except she tucks her wallet back in her bag and walks away as though everything is perfectly normal.

'Good to go,' Spencer says softly. He's got the cellphone out and is checking a text message. 'It works like we thought.' I am at once impressed when I see all of the card information recorded and at the same time appalled. I don't want to be a part of this, whatever *this* is. What have we done?

'He wouldn't ask us to do this if it wasn't important,' Spencer tells me yet again. I don't like that he has to keep reminding me. I also don't like that he doesn't seem to be appalled at all, but is intrigued by the way this system works. He nods at me. 'This is pretty fucking genius.'

'But it's criminal,' I remind him.

'Maybe. Tracker's FBI. There's got to be more to this than it looks.'

It's nice that he's got confidence in this, since I don't have any at the moment. The adrenaline rush that I'd felt only moments ago is gone. I want to get away as soon as possible. 'Let's go,' I say.

He shrugs and hands the backpack to me. I slip it over my shoulders, and the weight of it calms me down a little.

'Didn't you say that your grandmother lived around here somewhere?' Spencer asks. It sounds like an innocent question and, when I study his face, I don't see anything except curiosity.

Standing on this corner, I suddenly get my bearings. A rush of emotion overwhelms me. Until now, I'd been so focused on our mission, on getting that skimmer on the ATM, that I had subconsciously pushed aside the memories. But with the mission complete – for now – I have serious déjà vu. Perhaps because I *have* been here before, even though the last time was about thirty years ago.

Without thinking twice about it, when the sign begins to flash with a walking man figure, I cross the street, not really paying attention to Spencer, who is close on my heels. To his credit, he doesn't speak, but allows me to lead the way up rue Meslay. Oddly, I don't remember much about this street, which isn't a main thoroughfare. Storefronts all along the street on both sides show off displays of shoes, all types and sizes, one shop after the other.

'I guess this is the go-to place for shoes,' Spencer ruminates, stopping in front of one window. He points at a particularly high-heeled snakeskin in red. 'Looks like a place for strippers or drag queens.'

He's right, but I don't want to linger. Now that I'm here, I want to find it – the building I lived in during my time here with my grandmother. And suddenly, there it is. I'm surprised I recognize it, since most of the buildings look the same: tall stone buildings with large elaborate wooden doors and small balconies off the windows that aren't large enough for any other purpose than to sport some flowerpots in the summer and to chill the occasional bottle of wine in the winter.

I stop in front of the door. We don't have the key to go inside, but if we did, we would step into a dark foyer that leads to a courtyard in the middle. I close my eyes and picture the wrought-iron tables and chairs for the residents, the lush plants that made it feel as though it was my own personal playhouse. To the right, a wide, wooden stairwell narrows slightly as it leads up to the four stories of apartments. My grandmother scoffed at the 'modern' buildings that had elevators as she proudly carried her packages up to the top floor.

I am taken aback at the extent of my memories; how it seems only yesterday that I was here, running alongside my grandmother, chattering in French.

'There was a dog,' I say out loud, remembering it as more of an afterthought.

'Of course there was a dog,' Spencer says, although not unkindly.

'I can't remember his name. He was only around one summer. I'm not sure what happened to him.' It bothers me that I can't conjure any more than that. I want to relive it all in my head, and forgetting even the dog's name somehow makes it all wrong. And then: 'Why here?' I ask, looking directing at Spencer for the first time since we arrived.

'Why where?'

'Why did Zeke want us to put the skimmer on here, where my grandmother lived? What does that mean?'

He shrugs. 'I'm not sure, but maybe it *was* on purpose.'

It's probably not about me at all, just like Zeke's disappearance. But it still nags at me. 'I never told him where my grandmother lived,' I admit.

Spencer shakes his head. 'Yeah, but I keep telling you, Tina, he's FBI. He knows things.'

He's right, yet it continues to nag at me. Zeke does have access to more information than the average person – both through his job and his hacking. So why this particular corner? What message is Zeke trying to send to us?

I shake the thoughts aside when I can't come up with answers to the questions. 'OK, come on.' I start walking, but Spencer doesn't move. He's studying the cellphone. He doesn't look up, so I sidle over next to him and peer around to see what's got him so mesmerized.

It's a text message. Someone else has used the ATM, but when I see the name on the card, I gasp.

Spencer Cross.

THIRTY-FOUR

Spencer's shaking his head in disbelief, frowning at the phone. I'm confused, too, but I remember that hotel reservation made with the Spencer Cross credit card. That wasn't a debit card, though, and this one is. How many Spencer Cross cards are there out there?

Without saying anything to Spencer, I turn and jog down the sidewalk, back to where the ATM is. Maybe this is the reason Zeke wanted us to use the skimmer and phone app. Maybe he wants us to find out who's using Spencer Cross's card.

Maybe it's Ryan Whittier. He's used a Spencer Cross card before. I feel a little rush of adrenaline as I consider confronting him.

But when I get to the corner, no one is at the machine. I spin around, scanning the people on the sidewalk, the vehicles on the street. While there are several young men in the vicinity, I don't see anyone who resembles the Ryan Whittier in the article's photograph.

Does he exist at all? It's possible that the article was fake, especially since no one at Charleston College knows about him and there's no Internet footprint. But then I remember how the desk clerk at the hotel got skittish when I showed her the picture. It's possible she recognized him but for some reason wouldn't ID him for me. And why had she seemed frightened when she saw the picture of Zeke? Whatever is going on is eluding me, and Zeke certainly hasn't been much help. Did he know 'Spencer Cross' might use a card at that ATM once we installed that skimmer? If he didn't know, did he suspect?

I hate it that there are still more questions than answers.

All I know for sure is that Spencer Cross was with me and didn't use a debit card in that ATM a few minutes ago.

I pull my scarf over the hat on my head and yank off my glasses, throwing caution to the wind. Shrouding myself as much as possible, trying to keep my back to the cameras, I check out the ATM, running my fingers along the skimmer, which is still tight against the real one. I touch the keypad, as though I can somehow channel Zeke through it. I'm being silly.

I've forgotten about Spencer. I left him with the phone, contemplating who is using a debit card with his name on it. Yet when I turn, he's not there. I jog back around the corner of rue Meslay, but he's not there, either. How could he have disappeared? He was right here.

I reach the spot where we'd been standing, and the glow of the roach on the sidewalk confirms that I haven't been imagining any of this.

My paranoia rises until I finally see him. He's across the street, coming out of the Chinese restaurant. He shuts the door behind him and comes toward me, as though it's no big deal that he would wander off and not tell me. When he's reached me, I open my mouth to scold him about this, but something in his expression stops me.

'What's going on?' I ask instead. 'What were you doing over there?'

'I saw someone watching us through the window.'

I give an involuntary shiver, not liking that I hadn't noticed. I am too distracted by my memories here, so I am not paying as close attention to my surroundings as I need to be. I have to be more on alert.

'So, what are we supposed to do?' I ask.

He looks confused. 'Do about what? The guy in the window?'

'No, not that.' I indicate the phone, which he's still holding. 'What do you think it means?'

'What?'

He's being obtuse. 'It's your name.'

'But it's not my card.'

'I know that. But it's still got your name on it.' I pause a second. 'Did all the information download into the app?'

'Yeah. All the information is there.'

'Maybe we should try to find out if this card has anything to do with the other one that was used to make the hotel reservation. Maybe the accounts are linked,' I say. But before I can suggest heading back to the hotel to do just that, out of the corner of my eye I see the curtain move in the restaurant window. I reach over and grab Spencer's arm. 'You're right. Someone is watching us.' I pause. 'You said you went inside?'

Spencer nods. 'I figure if he's watching us, maybe he's watching everyone. Maybe he's seen someone at the ATM.'

'Maybe he saw who used this card,' I interrupt.

Spencer shrugs. 'Maybe. He wasn't very forthcoming, though, because there's a little bit of a problem.'

I know what that might be. 'He doesn't speak English?'

Spencer grins. 'Bingo. Want to come back with me?'

'You only want me for my French,' I mutter as we make our way to the restaurant.

'Unless you can also speak Chinese,' Spencer says.

I playfully punch his upper arm. 'I shouldn't help at all. You can play charades with him and see what he has to say. If anything.'

'Ye of little faith. Come on. Let's see if he knows anything.'

Why would this man in the Chinese restaurant be anything special? I still think we should go back to the hotel and get some real work done. I'd also like to find Zeke again, inside the laptop.

I've got a lot of questions for him.

It seems that Spencer, too, might have a lot of questions for the Chinese man who opens the restaurant door for us, because he's already turned to me and said, 'Show him a picture of Tracker and see if he's seen him.'

I want to be a contrarian and ask him why he thinks I'd have a picture of Zeke, but it will only waste valuable time, so I take out my own phone – not the one Zeke gave us – and open the photos app. 'We were wondering if you could help us identify someone,' I say in French, holding up the phone so he can see it. I accidentally tap the picture of Ryan Whittier, which opens, and then swipe to the next picture, the one of Zeke, and show it to him. 'Have you seen this man?' I ask.

He gives me a funny look, as though French might not be familiar to him, either, and instead of answering, leads us further inside. The walls are painted a deep red, and despite the white tin ceiling that reflects back the light from the hanging fixtures, it's somber. A large tank containing exotic-looking fish dominates the center of the room. Large Chinese watercolors and mirrors crowd the walls, making the room feel a bit claustrophobic and smaller than it actually is. There are tables with both red leather banquettes and chairs surrounding them. The tables are set with crystal water glasses, elegant china bowls, chopsticks and white linen napkins.

There are no diners. None at all.

He seats us at one of the tables and gives us menus, but he still hasn't said anything. Maybe he doesn't speak French. Spencer and I shrug at each other.

'Should we order something?' he asks.

I glance at the man, who looks at us expectantly. 'I think we have to.'

The menu is in French and Chinese, and after a little discussion we order pork dumplings and stir-fried noodles with shrimp, pointing at the items on the menu. The man then disappears through a swinging door behind us.

'I'm starving,' Spencer says.

'That's because you're stoned.'

'We haven't eaten hardly anything today,' he says. 'Don't tell me you're not hungry.'

'We just had pastries. Coffee.' But the idea of a real meal suddenly appeals to me. The man returns and puts a bottle of carbonated water on the table before disappearing again.

I don't know how long it will take, and I'm impatient, so

I pull the laptop out of my backpack. 'I want to see if Zeke's sent us any more messages,' I explain, putting the laptop on the table next to me and booting it up. The screen tells me nothing, and when I check the message app where he'd communicated with us earlier, there's nothing new there.

A plate with the dumplings appears on the table, and the man hovers, frowning at the laptop. He can't possibly have a problem with this, since there is no one else in the restaurant, but clearly he does. I stuff the laptop back in the pack. Spencer's already digging into the dumplings and, as I reach for one, the man finally speaks, startling me.

'He comes in here once a week,' he says in French.

'The man in the photo?'

'Yes. Him.'

'Is he alone when he comes?'

'Every time except once.'

'Was he with anyone?'

The man nods. 'Yes, a woman.'

I shouldn't feel the rush of jealousy that surges through me, but I do. I tell myself that it's work, that Zeke is here under-cover, that being here with another woman does not mean that our relationship means nothing.

Spencer is frowning. That's right. He doesn't speak French. He doesn't know what the man has said. I tell him.

'Ask him if he knows who she is. Maybe she paid with a credit card.'

So I do.

The man studies my face for a second, and it unnerves me a little. What is he looking for?

'I don't know her name,' he finally says. 'But she looks like you. A younger version of you.'

His words pinball around in my head. There is only one person I know who looks like me, enough so someone would make a connection.

My half-sister. Adriana DeMarco.

THIRTY-FIVE

'Do you have a picture of her?' Spencer asks when I translate for him.

I don't, but she's easy enough to find online. Adriana DeMarco is famous for being her father's daughter, and she has been in the newspapers. I call up a photo of her on my phone app and show it to the restaurateur.

His mouth breaks out in a wide grin. 'Yes, that's her,' he says, as though he is giving me something that I want.

I suppose he is, but not in the way he thinks.

'When was the last time you saw him?' I ask. 'The man.'

The man scratches his forehead and stares at the ceiling a second before answering. 'Last week sometime?'

'Was he with *her*?'

He frowns, as though he's thinking hard about this, then shakes his head. 'I'll get your food now.' He scurries back and through the doors to the kitchen before we can grill him further.

'What do you think this is all about? I mean, Adriana DeMarco?' I ask Spencer, who has finished off all the dumplings except one, which he puts on my small plate. 'Oh, thanks,' I say sarcastically.

'No problem.'

'She knows he's FBI,' I say. 'What is she doing with him?'

'You might ask what is *he* doing with *her*?'

He's got a point. Zeke vanished from my life, from Spencer's life. But he's seeing Adriana? 'Do you think this has something to do with the carding forum?' I want to think that it's that simple. He did get into Tony DeMarco's car right after putting that skimmer on the ATM.

Spencer shrugs, and I can see from his expression that he might, in fact, think the same thing.

'But wasn't the carding forum set up by the FBI?' I can't keep myself from playing devil's advocate.

'Maybe. Maybe not. That was the word online, but DeMarco's got his hands in a lot of shit,' Spencer says.

'So you think that he's involved in the forum?' I turn this over in my head a few times. 'We couldn't get him on the kiddie porn site, but maybe Zeke can get him on this.'

'It would explain why he got into that car.'

'Adriana knows he's FBI.' This is nagging at me. 'Yet she's meeting with him. There's no way she'd go against her father, so what's her game plan?' I mull this over as the food arrives. I scoop some noodles and shrimp onto my plate and absently eat, trying to figure out what's going on. 'She'd never believe Zeke's on her side.'

'Maybe he's not doing it willingly,' Spencer suggests.

It takes me a few seconds to realize what he's saying.

'You think she's behind the pictures of me? You think she's holding that over him? That she won't follow through with the hit if he helps her with the carding forum? That as long as he helps, I'm alive?' I don't like the thought of it, but it makes sense.

'And she has someone following you, taking pictures, proving that she knows where you are, that you are within reach if necessary. It's not as though she didn't know about you. About you and him.' He says it so matter-of-factly, not realizing the effect his words have on me.

I put my chopsticks down and take a deep breath. At one point, I thought I could approach Adriana. Maybe talk to her. I don't want to be blamed for my father's indiscretion, the fact that he got her mother pregnant and cuckolded his best friend. My father was not a good person. He stole from everyone he knew. I am as much one of his victims as any of them. Adriana is probably the least affected by him, since her father, the man who raised her, loves her and shielded her. Logically, she shouldn't have a reason to hate me. But nothing about this – or Tony DeMarco – is logical.

'I thought Adriana had nothing to do with her father's business,' I say, mostly to myself. 'If it's what we think, it would mean that she's definitely part of it.'

'He's been grooming her,' Spencer says, slurping up the last of the sauce on his plate. 'DeMarco. Ever since he got sick.'

'How do you know that?'

He makes a face at me and shrugs. 'I pay attention.'

I don't have a comeback to that. The implication that I haven't been paying attention is more than that: it's fact. I sequestered myself in Charleston after our showdown in Miami six months ago. I only knew that Tony hadn't died yet and that no one had tried to kill me.

'She's not going to like it if Zeke's reached out to us,' I say. But the more I think about it, that's why the subterfuge. Why he arranged for us to meet up with the woman on the houseboat. Who were those people who showed up there? DeMarco's flunkies? Did Adriana find out what was going on?

'If he's been here,' I say softly, 'there would be no reason for us to put that skimmer on that machine. He could have done it himself.'

'So why are we here?' Spencer asks. 'Why did he ask us to do it?'

'That's the million dollar question, isn't it?'

The sound of the door opening startles both of us. A young couple come in, their arms wrapped around each other, smiles on their faces. I can tell from Spencer's expression that he'd had the same moment of hope that I'd had: that it would be Zeke walking through the door.

'Are we going to sit here all night and hope he comes in?' I ask. I wouldn't mind that, but I doubt the restaurant owner would like it very much. Maybe there's a place somewhere outside. I am about to suggest that, but Spencer fidgets in his seat.

'I think we'd be better off going back to the hotel and working out this app.' He indicates the phone. 'While we've been sitting here, three more people have used the ATM.'

'Any names we might recognize?'

He shakes his head. 'No. I don't know if we're supposed to transfer all the information or keep it in the phone. Since that guy' – Spencer cocks his head toward the restaurant owner, who's talking animatedly with the couple who just came in – 'won't let us open the laptop here, we should make tracks. The hotel will give us a lot more privacy.'

He's got a point. The chances of Zeke wandering in here

now are slim, especially since he sent us on this mission. If he had us install the skimmer, then it's likely he's not going to be in the area or he could have done it himself.

Is he even in Paris anymore? While we tried to safeguard ourselves against him finding out where we are, he still knew we were here in order to ask us to run his errand. It's more than likely the same people who've been following me for the last few months are still doing so. And I am still oblivious to my surroundings.

The only clue we've got that he might still be in the city is the fact that he gave the woman on the houseboat the envelope with the skimmer and phone. But did he do that and immediately take off? We're in Europe. He could have hopped on a train and might be in London now. Amsterdam. On his way to Germany or Switzerland.

He could be anywhere.

We wave down the owner and pay our check. He seems rather relieved that we're going to be leaving. On impulse, I scribble my phone number down on his copy of the receipt.

'If you see that man or woman again, can you call me?' I ask.

He gets a deer-in-the-headlights look about him; he doesn't want to get involved.

'It's important,' I say softly.

After a few seconds, he reluctantly nods. I'll be lucky if he calls, but I would've kicked myself if I hadn't tried.

The sun has gone down by the time we get off the metro near the hotel. We haven't spoken since we left the restaurant, both of us deep in our own thoughts. I am wrapped up in my memories of Zeke, of what he may be into, and from the surprisingly determined look on Spencer's face, he is likely running code in his head.

As we turn to go down the street to the hotel, I see them. I grab Spencer's arm and pull him back around the corner.

'What's going on?' he demands.

I put my finger to my lips and whisper, 'Two men. Outside the hotel.'

He scowls. 'There are a lot of people around.' He waves his arm to indicate the passers-by.

I can't explain my suspicion and tell myself I'm being silly and paranoid. But when I peer around the corner again, my instincts are confirmed.

Standing in the light from the streetlamp, I recognize him. FBI Agent Tilman.

THIRTY-SIX

I met Agent Tilman last summer in Cape Cod when he questioned me about a hit ordered on Tony DeMarco. He worked with Zeke, and I went to work for Zeke in Miami to try to find out about the hit.

I tell Spencer about him.

'Are you sure?'

'Yes.' I have no doubt who he is. While my time with him was relatively short, it was an intense interrogation that's etched into my memory.

'This is so not good,' Spencer says in a low voice.

'Understatement,' I say.

Neither Spencer nor I can get that up close and personal with federal agents – with the sole exception of Zeke.

'I don't understand what's going on,' I say, turning to him, but he's already started off, and I catch up. 'Where are you going?' I ask.

He shakes his head. 'No clue. This is your city. Where should we go?'

It hasn't been 'my' city in years, but I don't remind him of that small fact. He's right that we need to find somewhere safe. There's just one small problem.

'If they're at the hotel, they have to know about Elizabeth and Max,' I say, referring to our aliases. 'We can't use those passports or credit cards now.' I've got the cash in my backpack, but it's mostly American dollars, not euros. I was going to get more euros, but in order to do that, I'll need identification.

'Don't worry about that,' Spencer says casually, indicating that I really may not have to worry about it. He's got connections everywhere. 'Where should we go?' he asks.

I'm having a hard time focusing. Something tugs at my memory: the police showing up at Spencer's house in Charleston. I'd been convinced that Madeline had sicced Tony's people on me. But having the police show up makes me think twice about that. Tony – or Adriana – wouldn't involve the police. There's a hit out on me. Tony would just have me killed. Did Madeline call the police? The FBI? But if that's the case, then how did they track us to Paris?

The only FBI agent I trust is Zeke.

We need to talk to him. He's the only one who can answer our questions. But we need a place to go to get online and hope that he is waiting for us. I'm regretting not putting a RAT in a link for him, so we could get into his computer instead of the other way around.

I try to be optimistic. He could be anxious, wanting to hear how the ATM skimmer installation went, hoping that we'll go back online soon so he can communicate with us. Too bad that Chinese restaurant owner had a no-laptop policy. We could find another restaurant, a table in the back, and try it that way, but it still seems too public, too risky. Until we know what's going on, we can't make it easy for Tilman to find us.

And then I remember.

I tug on Spencer's sleeve. 'The houseboat.'

He frowns.

'That woman on the houseboat,' I remind him. 'Zeke left the skimmer and cellphone with her. She knew about us, about him. That's where we need to go. We need to find out who she is, if she can help us. Zeke trusted her. Maybe we can, too.'

He's dubious. 'What if these guys are the ones who showed up at the houseboat while we were there? I mean, the FBI. Maybe it's not so much that they're tracking us, but they're after Zeke.'

I consider this for a moment. If Zeke is undercover and running that carding forum, then there wouldn't be a reason for the FBI to come looking for him. Unless something went wrong with the operation. Unless Adriana DeMarco wasn't part of the original plan.

'But why would they show up at the Hotel Adele? Do they think he's there?' I begin to wish that we hadn't left so quickly. 'What if he came there looking for us?' I hate the idea that if he did come, we weren't there. But then something else strikes me. 'How would he know where we're staying?'

Spencer shakes his head and sighs. 'Tina, he's the one who set up the passports and credit cards.'

He knows our aliases. It probably didn't take him too long to find out, either, since he's got our card information. And I know how easy it is to get inside the Hotel Adele's reservation system.

'If the FBI is looking for him, then it must be bad.' I'm thinking out loud now.

'Unless it's part of it.'

I'm not sure what he's getting at, and he sees my confusion.

'What if he's got to make it look good for Adriana? He can tell her that the FBI is looking for him, and she'll trust him more.'

It makes sense, but it's all speculation. Neither of us has a clue what's really going on. This doesn't jibe with our theory about why d4rkn!te is sending pictures of me to Zeke, either – how we've thought Zeke is being held hostage by those photos of me.

'Do you think there's a way to talk to them? The FBI, I mean. Maybe we could do a little social engineering, see if we can't get out of them what's going on with Zeke.'

Spencer is staring at me as though I've grown another head. 'You're out of your mind, Tina. There is no way I'm going to the FBI.'

I roll my eyes. 'Neither of us have to actually physically go to the FBI,' I say. 'There's a thing called the Internet, remember? We can email or message them anonymously.'

'Come on, Tina. How anonymous are we really? If we can get information, so can they. You do know that the feds set up Tor, so they know the ins and outs of it.'

He's right. The government created Tor for intelligence

gathering and everyone else who wanted more privacy and security jumped on board, too. But it doesn't mean it can't be cracked.

We've been walking, and we're at Place de Concorde. We can get the metro here. 'I still think we should go back to the houseboat,' I say.

Spencer is chewing on his lip, distracted by the thought of the FBI agents who are so close. He's on the fence about the idea.

'He trusted that woman,' I remind him again. 'Maybe we can trust her, too.'

'OK, sure, if you think so.' Although he's not entirely convinced.

I'm not a hundred percent certain this is what we should do, either, but I don't have any other ideas.

As we approach the houseboat, we see lights illuminating the windows, but they're covered by curtains so we can only see shadows inside. Again, I'm assaulted by memories and I force them aside, telling myself that Zeke is still alive. At least, last we knew.

'Do we just knock on the door?' Spencer asks.

Now that we're here, I'm even less certain about this, but since I convinced Spencer to come, I have to follow through. I boldly go up the plank to the door and knock loudly.

When I hear footsteps on the other side, I almost bolt, but the door swings open while I'm trying to decide. The older woman stands there, frowning at me. She peers around and spots Spencer.

Before I can say anything, she grabs my arm and pulls me inside, Spencer close on my heels. The door shuts firmly behind us. Without a word, she circles the room, dimming the lights or shutting them out altogether. She indicates that we're to sit on the couch, so we do, but I'm merely perching on the edge, my backpack between my legs, ready to flee again. She pulls over a wooden rocking chair and sits facing us, her eyes darting around behind us, checking out the windows as though expecting the boogeyman to jump out at any moment.

'Were you followed?' she asks in French, looking at me for an answer as though she knows Spencer doesn't speak the language.

'I don't think so. No.'

She doesn't believe me. Her doubt is palpable. 'Why are you here?'

'We have to find Zeke,' I say outright. 'Someone's after us.'

'Someone's after him, too,' she says, not bothering to deny that she knows whom I'm talking about.

'Where is he?'

She shakes her head. 'I don't know. I was hoping that you were him.' The disappointment is clear in her expression, and the worry has set in around her mouth, around her eyes. If I hadn't been worried myself before, I definitely am now.

Spencer leans forward, his elbows on his knees. 'Who are you?' he asks her in English. 'How do you know Tracker?'

I begin to translate, but she holds her hand up and looks Spencer straight in the eye.

'I'm Ellen Chapman.'

It takes a few moments for her name to sink in, but she doesn't wait for my reaction.

'Zeke is my son.'

THIRTY-SEVEN

I forget to breathe for a moment as this sinks in. This woman is Zeke's mother? I study her face and then I can see it. He shares her eyes, the slope of the nose. But I wouldn't have noticed if she hadn't told me.

'You're surprised?' she asks in English. She's not French, but her French is perfect. Like my own. I try to trace an accent in her English, but come up with nothing. 'Did you think he didn't have a mother?' she asks. A smile defies the worry, playing at the corner of her mouth, teasing us.

Honestly, I'd never really thought about it. About Zeke having a family. Spencer had mentioned Zeke's father once, an FBI agent who was able to get his son a shorter jail term when he got caught hacking as a teenager. But I'd never talked to Zeke about his family, not about his father or his mother. I know very little about Zeke's life outside of Tracker, outside of his obsession with Tony DeMarco, outside of how he feels about me.

I am embarrassed by this, by my lack of curiosity. I attribute it to the fact that I have lived without an identity for so long, guarding my own privacy, that I don't press anyone for information about themselves. I find that people usually end up telling me their stories without any prodding. It's at this very moment that I realize Zeke has never done this.

Zeke, however, knows all about me because of my father. He knows where I came from, what my life was like before I became Nicole Jones on Block Island. He also knows about my life now, that I was in Charleston, because he's been keeping an eye on me through Spencer.

Spencer. Zeke's closest friend, but I can see from his expression that he didn't have a clue about this, either. I am relieved that I wasn't the only one in the dark.

'You've had trouble?' she's asking, her face clouded again with concern.

I nod and tell her about the FBI agents at our hotel. 'We think Zeke was there, that they were there for him.'

'Why?'

'Why what?'

'Why do you think the FBI would be looking for Zeke at your hotel? Why wouldn't they be looking for *you*?'

'Because I don't think either Spencer or I are on the FBI's radar here.'

'Why not?' she asks.

Why not is right. I'm not sure I like this line of questioning, because it's making me think twice about everything. 'Where is he? Do you know?'

Again, she's distracted by something behind me, and I turn but see nothing.

'You can't be here.'

'You really don't know where he is?' Spencer asks.

She shakes her head. 'No.' But there's something in her

expression, something that makes me think she knows more than she's saying.

'But you had that envelope for us,' I remind her. 'He gave it to you.'

'He left it for me with his instructions.'

'Left it where?' I push.

Instead of answering my question, she says, 'He told me about you.' The way she studies my face makes me realize that whatever Zeke told her doesn't have anything to do with that envelope. I feel my cheeks flush under her gaze. 'It's OK,' she says, although I'm not certain that it is. I am sure that she knows what happened on this boat all those years ago, how I broke her son's heart and left him bleeding and for dead.

He went undercover back then. The FBI said he really was dead, and he disappeared. Is she blaming me for him vanishing again?

'You don't live here,' I say as reality dawns. There's no way she could live here.

'No,' she says, confirming this. 'But I got the envelope and a key and a note that said I had to meet you here.'

He knew we were on our way to Paris enough to plan this. The skimmer wasn't an afterthought. But where did he send the envelope? Where does she live? I'm about to ask her, but she speaks first.

'If he'd come in person, I would have refused,' she says, her gaze again settling in my face. I force myself to stay focused. She does blame me. For what, I'm not certain. Maybe all of it.

This annoys me a little, how she knows all about me and I know nothing about her. I should blame Zeke, but he's not here.

'Who were those guys who showed up while we were here?' Spencer asks, interrupting. I'm grateful for the distraction.

She is all business again. 'They were lost,' she says matter-of-factly. I try to see the lie in her expression, but she's good. Very good. I begin to wonder if Zeke's father wasn't the only agent in the family. But we're not getting anywhere here. She is being too obtuse. No answers mean that we're right back where we were at the beginning.

It's now that I notice the suitcase and bag by the door. 'You're leaving?' I ask.

'I shouldn't have stayed this long, but I had some errands to run.' This time I do see the lie. She was hoping Zeke would show up, just as I've been hoping. 'You two might want to get out of town, too,' she adds.

Spencer and I exchange a glance.

'Why?' I ask. 'We have to find Zeke.'

'It's not safe for you here. Take my word for it. He can take care of himself.'

I've heard this so many times from Spencer, and maybe they're both right, but I can't ignore the nagging feeling that this time might be different.

'Why, don't you think so?' she asks me. Concern laces her tone; she really wants to know, and her own doubts are obvious, despite what she says.

I don't hesitate. 'Tony DeMarco's involved. His daughter, at least. And they know who he is. What he can do. And when he does it, whatever it is they want him to do, they'll kill him.' It's the first time I've said this out loud, what I've been thinking, ever since we found out about Zeke meeting with Adriana, and the fear overwhelms me.

'They're after both of you,' Spencer reminds me, as though he needs to.

Ellen is nodding. 'He's right. And you're not safe here.' She walks over to the door and picks up her bag, looking at us expectantly.

'We don't have anywhere to go. We can't go back to the hotel; we don't have passports or credit cards. Just a bit of cash, but I'm not sure how far it'll go,' I say.

'You've got your laptops?'

'Yes.'

'You've got the phone? The one Zeke left for you?' It's the way she says it that makes me realize she knows exactly what that phone can do. What was in that envelope. We don't have to hedge around what Zeke's been doing.

'You think we can use those compromised card numbers.

But the moment we do, it'll raise red flags with the card companies. With the people who actually own these cards. Why can't we stay here? He gave you a key, didn't he?'

'No, you can't stay here. It's not safe.'

'And it's safer to use a compromised credit card?'

Spencer has been quiet through this exchange, and he lights up a joint. The scent of weed fills the small room. 'There's one card we can use and no one will pay any mind to it,' he says, reaching down into his backpack and pulling out his laptop. He opens it and boots it up. When he realizes I still don't get it, he chuckles.

'They can't come after someone who doesn't exist,' he says simply, a wide grin spreading across his face.

It takes me another couple of seconds, and then it dawns on me. I know what he's talking about. Who he's talking about.

Spencer Cross.

THIRTY-EIGHT

'You're talking about that credit card?' I ask, the one that Ryan Whittier used to pay for the hotel. Spencer Cross's card has been used at hotels all over Europe. One night only. 'You figure that if we use it one night here in Paris, who's going to notice?'

'First, we need to see if it's linked to the same account as the one used at the ATM earlier. Maybe it's even the same number,' Spencer says. He's got the phone next to him, the app open. 'Show me how you got inside the reservation system so we can pull the number.'

I scoot a little closer to him and give him instructions.

'There's a back door in here,' he says softly, as though to himself.

'Yeah, I found that, too.'

'Fucking weird,' he says.

'I figured it was because it's an old system network. It hasn't been updated.'

But Spencer's shaking his head. 'No. I don't think so.'

'My God, you're exactly like him.' It's said softly, only a little more than a whisper. Spencer and I both look up and see Ellen Chapman frowning, but it doesn't have anything to do with her not knowing what we're doing – at least, I don't think she does. It's more than that. There's something in her eyes, in the way she's watching us.

She's not just talking about me, but about both of us. How we're like Zeke. She's not thinking of him now as an FBI agent who can take care of himself, but as that long-ago teenager who hacked into the FBI server and ended up in jail, where he met Spencer. I wonder how much Zeke has told her about me, about Spencer, about the hacking. While she may know what happened on this houseboat, I'm not sure she knows the whole story. What I did, what Zeke – as Tracker – helped me to do seventeen years ago that resulted in both of us vanishing.

I'm not about to enlighten her, although she's probably already figured out that my time in front of a computer screen hasn't always been for the good.

'How long can we stay here?' Spencer's asking.

If she'd been expecting a different question, she doesn't show it and manages to compose herself again. 'Not long.'

'OK. I don't think this will take that much time anyway.' This last part is directed to me, and I watch him navigate the hotel reservations looking for Spencer Cross and Ryan Whittier.

Ellen Chapman shifts the smaller bag over her shoulder and tugs on the handle of the larger one to make it longer so she can pull it behind her. I am not so distracted by the screen that I can ignore her leaving. I get up and go over to her.

'Where are you going?' I ask.

'Home,' she says simply, not elaborating. I wonder where that is, if it's where Zeke grew up or if she's moved on since then. I want to ask if his father is alive, if they have Christmas and Thanksgiving together, but I would be tipping my hand, showing her that the woman her son has been involved with doesn't have any idea about his life outside of his job and hacking.

'Are *you* safe?' I ask her.

She smiles, and again I'm struck by the feeling that she is no stranger to keeping secrets. 'Yes. Thank you for asking.' She pauses. 'Don't stay too long. They've been watching this place ever since I got here.'

'Who? Is it the FBI? Or is it DeMarco's people?'

'Does it matter which?' she asks, then pulls the door open and steps outside. But she turns for a moment and adds, 'I hope we have a chance to meet again under better circumstances.'

Her tone doesn't give away whether she's telling the truth. Regardless, I want to say I'd like that, too, but she's already down the plank and vanishes into the darkness. I have a sudden urge to run after her, to make sure that she's OK, but I have the feeling that she wouldn't take well to that.

I go back inside, closing the door behind me. Spencer is hunched over his laptop, a joint hanging from his lips. His head shoots up when he realizes I'm standing there. 'I've got the card number, all the information.' He pauses. 'It matches the card from the ATM.'

We let that sit between us for a few seconds.

'So he was there,' I say softly. 'Ryan Whittier.'

'Maybe. Maybe not.'

'What do you mean?'

'We don't know that Ryan Whittier is using this card. *Someone* is. But it could be anyone.'

He's right. Even though this card was used to make a reservation for Ryan Whittier, he doesn't have to be the person who made it.

'Let's just make a reservation somewhere tonight and we can get out of here. We can try to figure it all out later,' Spencer says.

I'm all for that, because Ellen's warnings begin to resonate.

Spencer's navigating a travel website, looking for a hotel. I am suddenly so tired I can barely stand up. I pull back the curtain on the window and peer out over the Seine, the moon casting a glimmer of light that skips along the black water. It was a night like this, the night I shot Zeke. The night he showed up wanting to run away with me. Instead, I ran away alone.

My thoughts circle around, though, to the houseboat and

how Zeke's mother came to be here. Who owns it? Is it a
rental, like the one next door? Zeke must know, since he left
her the key. But how did *he* get the key? He can't possibly
have any nostalgic feelings about this place, but maybe it was
easier for him to send her here, to send me here. It was a
place I'd know, even if he were being cryptic.

But it again makes me wonder just how he knew where I
was. I've been careful online. He's inside my laptop with the
remote access Trojan, but Spencer and I set up a strong firewall. Zeke's talented, but so are we.

I begin to think, too, about how easy it was to set up a
meeting between his mother and me. That was no accident.
He didn't have to ask his mother to bring the envelope. He
could have asked a colleague, even paid a stranger a handsome
sum to do an errand for him. If he wanted his girlfriend – is
that what I am? I suppose I prefer to think of us as lovers,
since we're not teenagers – to meet his mother, it should have
been the normal way: over dinner or cocktails. Certainly not
on the houseboat where said girlfriend – lover – shot him and
left him for dead.

'How about the Ritz?' Spencer chuckles, interrupting my
thoughts. 'I used to stay at the Ritz back in the day.' He's
remembering those times as he clicks on the images of the
elegant hotel.

I am grateful for the distraction. I plop down next to him
and put my hand over the keyboard. 'You're kidding. We need
a nondescript place. Maybe we shouldn't even stay in Paris.
Maybe we should just leave. We can go to London. Amsterdam.
Somewhere.'

Spencer looks at me as though I've lost my mind. Maybe
I have. I pull out my own laptop and do a simple search for
our location. I discover the exact address and then put that
into the search engine. Spencer's watching me intently.

I take a couple of deep breaths as I wait for the page to
load. Finally, it does.

'It's a rental,' I say, mostly to myself.

Spencer peers over my shoulder. 'What are you looking
for?'

'Who rented this houseboat.'

'Dude had a key,' Spencer reminds me. 'He gave it to her. I think it's pretty clear who rented it.'

Still, I maneuver my way around the rental company's website, trying to find a way inside. The FAQs page is always a good bet, and there are no surprises here. Soon I'm in the source code, and I make myself an authorized user. It's not dissimilar to getting into the hotel reservation system, but there's no back door here. At least not one that I can see.

But no matter where I turn, there is no record of anyone renting the houseboat this week – or even in the last month. There's a reservation that will begin in three days, but that doesn't help.

'Why isn't there a record?' I mutter.

'He's FBI, Tina. I don't think he's going to advertise that he's rented a houseboat. He can get into a reservation system as easy as you just did and erase any sign of himself.'

He's right, but I can't explain why I want to know for sure. Why I want to see his name listed as making a reservation. I want to know just when he made the reservation. When he got the key. This wasn't a random, spontaneous thing. He set it up with his mother. Why didn't I ask her *when* he'd given her the envelope? The key? She had luggage. Two bags. She was here longer than just a day.

Why did he want us to put that skimmer on the ATM? What is so important about that?

I feel Spencer's hand on my arm. 'Stop, Tina. We need to get going. We can continue this later.'

We've come so far, but we only keep unearthing more questions. There are no answers. I'm sleepy; it's been a long day. Spencer's right. We can get out of here first and then figure out what our next move will be.

'Did you find a room for us?'

'It's somewhere near the Luxembourg Gardens. I've got the address.' He holds up the phone to indicate we'll use the GPS. He's put his laptop back in the backpack.

I admit defeat. I reach out to close my laptop but stop when the message appears.

But it's not a text. It's a picture.

Of the houseboat.

THIRTY-NINE

I don't think that Zeke has posted this picture in my laptop. There's no reason for him to do that. He already knows that we came to the houseboat. But as I look more closely, this is not a photograph from this afternoon. In the picture, it's nighttime. Is whoever's taken this outside right now?

'Someone's got hold of his computer,' I whisper to Spencer, as though whoever is snapping photographs is truly within listening distance.

As he takes stock of this, he grabs his laptop from his backpack and boots it up. He nervously taps his thigh as he waits until it finally springs to life. His fingers move across the keyboard, but suddenly he pulls his hands back as though he's touched fire, his eyes bright. 'It's d4rkn!te.'

I reach over and turn his laptop around so I can see the screen. It's not as though I don't believe him – I do. But I have to see it for myself.

It's like looking in the mirror. I can see everything on my laptop screen on Spencer's.

'Does this mean whoever's doing this knows we're on the other side of the screen?' I ask.

'Maybe.'

'So the person we're watching – d4rkn!te – has managed to insert a RAT into Zeke's computer and he can see into my laptop. In the meantime, we're watching the same thing through our RAT in d4rkn!te's computer. Do you think he has any idea we're watching *him*?'

'I don't know.' Spencer looks a little rattled by this, and probably for the same reason I am.

Someone managed to sneak a RAT into Zeke's computer.

Zeke is one of the best hackers I've ever known. I knew immediately when I had a shadow. The signs were subtle, but they were there. How could he not have known?

Unless he did. But then he's willingly letting someone else look inside my laptop. Why would he do that?

I tell Spencer about my suspicion, and he shakes his head. 'I have no idea.'

'Do you think that d4rkn!te is showing Zeke the picture to let him know that he knows where we are?'

'Might not be about us.'

I'm not sure what he means at first, and then it dawns on me. 'We haven't been here too long. But Ellen has.'

I think about that for a few minutes, and he's right. It's not just me. D4rkn!te is taunting Zeke with photographs of places where his mother has been, too. He's threatening him with knowledge of both of us. First, it was through the chat room, but now it's directly in his computer. D4rkn!te is getting closer – to all of us.

Does d4rkn!te know who Zeke is watching? He may not. We don't have anything on this laptop that would give us away. But what if he were able to see the messages that Zeke sent us? He could easily figure out from those who Zeke's been talking to. Thus the picture of the houseboat. He knows we can see it.

'Whoever it is, he's right outside.' The photo has been taken at night, and the lights are on in the windows. 'Do you think he knows Ellen has left? Does he know that we're here now?'

Not knowing who's out there watching us – me – is too frightening. I'm sure that it really was Zeke who had sent us those messages earlier, but now I begin to worry. Maybe we should have left with Ellen rather than be sitting ducks here on the boat. Or maybe whoever took that picture is following her and she's in danger and we're actually safer here. We have no way of knowing which.

Spencer is busy on the laptop. He's trying to locate d4rkn!te's IP address. But d4rkn!te isn't stupid and must be using Tor, a VPN, because it's going in circles. 'Talk to him,' he instructs.

'What?'

'Talk to him.' He cocks his head toward my laptop. 'He's in there. He's waiting for something. For *you*.'

My heart pounds and my hands shake. I'm having serious doubts about this. 'No. There are two of them. I'll be talking to Zeke *and* d4rkn!te.' I don't know if I can be clever enough to keep my identity at bay for d4rkn!te but have Zeke know who I am. If I weren't so anxious, maybe. But my head is spinning and all I can think about is escape. 'We have to get out of here,' I tell Spencer. 'I'll send a message when d4rkn!te doesn't know where we are.' But is there such a place? He knew I was in Charleston, in Folly Beach, on the train, and now here. Is there any escape at all?

Spencer is oblivious to my fear. He's still trying to find the IP address. 'You're not going to find him,' I say. Still, I watch him work, unable to do anything else, my thoughts about escape bouncing around in my head, but I'm not able to think of a way to get off this boat other than the way we fled earlier when the two men showed up. Is that an option?

'Tina.' Spencer's voice is low as he indicates his screen. 'Check it out.'

I can't believe what I'm seeing, until I look at my laptop screen. It's in both places. It's real.

Zeke. He's staring right at us.

The video chat program is open, and I can hear a muffled voice saying something but I can't make it out.

'What's that?' I ask Spencer.

He fiddles with the volume, but it doesn't help.

I watch Zeke's face for signs that he sees us, too, but I know he can't. The little piece of tape that I put over the camera when I bought the laptop keeps anyone from seeing what's on this side of the screen.

'What's going on?' My body is tingling with fear. Spencer's face is paler than usual, and he's breathing hard. I want to leave, get out of here. But the idea that someone is outside lying in wait for me to emerge from the houseboat is claustrophobic.

I've had enough time to study Zeke's face. He's thinner than I remember, with a thick growth of beard that indicates he hasn't seen a razor for a while. Is it by choice or has he not had the opportunity to shave? I don't want to think about the latter.

'I've done everything you wanted.'

His voice startles me. It's familiar but also strange because it's muffled. The microphone isn't working properly.

His words confuse me. I lean toward Spencer and whisper in his ear. 'He can't see us, but can he hear us?'

Spencer shakes his head. He puts his finger to his lips. He's right. We shouldn't say anything. They may have found us through the RAT in the laptop, but Zeke probably hasn't told them who we are. Whom he's watching.

'I did everything you asked me to do,' he says again.

'No. You didn't.'

I can't tell if this other voice is male or female. It sounds far away and has an echo-y effect. Whoever it is, he's being careful not to be visible.

Now that the shock of seeing Zeke has worn off, I study his surroundings, as though that will tell me what's going on. But there's nothing distinguishable. In fact, the lighting is throwing off a glare on the wall behind him, so I can't make out any details at all.

I turn my attention to the laptops we've got open, d4rkn!te inside one of them. Who is he? For a moment, I wonder if it's Adriana, but then dismiss that idea. While I have no idea whether she knows how to hack, I know how Tony DeMarco works and I have no reason to think his daughter is any different. Tony doesn't like to get his own hands dirty. If he's truly grooming his daughter to take over for him, then he will teach her that. No, Adriana is not d4rkn!te, but every instinct tells me that she does know who he is and he is likely working for her.

'Do you think it's Ryan Whittier?' I whisper to Spencer.

He chews on his lip as he considers that possibility. We still don't know exactly who Ryan Whittier is. However, I do think that Zeke might know. I peer more closely at the screen, studying his face for any clues he might manage to give me, but he is a blank slate. No, if there's going to be a clue, it's going to be in something he says. He may know that we're watching.

Spencer is sitting at the edge of the couch, as mesmerized by the scene as I am. I don't know what we're waiting for, but we both seem to know it's coming. As long as we're patient.

'We have to shut the thing down until it all dies down,'

Zeke says. 'We can start it up again, create a different site. I told you the base was too big. The FBI is going to be all over it. They'll be able to find anyone with that GPS in the phone.'

As I try to puzzle out what he's saying, Spencer's head pops up. He grabs his second laptop out of the backpack. I'd forgotten he has both of them. When it boots up, he begins typing.

I read over his shoulder and see what caught his attention. A 'base' is a collection of dumps all skimmed from the same source. Spencer's jabbing his finger at the screen, but I see what's going on now.

This isn't just about ATM skimmers. Whoever Zeke is working for hacked into one of the largest banks in the world and millions of people have had their accounts compromised.

FORTY

'**A**nd you thought ten million was a lot,' Spencer mutters under his breath, referring to *my* crime.

'How do we know this is real?' I whisper.

Spencer narrows his eyes at me, incredulous that I would question. He's messaging with someone called Charade, who's telling him about the hack and how no one knows who pulled it off.

No amateurs could do this, it's too much. Word is that the FBI did it themselves, to see if it could be done, to see how to do it.

I think about it for a second. Zeke – as Tracker – helped me with my hack. Seems that he may have taken a little trip down memory lane, but on a much larger scale. The number of credit cards is staggering. All of that information, everything that should be secure, is suddenly out there, being sold online to whoever wants to buy it.

If the FBI is behind the theft, it really can't put all that information out there. When Zeke helped me as Tracker, he circumvented the accounts and made sure that most of the money was recovered.

And then I realize what the cellphone app was for. Without it, the ATM information doesn't move directly into whatever server the hackers set up. Zeke created a sort of two-step verification for the ATM hacks. While it seems as though millions of credit cards were compromised, what if they really weren't? What if he'd anticipated this and the app was a way to keep it from happening?

I reread Charade's comment. It would make sense that Zeke would do this undercover. Maybe not for the FBI, but for someone else.

It *has* to be Tony DeMarco – or, by extension, Adriana. He got into a car owned by DeMarco. He met with Adriana at the Chinese restaurant.

'It's Adriana,' I whisper. Spencer nods. He's on the same page. Adriana knows who Zeke is. She knows he's FBI, and she knows he's a hacker. She's also got the resources to have me followed. She could hold him hostage with the knowledge that she can get to me at any moment if she wants to. She could have forced him by threatening my safety. My life. Yet Zeke being Zeke, he might have only made it seem as though he was doing her bidding to save me. At the same time, he's a hacker. And hackers are like magicians with a little sleight of hand: one minute you see it, the next you don't. Adriana wouldn't know what was happening underneath her own nose if he was feeding information to his people at the FBI at the same time.

Sorting this all out makes me realize that the houseboat photograph *must* be about me. None of those other pictures indicated that Adriana had any clue about Ellen Chapman. Adriana knows I'm here. *She knows I'm here.*

I think about the video chat. We wouldn't be seeing anything if Zeke hadn't set it up that way. He wants us to see what's going on. He wants us to hear the conversation.

Zeke knows that I might be watching.

I go over his words in my head and it finally hits me. I can't believe it's taken me this long to figure it out. 'They'll be able to find anyone with that GPS in the phone,' he'd said.

I fumble for the backpack and unzip the front pocket. The cellphone is in here – not the one Zeke gave us with the skimmer, but the phone I've had on me ever since I left Miami. The one with the GPS inside. The GPS that I did not disable because I wanted Zeke to know where I was.

What I have not realized until right now is that, by not disabling it, I gave myself away to whoever's been following me. And this compromised phone has pinpointed all of my locations.

I scan the room. The windows are all covered by curtains, and while Ellen dimmed some lights, they are still on. I remember how when we approached the houseboat we could see the shadows inside. We're exposed here.

I lean over and across Spencer and turn off the light on the table next to the sofa. I hadn't realized how bright it was until it's off, but we're still not sitting in the dark. The light over the kitchen sink is on, casting a warm glow. In better times, it might be nice, the boat gently moving with the river, a cup of hot tea, a good book. It reminds me a little of Block Island.

But this houseboat was never really home, just a stopping point. And now it's a prison.

We need to get rid of the phone.

As I take stock of our surroundings, I'm distracted by the laptop, by Zeke. He's still there. His mouth is moving, but I can't hear him. Something's wrong with the video chat. The sound has cut out. Whoever is with him might not know about the remote access Trojan, but he is clever, staying out of sight, only a shadow against the wall indicating that there is someone else there. As much as I try, I can't make out the exact shape, either. Man, woman, it's still anyone's guess.

And then, all of a sudden, the screen goes blank. Zeke's gone in a split second. I hadn't realized how relieved I've been to see him, even if I don't know exactly where he is. Maybe the laptop's merely gone to sleep. I hit a couple of keys and realize that it's run out of juice. The power cord is in the backpack, but do we have enough time? How long can we stay here? I still half expect the door to swing open and the bad guys – whoever they may be – to come in and take us at gunpoint. Or worse.

I want to shut off the kitchen light but I don't dare get up. Spencer is oblivious as he chats with Charade. I assume they know each other from Incognito, but can either of them really tip his hand and reveal anything of any substance? I check the third laptop, the one where we're watching d4rkn!te, and, by extension, Zeke. But that screen is dark, too, although not because of the battery. D4rkn!te has shut down. I'm not quite sure what to do now. How are we going to help Zeke? We don't even know where he is. We don't know who's holding him, who d4rkn!te is. And we have no way off this boat without being seen.

'Spence,' I whisper.

He doesn't respond. He must be deep in conversation with Charade. I look at his screen, and see that I am wrong. He's no longer chatting, but he's inside a program I don't recognize – until I do.

'Is that the app?' I ask.

He puts his finger to his lips and nods. I cock my head toward my laptop to indicate that complete silence isn't necessary anymore.

'What happened?' he asks.

'Have to power up,' I explain, leaning over to take the cord out of the pack. I plug it in and look around for an outlet, but remember that I don't have the adapters. They're back at the hotel. I sigh before I can stop myself, but Spencer doesn't react. He's checking out source code. He's so intent on it that I'm curious. When I look a little more closely at his screen and scan the code, I try to see what's got him mesmerized, but I can't figure it out.

He sees me frowning. 'Look,' he says, pointing at the code. 'It's the information from the Spencer Cross debit card.'

We've already seen this and determined that it's the same card number used to make the hotel reservation. I am about to remind him that this is old news, but then he toggles to another window and pulls up a similar program to the one I used to search for the bank that issued the Spencer Cross card. It really is too easy; even a novice could do this.

But then I see it. Spencer Cross's account number also belongs to Ryan Whittier.

'How did you find this?' I ask.

'I just looked for the account number. Not the name. Ryan Whittier came up.' He sounds as surprised as I am.

This card, however, isn't issued through the same bank as Spencer Cross's. Ryan Whittier's debit card is actually issued through a bank in Charleston. I puzzle over that for a few seconds. So there *is* a Charleston connection. And it gets even more interesting because the address associated with the card is listed at Charleston College.

So Ryan Whittier *is* a Charleston College student after all?

I've been convinced that the story was fake, but if the police had tracked this card, it's no wonder it was reported the way it was. But the college spokesman told me they'd never had a student there by that name. He'd practically hung up on me. The only explanation is that Ryan Whittier is a fake name with a fake address. Not to mention sharing an account number with a fake Spencer Cross.

Spencer has gone deeper into the card information. Unlike Spencer Cross, whose card balance is paid off through mysterious means, Ryan Whittier's card is paid through his debit account at the bank where he got the card. His account information suddenly pops up on the screen. A list of charges and ATM withdrawals indicate that Ryan is still in Paris.

And he last made a withdrawal at an ATM machine half an hour ago.

'Can we find out which ATM?' I ask Spencer. 'Is it the same one as before?' We should have stayed there. At the Chinese restaurant, or somewhere else in the vicinity, to see if he came back. 'Check the phone. See if he had another transaction there.'

But there's no record of any new transaction at the ATM where we installed the skimmer, except the last one made by Ryan when we were still in the neighborhood. I'm disappointed, but a little surprised. It's a busy corner. I can't help but think that *someone* would want to get some cash. I'm still uncertain why Zeke wanted us to put the skimmer on that particular ATM. There has to be a reason. And a reason why he was hanging out at that Chinese restaurant. He's been watching someone – or watching *for* someone. Is it Ryan Whittier?

I'm so caught up in my thoughts that I almost miss it. The sound of voices outside, getting closer.

Spencer's not quite so oblivious, though. In one swift second, he's got his laptops back in the backpack and indicates I need to do the same. When I'm done, he gets up and indicates that I should follow him into the bedroom. We step inside, and he shuts the door, but not all the way. We listen through the crack.

Someone is pounding on the door and shouting something in French, but it's muffled. I can't make it out right away. And then I do.

It's the police.

FORTY-ONE

The door is unlocked. At least, we didn't lock it after Ellen left, and I don't remember her locking it, either. All they have to do is turn the knob, and they're inside. I am frozen, uncertain what to do, but Spencer doesn't seem to have my paralysis. He's shoved the backpacks into a small closet and pulls his T-shirt off, exposing his torso.

'What are you doing?' I ask when he starts taking off his jeans.

'Get undressed,' he hisses.

I stand, frozen. I don't understand.

He's stripped down now to a pair of red-and-white striped boxers. I still haven't moved.

Spencer moves closer to me as the pounding continues. It's only a matter of time before they realize they can come in without any trouble.

'At least take your shirt off and get into bed,' Spencer whispers, and then he does just that, looking at me expectantly as he holds open the covers for me to climb in next to him. I get it now. I take off my shirt and toss it on the floor, slip off my sneakers and shimmy out of my jeans. I crawl into the bed beside him, and he wraps the blankets around me.

They're inside now; I can feel the vibration of their heavy

footsteps against the wooden floorboards. Spencer climbs on top of me. 'We have to make it look good,' he whispers, his breath hot against my neck. I'm not keen on this, but he's right, now that I understand what he's up to.

Because when they burst into the bedroom, it certainly looks as though something very intimate is going on, with the clothing scattered on the floor and a clear view of Spencer's bare back. He twists around a little and scowls.

'What the fuck!' he says loudly.

I peer over his shoulder to see two police officers staring at us, uncertain what to do. I'm relieved that Agent Tilman is not with them; he would most certainly remember me from our encounter six months ago.

'We are looking for two Americans,' one of the officers says in a thickly accented English.

Neither of us has a passport to prove who we are, or any other type of identification.

'I found this one in the bar up the street,' I say in French, 'but I didn't know he had a friend, or I would have asked him to join us.'

Spencer's hand tightens around my waist. I don't think he understands what I've said, and I hope to keep it that way. I don't dare look at his face, fearing that I might somehow give us away. I pray that they don't pry, that they don't ask which bar because I don't know of any in the area, or even how close we are to a bar.

However, the officers look a little flummoxed, and one of them actually blushes.

'Sorry,' says the one who's blushing, cocking his head to indicate that he and his partner should leave. The other one hesitates, and I stop breathing for a moment, worried that he is going to argue, but then he gives a shake of his head and they disappear around the corner.

Spencer doesn't move.

'Get off,' I whisper.

'They haven't left yet,' he whispers back. 'Have to make it look good.'

He's right. The officers are talking, but I can't make out what they're saying. Finally, I hear the door shut. Spencer rolls off and settles into the bed next to me. We both stare at the ceiling, holding our breaths as if waiting for them to burst back in and shout 'Surprise!' or worse.

'Do you think they're really gone?' I ask.

Spencer shakes his head as he pulls out a joint. His hands shake, indicating that he's been rattled, or maybe he's having a delayed reaction. He leans over and takes a lighter out of his jeans pocket, lights the joint and takes a drag before offering it to me. It doesn't feel like a time to say no. Maybe it will settle the butterflies in my stomach and my pounding heart.

'I'm not going to tell Tracker about this,' Spencer says, and I can hear the question in his tone: *Are you?*

'I don't think he needs to know. And I don't think we speak of this ever again.'

'Never happened.'

I can't help it, though. 'It was actually pretty brilliant.'

Spencer grins. 'What did you say to them?'

'You'll never know.'

'He turned all red.'

'Yeah, he did.'

Spencer swings his legs over the side of the bed and gets up, circling around to the window. He's still only got his boxers on. He pulls back the curtain slightly and looks out.

'I don't see them,' he says, then comes back and picks his jeans and T-shirt up off the floor, going into the other room.

I take that as my cue to get out of bed. I reach over, grab my shirt and tug it over my head. I sit for a moment to catch my breath. I hear him moving around in the other room, so I quickly put on my jeans and sneakers. The backpacks are still in the closet, so I fetch them and go out to meet him.

'We have to get out of here while we can.' I realize I haven't told him about the phone, so I do. 'We can throw it in the Seine on the way out. No one will be able to find us without it.'

'We should have thought about that sooner,' Spencer says. 'I can't believe we didn't.'

'Yeah, it was pretty stupid. I should've disabled the GPS right away.' Neither of us says what we're thinking: that we never thought Zeke would be able to be compromised like this. I realize now, too, that if someone had been following me through the GPS, then he must have had access to Zeke's phone all along. Either physically or he hacked into it. Is it d4rkn!te?

I can't get the image of him on the screen out of my head. He gave us a clue to save ourselves, but he's still being held somewhere and we don't know where. It's possible that he was giving us more clues when the sound kicked off. Technology can be so fickle.

I notice now that Spencer is circling the room, looking in cabinets and under sofas. 'What, are you casing the place?' I joke.

He stops for a moment and faces me. 'I think this is a drop address.' And then he goes back to his search.

'What are you talking about?'

'Jesus, Tina. Do you *not* know anything?'

I guess I don't. I wait for him to explain. Instead, he exclaims, 'Aha!' and leans over behind the kitchen island, coming back up with a pile of boxes. He stacks them on the counter. They're full of brand-name electronic devices. 'Still don't get it?' Spencer asks.

I shrug.

'OK, here's the deal. When people go on a carding forum, they're buying dumps, which means they're buying a shitload of credit card information.' He pauses. I think I know where he's going now, but I let him have his moment. 'They've only got a short time to use that card information, so they go online and order shit.' He does a game-show model wave over the boxes. 'This shit. But they have to have it delivered somewhere, preferably not their own residences where they could get caught.'

'And you think that this is a drop address.'

'Could be why the cops showed up.'

He's got a point. 'So then why didn't they stay? They could have forced us out of bed. Searched the place.'

'What did you say to them?'

OK. Maybe I embarrassed them to leave, which means that perhaps they'll be back – and sooner, rather than later. But then I have another thought. What about Ellen Chapman? Is she part of the scam? The more I think about it, about her and the way she acted with us, it might not be too far from the truth. She might be undercover, too. 'Do you think Ellen Chapman is FBI?'

He doesn't seem fazed by the question. 'She could have been here just for us. Dude told her to give us that envelope.' He busies himself by checking out the boxes. 'This is some good shit. Too bad we're traveling light.' It's the way he dismisses it so lightly that makes me pretty sure that he might know far more about Ellen than he's saying. I let it go for now. It's time to leave.

'Put that stuff back. Even if those cops weren't here for us, we need to make tracks. *Someone* posted that picture of the houseboat. We're not safe here.'

I barely give the room another glance as we let ourselves out. I drop the cellphone off the gangplank as we leave. It hits the water with a soft 'plop.' We glance around, hoping that will be the end of it. The coast seems clear, but things are rarely the way they seem these days.

FORTY-TWO

We're waiting for the train in the metro station, on our way to the hotel where Spencer made the reservations with his fake credit card. A train rumbles to a stop in front of us, and I step forward and pull up on the handle to open the doors. I sit, but on the edge of the seat, watching the platform. I thought I saw Zeke that one time, but not now. The train begins to move, and while Spencer relaxes back into his seat, I am still too tense.

Spencer's fingers tap nervously against the zipper on his backpack. His addiction is worse than mine; I can wait until wherever we're going to go online. I'm tense for other reasons, despite the weed.

We need to get off at Cardinal Lemoine, and I almost miss the stop. Spencer is nodding off, so I shake his shoulder and we disembark. The hotel isn't too far from here, just a walk up the hill. We are not far from the Panthéon and Jardin du Luxembourg, and since it is a touristy neighborhood, we may be able to blend in.

The hotel is behind two large wooden doors that I push open to reveal a cobblestone driveway. We walk into a lush courtyard with buildings on both sides. The lobby is to our left. 'Let me talk,' I say as we go inside.

It's ironic, really, that we've used Spencer Cross's credit card for the room. When the desk clerk asks if we want to keep it on the card we used to make the reservation, I say OK, hoping they don't want to see it. Our luck continues as she just hands me a key and says our room is in the building opposite; do we need help with bags? I don't point out that the backpacks are all we have; I merely tell her that we can find our way.

When we're finally in the room – the wallpaper is covered with small pink flowers and the bed has an old-fashioned white bedspread on it – Spencer plops down on the mattress, the backpack landing with a thud on the floor. I shrug mine off and sit in a plush armchair across the room.

'I hope no one is tracking Spencer Cross tonight,' I say.

He stares at the ceiling. 'Fucking weird day, Tina. And we still don't know what's going on.'

He's right. We're going in circles. He lights a joint, takes a drag and hands it to me. After a few minutes, I lean my head back on the chair and close my eyes, letting the weed do its magic.

Sometime in the night, I wake up and move to the bed. I ignore Spencer's soft snores and go back to sleep.

'Wake up, Tina.' Spencer is hovering over me, waving a coffee cup. His hair is wet, and he's cleanly shaved.

The scent of coffee hits my nose, and I scoot up and take the cup, noticing the tray with a French press and some baguettes and jam. I indicate that I want some as I drink, and Spencer hands me a plate.

'I'm going to go out on a limb and say that I doubt anyone's followed us here since we dumped the phone,' I say between bites and sips of coffee.

Spencer has opened one of the laptops. 'Let's see what d4rkn!te is up to,' he says. 'He's got to give himself up sometime.'

Hacking can take time. A lot of time. We're used to being patient, but do we really have that much time now?

'What about your friend Charade? Can you reach out again? See if you can't find out more about the base.' I'm not sure that has anything to do with all of this, but it might. I'm grabbing at straws. Anything I can.

Spencer has already opened his second laptop and is doing what I've suggested. We've got three laptops, which means we're not restricted to just one search at a time. I reach for my backpack and pull out mine. Oh, that's right. It needs to be powered up. I sigh loudly, and Spencer tosses something at me. It lands next to my feet. An adapter.

He shrugs. 'I got it from the concierge. Dude spoke English.'

I pull out the power cord and plug it into the wall, connecting it to the laptop, which springs to life when I hit the power button. I don't know why I'm surprised when the message pops up on the screen. It's not as though I don't know that Zeke has access to my laptop, but it's the question that throws me a little.

Did you get rid of the phone?

From what we witnessed last night, I wasn't sure that Zeke would have access to his laptop again. But this question makes it clear that he's at the helm. At least, that's what I'm supposed to think.

I still can't trust this completely.

'Spencer.'

He's sitting in the armchair across from the bed, engrossed in something on his own screen, and doesn't even look up when I speak.

My fingers hover over the keyboard for a second before typing, *Yes*.

Good.

My heart does a little leap. He's online. He's OK. No, it's too easy. I remind myself that I still can't completely believe this is really him. I toggle to the bookmarked poem. Where did we leave off? I can't remember, so I just pick a line: *Any man's death diminishes me.*

Because I am involved in mankind.

It's the next line, but before I can respond, he adds: *Not very romantic, is it?*

I don't want to admit that I have no idea what this poem means. *Where are you?*

If I tell you, I'll have to kill you.

I want to remind him that this isn't exactly time for teasing, but I am relieved to know he's OK.

What do you know?

Do I dare say anything? It still might not be him.

'Spencer,' I say, more loudly this time.

His head shoots up, a frown on his face. 'What?' he snaps.

I point at my screen.

He comes over and reads the messages. 'Hold off for a second.' He grabs the laptop he was working on. 'If it's really him, he doesn't know about d4rkn!te's RAT, otherwise he wouldn't be asking you anything. He wouldn't even engage.'

He's got a point. I'd forgotten about the RAT because I was too happy to have contact. 'We need to warn him.' But I'm not exactly sure how to do that without completely tipping our hand. I want to make sure he stays safe, wherever he is.

Are you there?

Spencer and I exchange a look, neither of us certain what we should do. And then I have an idea.

Remember why I had to leave Quebec? It's the only thing I can think of. If it is Zeke, this will remind him about the shadow in my laptop, the one that forced me to leave my sanctuary and return to the States despite the price on my head. I'm taking a chance that d4rkn!te does not know about my time in Canada or why I had to return.

Let me look into it.

He understands.

'He'll find it,' I tell Spencer. 'Right?'

Spencer nods.

'What are you so focused on?'

He pulls his laptop over and shows me. D4rkn!te is in the chat room. He's not engaging with anyone.

'If he's here, do you think he's not watching Zeke?' I ask.

'I think he's probably watching him.' He doesn't have to say any more. D4rkn!te most likely has a setup like Spencer did in Charleston and Miami. He's savvy enough to post pictures of me, installing a RAT in Zeke's computer without him knowing. Savvy enough that we can get into his laptop but find precious little about who he actually is – or where he is.

'Maybe we can test it.'

I'm not sure I like that idea, but before I can say anything, he pulls out his second laptop and, with a few keystrokes, is signing into the same chat room that d4rkn!te's navigating. To my surprise, he uses the screen name Tracker.

Now, this could be a huge mistake. 'What are you doing? If he's watching Zeke, then he *knows* what he's doing.'

'Trust me.'

I've trusted him for days, months, but I'm still uncertain about this. We don't know how volatile d4rkn!te is, and this could be putting Zeke in even more trouble. But Spencer doesn't seem concerned. He's got one eye on this laptop and the other on the one that's inside d4rkn!te's computer.

I'm a little surprised that d4rkn!te hasn't discovered the RAT yet in his own computer. Unless he's so confident in his own skills that he thinks no one could ever hack him. His arrogance might be his Achilles heel.

I say as much, but Spencer is distracted as he watches d4rkn!te in the chat room. 'Interesting that I'm here as Tracker, and he knows it, but hasn't tried to communicate. He's getting involved in some of the threads, but it's like he's deliberately ignoring me.'

I reach over and pat his arm. 'Don't feel rejected. He doesn't know it's you.'

He doesn't have time to respond before a message pops up on my screen. It's Zeke.

How did you know?

We've got a RAT in his computer, I type.

You managed that?

Yes, and never mind how. But we can't get through his firewalls to find his IP address. Where are you?

What's he doing?

Why is he so focused on d4rkn!te? *He's in the chat room. Spencer's in there as Tracker.*

Tell Spencer to get out of there NOW.

Spencer's focused on his screen. 'Spence?' I indicate Zeke's message. He frowns, but in a second, signs out of the forum.

He's out, I type.

Do you know who he is?

No. Except he's been stalking me. His screen name is d4rkn!te.

He's a terrorist.

FORTY-THREE

I stare at the screen, my head spinning with questions. Terrorist? I have visions of 9/11, planes crashing into buildings, mass shootings. But involvement in a carding forum doesn't seem quite at that level. It's a crime, but non-violent. Maybe the stalking puts d4rkn!te on the edge, but even *that* isn't terrorism. However, Zeke – the FBI – is involved, so perhaps my definition of terrorism isn't quite as black and white as I've thought.

Are you in danger? I write.

Nothing online. He might not have been the only one watching.

I hadn't thought about that. *Can we meet?*

No.

Why not?

I can't manage it right now. Stay put. It shouldn't be much longer.

I want to ask if I'm in danger, if d4rkn!te is still following me. I give an involuntary shiver just thinking about it. And then my thoughts stray to the cellphone. To the app. As I consider the information that's been transferred from the ATM, it's clear that it's extremely valuable – and possibly could bankroll terrorist activities.

Does Zeke have access to the information we have in the phone or are we the only ones who have it? But before I can ask, his next message pops up.

Just remember, I love you. And then he's gone.

I stare at the screen.

'I don't know who he is, but he's good,' Spencer's saying. He's still trying to track d4rkn!te. 'No matter what I try, it doesn't work.' He realizes I'm not paying attention. 'What's wrong?'

I don't say anything. He peers at the screen over my shoulder and reads the exchange with Zeke.

'What the fuck,' he mutters. 'A terrorist?' His reaction is more disbelief than the shock I felt. 'I mean, he's obviously not one of the good guys, but a *terrorist*?'

'Zeke's in trouble.'

Spencer rolls his eyes at me. 'Dude is FBI, Tina. How many times do I have to remind you? This is what he's trained to do. He's supposed to go after terrorists.'

'He's never said that before. He's never told me he loves me.' A chill runs through me. Under normal circumstances, I would be elated, but this is not normal. It's almost like he's saying goodbye. For good.

Spencer is frowning.

'We have to find him,' I say.

'He says it shouldn't be much longer, whatever it is he's doing.' Spencer chews on the corner of his lip. 'We should trust him.' But I can tell that even he is having a hard time with this. So much for 'dude is FBI.'

I'm at a loss. I don't know where to turn. The only thing we've got is the phone with the card information, but we don't know what to do with it. Maybe that's the point. Maybe no one is supposed to know where the information went. I don't like the idea of that, though, either, since now we're in possession of information that is extremely valuable to the wrong people.

'Do you think this is what happened to Ryan Whittier? A terrorist got to him?' I ask.

'We're not even sure that Ryan Whittier exists,' Spencer reminds me.

I know that, but I play devil's advocate. He used the ATM and vanished. Zeke's face is in that photograph. He can be identified. By terrorists.

But then I remember Adriana DeMarco. She's involved in this somehow.

I don't realize I'm thinking out loud until I notice Spencer watching me closely.

'What?' I ask.

He shakes his head. 'Nothing.' He turns back to the laptop.

Why isn't he more curious about this? He doesn't seem concerned at all.

'You didn't know about this, did you?' I ask, insinuating that maybe he did, in fact, know.

'Come on, Tina,' he says, although it's not really an answer.

'What if d4rkn!te is FBI, like Zeke? Do you think that he could be? We've thought Zeke could be a double agent, but maybe it's really d4rkn!te,' I speculate. The more I think about it, the more I wonder. Terrorists can play both sides of the fence.

Spencer doesn't say anything. He's got the chat room on one screen, d4rkn!te's screen on the other. But he doesn't really need both right now. D4rkn!te is in the chat, although there isn't a lot of action on his part.

I can't stand it. I have to move around a little, get rid of my nervous energy. Being cooped up in this room with someone who's ignoring me is getting to me.

Even though d4rkn!te might be a terrorist, if he's lurking in a chat room he's not outside the door, lying in wait for me. Anyway, we got rid of the phone with the GPS. I have to get out of here, get some fresh air, even if it's just in the little courtyard outside. I tell Spencer where I'm going, and he barely looks up from his screens. I snatch the phone on my way out, in case I need to call for help. I don't think he even notices.

I let myself out and go down the stairs. The courtyard is lush with flowering plants and tall, willowy trees whose branches cast shade over a few small tables on a patio. I slide into one of the seats and begin to fiddle with the phone. There are several text messages now that indicate people have been taking money out of the ATM at the corner of rue Meslay and rue du Temple. I scan the information but don't see any names I recognize.

I open the app's source code – a relatively easy thing to do with only a few steps on the phone – and scan it. I have no idea what I'm looking for, and it looks like pretty standard code. Until I spot it. The exact same back door that I found in the hotel reservation site for the Hotel Adele. I stare at it for a few seconds. I've assumed that Zeke developed this app, so he is presumably the one who installed this back door. Did he also put the back door in the reservation site?

I try to think like Zeke. Piece together anything I can from the last six months to try to pinpoint where he might be right now, what might have happened to him. He left me in Miami to go to work. Two months later, he's putting a skimmer on an ATM. Spencer stops hearing from him. Someone starts following me, taking pictures of me, and then I have to leave because Madeline Whittier discovers that I'm Daniel Adler's daughter, the woman who stole her money.

Whittier. The simple online search for her also brought up the article about the missing Ryan, who allegedly hails from Charleston, where Madeline lives.

I didn't have time to ask Madeline if she has a relative named Ryan and I've been so distracted by everything else that's been going on that I let it slide. But maybe it's time to be a little more proactive.

I may not have my laptop, but I've got a phone. I bypass the general and news searches this time and opt for the images.

The first picture that comes up is the one that was in the article online, the one that shows the baby-faced Ryan Whittier. There are other Ryan Whittiers, too, of all shapes and sizes that don't resemble the one I'm familiar with. It's like that old TV show *To Tell the Truth*: which one is the real Ryan Whittier – or at least the one I'm looking for?

This is a futile exercise, until a familiar face jumps out at me. I've scrolled almost to the bottom, so it's not a surprise I haven't seen it until now.

A picture of Madeline Whittier – and Ryan Whittier.

FORTY-FOUR

It's as though my worlds are colliding. I touch the image and it fills the screen. Madeline is wearing a long evening gown and Ryan is sporting a tuxedo. She has her hand on his arm, her diamonds glittering. She's smiling at him, but he isn't looking at her. Rather, he's looking directly into the camera. His gaze is unsettling, half bored and half something that I can't put my finger on. I find a link that goes to a story about a black tie charity affair in Charleston. But other than the photograph caption, which describes Madeline as a major donor and her grand-nephew Ryan, there is no mention of either in the actual story, leaving me with yet another dead end.

Or is it?

I realize what is nagging at me about this picture. I call up the article about Ryan's disappearance, the one with his photograph. It's the same image, but this one is a close-up of his face. I toggle back and forth between the two to make sure, but I don't really have to, it's merely for my own validation.

If Madeline hadn't recognized me, I could have called her now and asked about her grand-nephew. But I do know someone who might have some information.

I check the time and wonder if it's too early back in the States to call Randy. If anyone knows anything, he would. Is it a good idea to contact him, though? Madeline has probably told him all about me by now. Yet I can't help but wonder if she would keep it a secret. She wouldn't want it to get out all over Charleston that she was taken in by a con man, that she bought a painting by said con man's daughter who hacked into her bank account and stole from her. Madeline Whittier seemed to be all about her status, and that would definitely change things for her in Charleston society.

I have to take the chance. It is a little early, but Randy is an early riser and goes running in the mornings. I hope I'll be able to catch him before he goes out.

I punch in the familiar number, embedded in my memory over the last months. I get a sudden rush of homesickness – not that I spent a lot of time in Charleston, but for my simpler life there, the beach, my watercolors.

'Hello?' His voice is tentative; he doesn't know this number. I'm not even sure what it is.

'Randy? It's Tina.' I hope he doesn't hang up.

A long pause, then, 'Where are you?'

'I'm sorry I had to leave so quickly, but I had a family emergency' – this sounds like the best excuse – 'and had to rush off.'

'Is everything OK?'

'Still touch and go.' I let him think it's something medical. 'I have a question, though, that maybe you can answer.'

'OK.' His tone is still hesitant, but the fact that he's still on the phone means Madeline hasn't gotten to him.

'I had tea with Madeline the other day.'

'I know. She said you rushed off.'

I wait a few seconds to see if he says anything more, but he doesn't, so I continue. 'Yeah. I had to go, but before I left, we were talking about her grand-nephew Ryan.' I hate lying, but it's the only way.

Silence, then, 'What do you know about him?'

'Not much, except he went missing a few months ago. I wanted to know if they ever found him.'

'Why?'

That's a good question. I think quickly. 'I thought I saw him. Before I left.'

He snorts. 'Tina, you didn't see him.'

'You know what happened to him?'

'I'm a little surprised Madeline talked to you about this. She never talks about Ryan.'

'She had a couple of mint juleps before tea.'

He laughs, and I realize how much I've missed him and am sorry that I'm lying to him like this. 'I suppose that's one way to get her to talk. She didn't say much except that you rushed off, and she wanted to know if I knew where you were. I told her I didn't.' He pauses. 'She left town, too. The next day.'

Curious. I'll have to get back to that. But right now: 'What

happened with Ryan? Did her trip out of town have anything
to do with him?'

'No.' Randy sighs. 'Listen, she'd be pissed if she found out
I'm telling you anything, so I didn't say a word, OK?'

'Mum's the word.'

'Ryan didn't go missing. He went into hiding. The FBI is
looking for him.'

I tighten my grip on the phone. 'The FBI?'

'He got into something, some sort of computer hacking.'

My throat has gone dry, and I cannot speak. I close my eyes
and picture the ATM, Zeke's picture snapped just before Ryan
Whittier used the machine. What was the real purpose of that
article? Was it to locate Zeke or Ryan Whittier? Or both?

'Tina?'

'I'm here,' I finally say. 'Do you know who he's hacking
for? I mean, is he working for anyone or hacking for himself?'

'You won't believe this,' Randy says with a chuckle.

'Try me.' I might believe almost anything now. But what
he says next is something I truly do not expect.

'Remember the guy who was the whistleblower against the
government? The guy who showed that we weren't vetting
the refugees like they said they were and then there was that
terrorist attack?'

Now I really cannot breathe. I'm still holding the phone
against my ear, but I lean over and put my head between my
knees. I know who he's talking about.

'Spencer Cross, that was his name. Remember him?' Randy
is asking. 'That's who Ryan was working for. Spencer Cross.'

FORTY-FIVE

Instinctively, I glance up at our hotel room window. Spencer
is in there, trying to find d4rkn!te's identity to keep me
safe. I have spent the last days with him. He is my friend,
and I trust him.

And yet.

No. I can't question him. There is something larger at play here. It's too much of a coincidence that Madeline Whittier happens to be Ryan Whittier's grand-aunt.

But still. Spencer has a house in Charleston. How do I know that he doesn't know Madeline Whittier? That he doesn't know her grand-nephew Ryan? He was the one who subliminally suggested that Charleston might be a good place for me to go. It was remarkably easy to escape the city, too. He knew exactly how to do it.

Spencer managed to put a RAT in d4rkn!te's computer – something Zeke was even impressed with. What if it was easy because he had access all the time?

How easy would it be for Spencer to lie to me?

I shake off the thought. He can't possibly be involved in this. Can he?

This is crazy. Until I know something definite, I have to trust Spencer. Being on the run for so long has made me too cynical, too suspicious. Spencer has been by my side for the last few days; he would never betray Zeke – Tracker – like this.

'Tina?'

I realize I'm still holding the phone and Randy's on the other end. 'Sorry, I got distracted. I really appreciate you telling me this.'

'What's going on? Are you OK?' Worry laces his voice.

'I'm OK,' I assure him, although I'm not a hundred percent sure of that right now.

'When will you be back? I've sold a couple more of your watercolors.'

'I'm not sure. I'll be in touch. But one thing, Randy: please don't tell Madeline that you spoke to me.'

He laughs. 'I'm not going to say a word. She'd kill me if she knew I told you about Ryan. She's got an image to uphold. And you have to promise you won't tell her I told you.'

'No worries there,' I say, sure that I'll be able to keep that promise since I won't be returning to Charleston. 'Take care, and thanks again.' I end the call after saying goodbye and remain sitting, staring up at the hotel room window again.

Spencer's name has been linked to all of this from the start because of the hotel reservation. But if he were really involved, he wouldn't be so obvious about it and use his own name. He's not stupid.

Thinking this through makes me breathe a little easier, and I'm embarrassed that I even suspected him of anything at all. I study the phone in my hand, then open the browser app. The photograph of Madeline and Ryan Whittier pops back up on the screen. I go back to the search engine and click on images again. I see the picture, and I swipe the screen, scrolling through photographs of Madeline at various events in Charleston. I am about to stop, but see the same picture again with Madeline and Ryan. This time it's on a different site. I tap it and another article about the event fills the screen. There are more photographs here from what seems to be the same event.

One of them makes me catch my breath.

It's Madeline and Ryan again, but they're standing with someone else. Someone I recognize.

Adriana DeMarco.

She is laughing at something Madeline has said, her hand caressing Ryan Whittier's shoulder. He is watching her with a contemplative expression.

My suspicions about Madeline knowing Tony DeMarco are confirmed. The pieces are starting to fall into place, but there are still a few missing.

I am so deep in thought that I don't notice him coming up the cobblestoned driveway until he's right in front of me.

'Miss Adler?'

I squint up against the sunlight, shielding my eyes with my hand. When I recognize him, I freeze.

FBI Agent Tilman.

I don't know what confuses me more: his actual presence or the fact that he knows my name. My real name. It throws me off a little, and every muscle in my body is taut. I'm trapped. Ready to run.

I force myself not to look up at our room's window. Agent Tilman can't know that Spencer's here. Although it seems that he's here for me, and his next words verify it.

'Please come with me.'

This is it. It's over. Seventeen years of being on the run, and finally the FBI has caught me. I'm not sure what they'll charge me with; the statute of limitations on the bank job passed years ago, but putting skimmers on ATMs is still a crime. I wonder how many years I'll get. Maybe I can find a lawyer who will argue that I was only helping a friend, an FBI agent who's undercover. Maybe I could get points for that.

Agent Tilman is looking at me expectantly. And then I wonder just what he's doing here. How did he know where I was?

'Did Zeke call you?' I ask. That doesn't make sense, though. Zeke doesn't know where I am. At least, I don't think so.

'I did get a call,' he says. 'But maybe we should wait to talk until we get there.'

'Get where?'

'The embassy.' He pauses. 'You should get your things.'

A panic rises in my chest as I think about Spencer in the room. 'I don't have anything.'

He cocks his head as his eyebrows rise into his forehead. 'Of course you do. Let's go to your room and get your things.'

I stand up slowly, biting my lip as I try to think of a way out of this. But I can't. He follows me closely into the building and up the stairs. As we approach the room, I say loudly, 'I don't know what you want, Agent Tilman.'

'Just open the door, Miss Adler.'

I turn the knob, but it's locked. I pull out my room key and open the door. The room is empty; the beds are made. My backpack is perched against the wall underneath the window, which is open.

Agent Tilman steps around me and goes to the bathroom, checks inside and then swiftly pulls open the closet door.

But Spencer's not here. There is only the faintest scent of weed in the air that indicates he was here at all. I'm glad he managed to escape; it's clear Agent Tilman didn't think I was alone.

I lift up my backpack and shift it onto my shoulder. It's lighter than it should be. My laptop isn't inside. I'm almost certain why Spencer took it with him. There wasn't enough time to clear it.

Agent Tilman gestures that I should walk with him. My legs feel unsteady, as though I'm being led to the guillotine. In a way, I am. My heart is pounding so hard I'm sure Agent Tilman can hear it.

A car is waiting at the curb, and he opens the door. I climb in. They'll deport me and then put me in prison back in the States. I wonder if I'll have to go back to Florida, to Miami. I sit back further in my seat and turn to the window, watching the landscape go by and wondering how long it will be before I have my freedom again.

FORTY-SIX

A gent Tilman hands me a cup of coffee, and I don't know what to do but take it. I'm seated in a plush chair in a fairly comfortable office, so unlike the inter-rogation room where we last met on Cape Cod. He is seated across from me, sipping his own coffee. I'm on edge, uncertain what this is all about. This isn't how I thought it would be once we got here.

'Are you OK?' he asks me. He actually seems like he wants to know. Like he cares.

I shrug. He smiles at me and takes another sip from his cup. He's around my age, maybe a little older, with some gray around his temples. He's dressed in a suit with a blue tie loosened a little around his neck.

I notice the laptop now. The one on the desk behind him. I shift a little, folding my hands in my lap to keep them still.

'You want to see it?'

I didn't realize I was that obvious, but Agent Tilman reaches over and picks up the laptop, handing it to me. I take it, awkwardly, uncertain. 'Open it,' he says.

'I'd rather not,' I say, putting it on the table between us but keeping an eye on it.

'Can you do that? Not go online?' he asks, although not unkindly. In fact, he seems more curious than anything else.

I nod and smile despite myself. 'Yes. I've done it before.'

'But what if we need you to help?'

I don't understand, and he sees my confusion.

'Miss Adler, Tina, if I may, we're looking for people like you.'

He makes it sound like I've got some sort of illness, and perhaps I do, but I still don't completely understand.

'The FBI is recruiting people who can go after cyber-criminals. Hackers.'

'But *I'm* a hacker,' I say before I can stop myself.

'That's why we need you.'

He makes it sound so noble.

I want to ask him what he knows about me. How much Zeke has told him. Because Zeke must have told him about me, if I'm here. But something nags at me.

'How did you know where I was?'

Agent Tilman smiles, and I try to see the trap in it, but it seems sincere. He cocks his head toward my hand. I'm still holding the phone. It dawns on me then. Zeke seems to have a thing for GPS. 'You tracked me,' I say.

He nods.

Does Zeke know about this? Does he know that he's not the only one who could track me? And what about Spencer? Zeke knows that Spencer has been with me. Spencer is far more vulnerable than I am, and Zeke would never reveal his location to the feds.

Unless Zeke didn't have a choice.

The thought makes me take pause.

'Why should I help you?'

Agent Tilman nods thoughtfully. 'We know who you are, Miss Adler.' The way he says it convinces me that he certainly does know, which concerns me. 'If you help us, if you are willing to work with us, certain incidents can be forgotten.'

I wonder if he knows about the bank job or if he's talking about me shooting Zeke all those years ago. I was the reason

Zeke had to go underground; he had to have told them some story about it. I'm not going to give voice to any of it.

'What, exactly, do you want me to do?'

'Are you saying yes?'

I'm not sure I have a choice, so I say, 'Maybe.'

He studies my face for a second, and I force myself not to look away. His eyes settle on my cheek, where the bruise is. Before I can catch myself, I reach up and touch it. It's still tender.

'It hurts?' he asks.

I nod.

'What happened?'

I can't tell him about the train. How I jumped off. I merely say, 'I fell.'

He's quiet for a few seconds, then says, 'There's someone we're looking for, and we could use your help.' He pauses. 'His name is Ryan Whittier. At least, that's the last name we have for him.'

I worry the edge of the cellphone.

'You don't seem surprised to hear the name.'

I shake my head. 'No, I guess I'm not.'

'Then you might know that he goes by the screen name d4rkn!te.' I sit up a little straighter in my chair. I didn't know that, but it makes perfect sense and I can't believe I didn't connect the dots when Randy told me Ryan Whittier was a computer hacker. I force myself not to look surprised. 'And he's working with Adriana DeMarco. That's a name I believe you most definitely do know.'

It all makes sense now. Adriana is the reason why they've chosen me for this particular job.

'Where is he?' I ask.

'We're not sure. Which is where you come in.'

'No, not Ryan Whittier. Zeke. Zeke Chapman. Where is he? Why isn't *he* here talking to me?'

Agent Tilman's expression doesn't change. 'Agent Chapman is undercover with this operation. I'm afraid I cannot disclose his location.'

'But you know where he is?'

'If you help us, you'll be helping him, too.'

I shouldn't have expected him to tell me anything. I grew up with federal agents poking around my house, watching my father, my whole family.

'What do you want me to do?'

FORTY-SEVEN

Until now, Agent Tilman has maintained a steady expression, but I can see the relief in his eyes.

'We want you to go online and draw d4rkn!te out. See if you can get him to come out of hiding, wherever he is. See if there is a real link between him and the DeMarcos.' He pauses. 'And anyone else.'

It's the way he says it that makes me think he does know about Spencer, what Randy told me. He can't know that I know anything about that, though. I wonder how much Zeke has told him about my involvement with the skimmer and my own search for d4rkn!te.

'You want me online to find d4rkn!te? Can't Zeke do that?'

'Agent Chapman isn't the only one involved in this operation, Miss Adler. Something like this takes a real team. You would be part of that team, with your one job to do.'

He's put me in my place. I'm merely a hacker for hire.

'Do I get paid?'

'You will be compensated.'

'And afterward?'

'If you're successful and interested, we might be able to arrange an agreement.'

Zeke tried to get me to work for the FBI six months ago. He thought I should go legit. Is this his backhanded way of doing that?

I push the thought aside, weighing my options, which seem rather limited right now. 'I need my own laptop,' I tell him.

Agent Tilman cocks his head at the laptop in front of me. 'You can use that one.'

'It doesn't have what I need.'

'How do you know that?' The way he says it intrigues me despite myself.

I reach over, grab the laptop and open it. 'I'm not sure what you all think I can do,' I say, but I know exactly what I need to do, since I don't have the RAT. I have to try to trace him through the chat room.

And then it strikes me why Zeke told them about me. He knows that Spencer and I have been watching d4rkn!te through a remote access Trojan. He thinks I can track him through it. But what Zeke doesn't know is that the RAT was on Spencer's laptop, not mine, and Spencer has somehow managed to vanish into thin air with all three of the laptops.

Agent Tilman leans over, his elbows on his knees, and I begin to navigate to the forum. 'You have to be careful.'

He doesn't have to tell me that. The DeMarcos have a hit out on me. I wonder if he's aware of that, then decide that he is. If Zeke was telling him about me, then maybe he mentioned it, maybe that's the reason he gave for me to be on the run, rather than hacking into a bank and stealing millions. Zeke really can't talk about that, either, since he was part of it.

Maybe I should be more frightened of the consequences of being here, but the longer he talks to me, the more I think that it might be OK.

Something he said pops into my head. I attribute the delayed response to the fact that I'm still a little bit in shock about being here. 'You want to know if there's a link between d4rkn!te and the DeMarcos?' I ask.

'That's right.'

'If d4rkn!te really is Ryan Whittier, the proof is right here.' I tap the top of the laptop.

He frowns, and with only a few keystrokes, the photograph of Madeline and Ryan and Adriana is on the screen. I turn it around so he can see it. But he's not impressed.

'We need to find something online, proof that they're in business together,' he explains. 'We know that they know each other.'

'You think they're in business together? Not Ryan working for DeMarco?'

Agent Tilman's expression hardens. 'Ryan Whittier doesn't work for anyone unless it's in his own interest.'

'I heard he's a terrorist.'

My words sit between us for a few seconds. His expression does not change.

'Where did you hear that?' he asks matter-of-factly.

I have no idea if Zeke has told him that we've been in contact online, so I merely shrug and turn the laptop back around. The Tor and VPN software is up to date. The laptop probably belongs to the cybercrime team. I could find out easily if they're watching what I'm doing, but I don't bother. I'm certain that they are. This is a test.

As I look through the software on this particular laptop, I see that Agent Tilman was right. There are things on this laptop that I could only dream of hacking into. I seem to have access to a lot of FBI software – software that can get past encryption and databases that I wish I had time to explore.

The bookmarks turn up a link that looks familiar, and when I click on it, I'm on the homepage of the carding forum. This shouldn't be a surprise. If what Spencer said is true, Zeke is an administrator and he's FBI. As Tilman said, there's a whole team working on this.

I type in the user name and password that I used before and begin to lurk. I don't spot d4rkn!te anywhere, though. Agent Tilman is watching me, and I squirm a little under his gaze. He notices and gets up.

'I'll go get some more coffee. Would you like some?'

'Yes, thanks.'

He leaves the room, but I know I can't really be alone. Can I? I look for signs of cameras, but that's silly. Of course, they would be hidden, tiny enough so no one is the wiser. I might be able to locate them, but what's the point? As I sit, feeling the FBI's eyes on me, I begin to question everything again. Why would Zeke expose me like this? Why not let the FBI use its own resources to find d4rkn!te? Zeke tried to keep me on his 'team' in Miami; he knows how much I hated it.

I toggle to another screen and sign into the chat room. The familiarity of it wraps itself around me and I begin to relax a little as I lurk.

Suddenly, I see him. But it's not d4rkn!te. It's Tracker.

And therefore never send to know for whom the bell tolls.

A quick check tells me that this is almost the end of the John Donne poem. Is this Zeke? I don't trust it; it would be too easy for someone to have read our previous messages and caught on, just like with the French phrases. But still, I wonder. I type the next line of the poem.

It tolls for thee.

Meet me for some Chinese.

What is he talking about? And then it strikes me: he wants to meet at that Chinese restaurant. But how does he know I was there? I flash back to tucking my cellphone number in the owner's hand. But would he share it with Zeke? I glance up at the door. Agent Tilman still hasn't returned.

Another message pops up.

See you in an hour. Come alone.

And then he's gone.

FORTY-EIGHT

I shove the laptop onto the table without closing the cover. The door swings open, startling me, and Agent Tilman is standing there, coffees in both hands.

'What's wrong?' he asks.

For a moment, I am tempted to lie. I've spent the last seventeen years lying, and it's easy for me. But I hear myself say, 'He wants to meet.'

'Who? Is it Ryan Whittier?'

I want to believe it's really Tracker – Zeke – but I honestly don't know. 'It might be Zeke,' I admit. I tell him about the John Donne poem, how we've managed to identify ourselves to each other.

Agent Tilman looks dubious. 'But you're not a hundred percent sure that it's him.'

'You never know who's on the other side of the screen.' The statements were cryptic, and I wouldn't expect Zeke to give himself away. I say as much. But something is bothering me.

'What is it?' he asks.

'If he told you to find me, why is he reaching out to me like this? Why does he want to meet? And why is he saying I should come alone? Doesn't he know that I'm with you?'

It's his turn to look uncomfortable. 'No, he doesn't know.'

'What's really going on here?' I don't like the sound of this.

'That phone you have is his.'

I can feel it in my back pocket. 'That's right. He gave it to me.' And I begin to understand. 'You were tracking *him*. Not me. But *I'm* the one you found at the hotel. You don't know where he is, do you?' His search of the hotel room makes more sense now. He doesn't know about Spencer, but he thought it was possible Zeke was with me. 'Do you think he's in trouble?'

'When did you last see him?' he asks, ignoring my question.

'Six months ago,' I answer honestly.

'So how did you end up here?'

I decide to be as truthful as I can, without bringing Spencer into it. 'D4rkn!te was posting pictures of me, sending them to Zeke online. He was stalking me and I think threatening Zeke. I had to leave town.' I don't bother telling him where I'd been and he doesn't ask. 'I saw an article online with a picture of Zeke. He was in Paris. I decided to come here to see if I could track him down. I thought maybe he was in trouble.' And it seems that I was right.

He frowns, mulling over my story, and finally says, 'OK. I'd like you to meet him – or whoever has contacted you. But to be on the safe side, let's do it my way.'

That's how I end up in a small room with a woman agent taping a wire to my torso. 'We'll be able to hear everything,' she says. They've told me that this is in case it's not Zeke, although I have a feeling they'd do this even if it were, considering. My experience with hackers is that they're not dangerous, but d4rkn!te does worry me. He's the one who was posting the photographs of me, and whether he was my actual stalker or not, it's still a threat against me. Not to mention that he's apparently a terrorist and working with a woman whose father has a hit out on me.

'So if d4rkn!te is a terrorist, exactly what does that mean?' I ask Tilman when we emerge.

He frowns, not understanding my question.

'Is he the type who's going to shoot up a restaurant? Is he going to drive a car through a crowd? Is he going to have a bomb?' My voice gets softer with each word, until I'm whispering.

Agent Tilman hesitates a moment. Finally, 'You'll be fine.'

It's not very reassuring. I hold onto the idea that d4rkn!te – Ryan Whittier – is a hacker. A cyberterrorist is more likely to launch a denial of service attack on a network of computers than kill someone.

They make me test the microphone, which is tucked in my bra.

'We'll be right there with you,' Agent Tilman says when they've decided everything's working, and he hands the cellphone back to me.

I'd almost forgotten about the phone, but when they were wiring me, I took it out of my back pocket and gave it to the woman agent, who doesn't seem all that curious about me. Does everyone know who I am? Or am I merely one of many who they wire up and send out to catch the criminals?

They are following me, but I don't see them. They're invisible, just like whoever was stalking me in Charleston, taking pictures of me. The metro rumbles to a stop. It's incredibly crowded, and I force my way through, the wire tugging at my skin, pinching it. I stumble up the stairs and come out into the sunlight. I blink a few times, get my bearings. The restaurant is just up a block or so. As I cross the street and approach it, my eyes dart from side to side, wondering who is FBI, who is watching me.

Maybe that's why I'm not afraid, because I know I'm not alone.

I step inside the Chinese restaurant and the owner gives me a tentative smile. He recognizes me from yesterday.

'I have not seen your friend,' he tells me.

'That's OK,' I say.

'Are you here to eat?' he asks.

I glance around the restaurant and see that it is as empty as it was before. I wonder how he stays in business. I'm aware that I'm breathing even easier now, since it's clear that whoever wants to meet isn't here yet.

The owner is hovering.

'Yes, please,' I say, and he leads me to a table off to the side. I make sure to sit facing the door. The tape on the wire tugs again at my skin and I squirm a little, trying to get more comfortable. I order some *shumai* and noodles and a beer. He scurries to the back, leaving me alone.

I fiddle with the cellphone for lack of anything else to do, and when the restaurant door opens, it startles me. A couple comes in, and the owner materializes and brings them to another table far enough away from me so we can all have some privacy. I glance back at the phone. The picture of Madeline, Ryan and Adriana pops up when I open the search engine app. I hadn't closed it out. I study it a little more closely, but it still doesn't tell me much except that they all know each other.

'Oh, yes, your friend.' The restaurant owner sets two plates of food in front of me. He's looking at the phone screen out of the corner of his eye.

I frown. 'No, that's not my friend. But that's the woman who was with him,' I remind him.

He frowns. 'Yes, and that is the friend you showed me before.'

It takes me a second before I realize that I'd shown him the picture of Ryan Whittier *before* the one of Zeke. And something dawns on me. 'This is the man who met with her,' I say, pointing to Adriana, 'here?'

A broad grin crosses his face. 'Yes, yes, that's him.'

It wasn't Zeke. He hadn't met Adriana here. But Ryan Whittier had. That would explain why Zeke wanted the skimmer on the ATM at the corner. Ryan might live around here, or at least he's staying around here. It's probably not so much about getting the card information – we already know that it's bogus, since it's the same as the Spencer Cross card – but knowing when Ryan might be in the vicinity.

'Ryan Whittier met with Adriana DeMarco here,' I say out loud, even though the owner has left my table and is now taking the couple's order. Agent Tilman is listening, though, so he'll know what the exchange is all about.

As I think about it and nibble on the *shumai*, I begin to feel the first twinge of fear. I don't think it was Zeke who set this meeting up. My hands begin to shake, and I drop a soy sauce-drenched *shumai* in my lap. I only have the beer, and the owner has again disappeared, so I head to the restroom for some water to wash my jeans. It's just past the door to the kitchen, within sight of my table. When I go inside, I quickly lock the door behind me.

The stain is not as bad as I thought, although after scrubbing with a little cold water, it looks worse. Nothing I can do about that, so I wash my hands and run them through my hair, the curls bouncing back around my face. I reach underneath my shirt and feel the wire. They can hear me, but I can't hear them. It's a little disconcerting. I take a few deep breaths and pull the door open.

I am wondering how long I can stay here without anyone getting suspicious, and if Ryan Whittier is really going to show up, when a hand clasps itself around my mouth as I'm pushed back into the restroom. I feel a hand reach up under my shirt, yank on the wire and watch it fall to the ground. I twist around, jabbing my elbow into his gut. I hear him grunt, but his grip is strong. His free hand roughly pats me down, and he discovers the cellphone in my back pocket. He pulls it out and slips it in his jacket pocket.

I still haven't seen his face as I'm dragged through the kitchen and out of a back door to a waiting car. He pushes me inside and the door slams shut behind me.

FORTY-NINE

I scramble around in the seat, slipping a little on the leather, and grab at the door handle. I yank at it, but nothing happens. Where is the FBI? They were supposed to keep this kind of thing from happening.

'You can't get away, and they won't find you now.'

Her voice startles me. I didn't even notice her sitting on the other side of the seat because I was too intent on escape. I've only come face-to-face with her once before, but it was at a distance, and we've never even said hello to each other. I did see her on the sidewalk outside her apartment in New York, but she didn't see me.

Her face is my face. At least, my face from years ago, when I first found myself on Block Island, alone and hiding. I cut my hair, threw away the contact lenses, started to bike, to paint. My life was created out of a crime.

But the longer I study her, the differences begin to emerge. Her cheekbones are higher; my hair is curlier. Our eyes are shaped the same, but they are different colors: mine are hazel, hers are green. My lips are fuller. I'm a lot leaner; she is softer around the edges. But that's the way I used to be, too. Before the biking.

Adriana stares me down, but oddly, it does not make me as uncomfortable as it's supposed to. Instead, I am filled with a sense of calm. While our father may have been a con man who bilked his clients – and Tony DeMarco – out of millions, I have his genes. I am as much a criminal as he was. And she is proving her own mettle as his daughter as well.

'What do you want with me?' I ask.

'You can't figure it out? He says you're smart.'

He. She means Zeke. 'Where is he?'

Her eyes flicker toward the driver behind the glass, but I doubt he can hear anything back here. The car is maneuvering the narrow streets, passing restaurants with tables set up outside, passers-by leisurely window shopping, the sun reflecting off the windshield. The world is going on outside as though nothing is wrong.

'Why do you think I know where he is?' she asks, her voice startling me out of my thoughts. I'd spoken to her before on the phone, and the similarities in our voices had struck me then as they do now. I tell myself that I cannot be distracted. The hit that hasn't been lifted on me hovers between us, but the fact that I am still alive gives me a little hope that I can still save myself – and Zeke – in some way.

Maybe I'm just naive.

'He's working for you,' I say matter-of-factly. 'You've been threatening him with those photographs of me. And now you've kidnapped me, so something must have gone wrong.' I am surprised by how calm I sound, when inside I feel as though I'm about to explode.

Her jaw tenses, and she studies me a little more intently, as though I might still be wearing a wire.

'He's an FBI agent. How could he be working for *me*? And why do you think this is all about *you*?' Her tone is belligerent. I chalk her attitude up to her age. I remember the brash arrogance I'd had up until the time I shot Zeke. Hers is no different.

And then she adds, 'Oh, that's right. He helped you steal all that money. I wonder what the FBI would say about that.'

The threat hangs between us, and I understand more what's been going on the last months. It's not only the photographs of me, the threat against my life, but the threat that she would reveal him and ruin his career. Possibly land him in prison.

But she can't prove it. We didn't leave a trail, and anyway, Zeke put the money back after we stole it. Well, except for those couple million dollars that disappeared.

I wonder again about Agent Tilman and his people. I hope that they were close enough to be able to follow us. I have no idea where she's taking me, but I have a reasonable suspicion as to why I've ended up here. The threats must not be working anymore.

'How is your father?' I ask.

The unexpected question startles her, and her face changes slightly before she can stop it. 'He's dying,' she says softly.

'I'm sorry,' I say, and I am surprised now because I think I mean it. I'm not sorry that the man who has ordered a hit on me is dying, but I *am* sorry that she is going to lose her father. I wasn't able to see my father before he died; I was sequestered on Block Island and wasn't able to say goodbye. While I know what kind of man he was, I still wish things had been different. So much so that I sent him a postcard and gave away my location, resulting in having to run for my life.

'Your father offered me a job,' I say for lack of anything else. 'He wanted me to hack for him.' I wonder if I'm saying too much.

'He told me about you,' she says. 'He told me I had a sister. He told me about your father. My mother.' Her voice is low, but there is an edge behind it. She blames me for my father's indiscretions. There's nothing I can do about that. I might blame me, too, for lack of anyone else.

'I didn't know about you,' I feel compelled to tell her. 'Not until about a year and a half ago. I had no idea.'

It doesn't make a difference. She is comfortable with her hatred toward me, toward my father. It is this hatred that worries me. That makes me think she will have no qualms about actually having me killed. This has little to do with Zeke or the carding forum, or the base that was compromised. It's merely convenient that threatening my life has been a way to get him to do what she wants. The end game will be the same either way. From the way Adriana is watching me, it is most definitely more about her father's revenge on me and her need to give him that before he dies. I will die in the city where I was happiest as a child. There is a certain symmetry to that, if I would, in fact, accept that fate.

I'm not ready to do that.

'Zeke,' I say, the sound of his name on my tongue giving me a little more strength.

'If you want to see him again, you'll do what I say.' Her tone is harsh, and I doubt that if she has her way, I will ever see Zeke again.

I say nothing, settling back against the soft leather and staring out the window, the city passing us by. She's not going to tell me anything, so I'm not going to bother with any more questions.

We are on the outskirts of the city now, I think perhaps in the tenth arrondissement. I spot water, but it's not the Seine. Maybe a canal, but I can't remember names. It's been too long. The charm of Paris has slipped away a little, with concrete buildings sporting brightly colored graffiti. I have no idea where we're heading until the car slows to a stop in front of what's clearly a warehouse that's been renovated into a sleek office building.

Adriana opens her door and steps out. I reach for my door handle, but the door is yanked open before I touch it.

'Get out.' The voice is harsh, male.

I climb out of the car and stand, the sun so bright I shield my eyes with my hand. Adriana is walking around the back of the car and steps up onto the sidewalk. She doesn't wait for me but moves to the building's entrance. For a second, I've got an opening and I might be able to get away, until the shadow moves in front of me. I lift my hand and look at his face.

I recognize him. He's the guy who sat next to me at the bar in Charleston that night before my escape.

FIFTY

This man is the one who is going to kill me. His eyes are like a shark's, black, dead.

He grabs my elbow and steers me toward Adriana, who's pushed her way through the glass doors. Again, I consider trying to flee, but that's when I feel the gun discreetly stuck in my side. I glance around, but there's no one on the sidewalk.

The FBI has not ridden up on white horses or even in a cab to save me. Realistically, I am expendable to Agent Tilman. He used me. It was a good idea, in theory. Use the hacker who has everything to lose; she can't say no. If it doesn't work out, then no one is the wiser. The sad thing is that he's not going to get Adriana or Ryan Whittier. Where is *he*, anyway?

Panic encompasses me, and my knees give a little. The gun slips a little as the man forces me to straighten up. I try to push the fear down and clear my head, to focus on my surroundings.

It's an office building, but there are no signs on the walls directing people to specific businesses. The floor is a sleek marble; a gigantic floral arrangement perches on an elegant table across from the bank of elevators. It looks very new. Maybe that's why there's no one here. No one except us.

The doors to one of the elevators open and the man shoves me inside, next to Adriana. She pushes a button, and I watch the flash of numbers until we stop on the fifth floor. He hands her the cellphone that he took out of my pocket. The doors slide open and I am pushed out, stumbling, trying to keep my balance.

My suspicions that this building has been renovated are confirmed, and this space is not finished yet. Pillars mark where offices will be, and instead of walls, plastic sheeting separates the spaces. The floor is covered in paper with a layer of chalky debris, footprints smudged on top of one another. The man uses the gun to guide me through one of the plastic sheets. Behind it, four large computer screens perch on a long table, a couple of swivel chairs in front. As we get closer, I'm embarrassed at how my fingers begin to itch. Even being held at gunpoint, afraid for my life, my addiction overwhelms me.

Adriana sees it. She's watching me, and she nods slightly. The man lets go of my arm, the gun no longer against me. For a second, I wonder if I can flee, but this man would have no qualms actually shooting me, and he and Adriana could leave me here to die. Just as I'd left Zeke all those years ago on the houseboat.

Zeke. I glance around, but there's no sign of him. No sign of anyone else, except a can of Red Bull next to one of the keyboards in front of the screens. Is this where he was when we saw him on video? It's possible, and looking at the setup, likely. But if he *was* here, where is he now?

Adriana cocks her head toward them. 'Go ahead. Check it out.'

'No, thanks.'

'I know you want to.'

I do, but not exactly for the reasons she might think. If I look at the screens, I might be able to get some clue as to whether Zeke has been here. Still, I resist.

'Tell me where he is. I want to see him.'

Adriana's eyes flicker over to the man with the gun, then back at me. 'He wants to see *you*, too.' There is a venom in her tone that tells me more is going on here than I originally thought. Zeke met Adriana when he was undercover. He said that the nature of his assignment was to get her to trust him, and he insists that there was never anything more than a platonic relationship. From the way she's looking at me, though, it's clear that she wanted it to be more. There was only one thing in the way: me.

I've been the target of a woman scorned before, and I managed to survive.

'Does your father know what you're up to?' I ask.

'Did *your* father?'

It's a loaded question. My father knew what I could do, and he set me up. Does she know what I was willing to do to get him to notice me? If she does, then she's answered my question. Tony DeMarco may not have asked her directly to do this, but she's willing to do it for his approval. My sister and I are not so different, which is why I say, 'You don't have to do this.'

She doesn't understand what I'm saying.

'I spent a long time in hiding,' I tell her. 'Believe me, it's not an easy life. Always looking over my shoulder. Taking on different names. Are you willing to do that? Is this all worth that? Is he worth that?' I pause. 'He's dying, Adriana. Go be with your father. Give this up. No one will ever know. You can go back to your businesses. Your legitimate businesses. He'll still be proud of you.'

My words affect her in a way she's not expecting. She wavers, and for a moment I think I've gotten through, that she is going to do as I say. But it's too late. Even I can see that.

The FBI is already in the picture, maybe in the periphery, but they're still there. Zeke's work will not go unnoticed, despite what might happen to him. To me.

I want to ask her what she wants of me, why she brought me here. Why not just kill me? There's something more at play, but I can't figure it out.

And then I spot the camera. It's up in the corner, angled down, right on me. Anyone watching will see the gun pointed at me.

Is Zeke on the other side? Is that what this is all about? Photographs showing that they're within an arm's reach of me are no longer doing the job. Now they have to bring me physically at gunpoint to prove that they mean business.

And as though they know what I'm thinking, the screens light up, code splashed across them.

'What's going on?' I ask, but I already know. Someone is remotely accessing these computers. It has to be Zeke. And then I have another thought. I turn to Adriana. 'You don't know where he is, do you?'

Her jaw tenses, but she says nothing, nods at the man behind me, who jabs the gun into my side. I flinch and catch my breath. But I'm distracted by what's happening on one of the screens. It's like a player piano; no one is at the keys but music comes out anyway.

I push my glasses up further on my nose and focus on the code splashed across the screen. I tune out everything – Adriana, the gun – as I study it, a language that I am even more fluent in than French.

I half expect this to be the source code of the app, but it's not. It's the source code of the message program in *my* laptop. The messages Zeke wrote to me are there, but they're mixed up in the code, so anyone like Adriana who doesn't know the language wouldn't be able to see it – not right away, anyway. This computer is still linked to mine – and Spencer is on the other side.

'What is he doing?' Adriana asks.

Even though she doesn't know how to code and can't read it, she suspects, like I do, that Zeke's on the other side of the screens. The problem is, does Zeke know about Spencer? Will he try to reach out to him? I want to warn him somehow, send him a message that he shouldn't engage, just in case. But unless I can get to the keyboard, my hands are tied.

'Tell me what's happening.' Adriana's tone is harder, more insistent. She wants me to interpret, make sure that he's doing what she wants. Her concern probably has to do with the card information. The information was never transferred. She has to make sure that she gets it. After that, she'll kill me.

I take a step toward the computers, and the man grabs my arm. Adriana gives a short shake of her head, and he lets me go. She nods at me, and I move to the chair and take a seat. I run my fingers along the keys, feeling their strength. This is what I do; this is how I've been able to save myself. I can't lose it now. I have to survive.

Because they've got this computer setup, it's possible Adriana doesn't know that everything can be controlled by a cellphone. A cellphone that she just happens to be holding.

I try to concentrate on the code but Adriana is pacing a few feet away; the man with the gun stands stiffly on the other side of me. They've got me boxed in. Even if I were considering taking off, one of them would be able to tackle me and take me down. Not to mention that gun might be put to use.

I switch from this screen to the one next to it. There's more code, and it takes me a few moments to decipher it. This is the code for the app. It looks like what I saw on my phone before Agent Tilman showed up at the hotel. And then I see it again.

The back door.

FIFTY-ONE

Zeke put this here for a reason, but I haven't been able to figure it out. It was also in the hotel reservation system. I read the code a little more closely.

There are hundreds, no, thousands of accounts stored here. This is the base, and it's all in limbo.

And then I have an idea. I once circumvented millions of dollars from several bank accounts to other accounts in other banks all over the world. All I have to do now is figure out how to first send this information to the server so Adriana will think she's finally got it – and then make it disappear.

I study the code and try to think the way Zeke – no, Tracker – would when he created the back door. I take a deep breath and close my eyes, shutting out everything. I let it all slip away as the code begins to run inside my head.

What do you see?

I ask myself the same question Tracker always used to ask me when he wasn't Zeke, when he wasn't anyone except my best friend who always pushed me to do my best work. And when I open my eyes, I know what I have to do.

The back door leads into the server, where the card information will be deposited and stored. But where will I send it from there? The answer comes to me so suddenly that I'm annoyed I didn't think of it sooner. What if I sent the information back where it came from? Into the card accounts.

It will be tricky to do that, since the information has come from cards issued by different banks. People use ATM machines indiscriminately. They don't choose an ATM at their own bank. This is what makes this hack more genius than merely going after one large institution.

And as I consider the genius of it, the back door in the app makes even more sense. I can recode it and reverse it. My fingers move across the keys as I create source code from what's already there. I shift a little in my seat and wish I still had the phone. Because of the two-step verification system that Zeke's set up, it would be easier to use the app for the final transfer, but I can't exactly ask Adriana to give it back to me or I'll tip my hand.

I glance around at her. She's doing something on a phone, but is it mine or hers? For a second, I worry that she's going to discover the app, but remember that Zeke set it up inside the music app and, even if she opens it, she won't be able to figure out what it really is.

The man with the gun is hovering next to me, the gun leveled at my head, steady, almost as though he's a statue. I want to point out that he's a stereotype, but he might not get it.

'How long were you in Charleston?' I ask.

He hasn't expected me to speak to him, and the sound of my voice startles him. I can tell only by the slight furrow of his brow before he composes himself again.

'You were at the bar,' I point out. 'How long were you following me?'

He barely blinks, staring at me, unnerving me. He remains mute.

I'm having trouble with the app. The two-step authentication is making it more difficult than it should be to reroute the information. I'm distracted by the empty can of Red Bull next to the keyboard. I wonder whose it is. I don't know that I've ever seen Zeke drink the stuff, although the young hackers we worked with in Miami seemed to thrive on it.

When I turn my attention back to the screens, what I see makes me catch my breath. It's not on the screen with the app code, but the other one, the one with my laptop message program.

In between the code, there's a message for me.

He's watching you.

A small shiver shimmies up my spine. Who's watching me? Who sent the message? Whoever did may still think I've got my laptop.

Spencer's going to see the message if he's monitoring it.

I glance up at the camera in the corner. D4rkn!te has been watching me all along. If he were the one who sent the message, would he admit it? Would he say '*I'm* watching you'? No. It's a warning. Zeke activated these screens. He's watching remotely, and he is able to see me.

I want to reply, but in case it's not him, I don't dare. If he's really monitoring these computers, he already knows what I'm planning to do.

I have to disable the two-step authentication program. Easier said than done. This isn't a typical program that can be turned off and on at will through account settings. Zeke created the source code. I don't even know what to look for or where. I go back to the screen with the app code and scan it, looking for anything that's unusual, anything that might jump out at me. But I don't see anything.

It doesn't help that I know I'm being watched.

It's got to be here.

I close my eyes and let Tracker in. *What do you see?*

When I open them, it's as though I'm seeing it for the first time. The two-step verification code is buried discreetly, but it's there. As I study it, I realize I don't have to disable it. I can use the program the way it's supposed to be used, even though I don't have the phone.

I am so intent on what I'm doing that the small *ding* startles me. It's similar to an alert sound on a computer, but that's not it. And then I realize that it's the elevator. I roll back in my chair a little, trying to see what's going on when I hear Adriana scream, 'Now!'

I don't wait around to find out what she means. I hit the final key and scramble out of the chair and push my way through the plastic sheeting, the gunshot echoing in my ears as I run.

FIFTY-TWO

'm on autopilot, my shoes slipping on the chalk-covered paper on the floor, but I manage not to fall as I head toward the bright red 'Exit' sign. Another gunshot sounds, and I weave back and forth through the plastic. This may have been the stupidest thing I've ever done in my life.

I hear shouting behind me, but I focus on the sign, the door where I'll make my escape. I reach it and push it open, skipping down the stairs, praying that I won't trip. The door slams shut above me – I'm on the fourth floor now – and then I hear it open again and heavy footsteps coming after me.

I can barely catch my breath, again regretting biking and not running. Maybe I need to switch up my exercise regimen.

Third floor.

Halfway to the second.

The footsteps are gaining on me.

I have no endgame, except that I want to be able to get out of here alive. It pushes me forward.

First floor.

The door won't budge. I yank on the handle, trying to force it, but nothing. The footsteps are closer, and I turn around, my back against the door. I slide down into a stoop, waiting.

I have no gun, no way to protect myself. Adriana DeMarco's revenge will be realized right here.

I can see him now, in the stairwell just above me. Even though I know it won't do any good, I jump up and try the door again.

But I have no more luck this time than before.

He's coming toward me, facing me, the gun aimed right at me. Above him, on the stairs, are two police officers, their guns drawn. And just as he reaches me, the door swings open, startling both of us. He grabs me around the neck and drags me backward, waving his gun around.

I can't breathe as I focus on who's come through the door. Zeke.

'Let her go!' he demands, his gun leveled at both of us.

I'm in the way. If I weren't in the way, he could kill this man who wants to kill me. I try to turn my head, but his arm is wrapped so tightly around my neck that it would take nothing to break it, and I would be dead.

I hear a cracking sound; suddenly, the man's arm goes slack, and then it's gone. I haven't realized he's been holding me up until I drop down on my knees. The concrete stairwell is hard beneath them. My entire body is shaking. What just happened? What's going on?

The officers on the stairwell are no longer there. They're behind me, looking at the man who just moments ago was going to kill me. I twist around, but then Zeke's arms are around me, and he's moving me away. 'Don't look,' he whispers in my ear, his breath tickling my neck.

We go through the doorway. We're in the lobby of the building and there are people – police – everywhere. Not like when I came in earlier. I can't think straight. How did they know where I was? And then I realize: the cellphone. Agent

Tilman gave it back to me, knowing full well that there was a GPS in it. That's how he'd found me in the first place. Where was the phone now? Oh, right. Adriana.

Adriana. My heart pounds as I think about how close she came to having me killed. But before I can ask about her, Zeke puts his finger to my lips and traces them. 'Sssh,' he whispers, and I think he's going to kiss me, but then I realize it's more practical than that.

His beard scratches against my cheek. 'Did you transfer the information?' he whispers.

I shake my head. 'I reprogrammed it. All the information looks like it's going to the server, but it won't. I got the idea from the bank job. You know, how you funneled all the money back into the original accounts. That's what I did.'

'You're a genius.'

I don't feel like I've done anything except cause trouble. What business did I have even coming here? I put him in danger. I put myself in danger. Adriana. 'Where is Adriana?' And I remember: 'I heard her scream.'

'We've got her, don't worry.'

Relief rushes through me, and I take a deep breath.

'Where have you been?' I ask. 'I've been so worried about you.'

He reaches up and touches the bruise under my eye, his lips brushing mine. 'You shouldn't be.' He gives me a small smile. 'I'm FBI.'

That's what Spencer keeps saying. 'That doesn't mean you're immortal.'

'No?' His expression grows dark and the smile fades. 'I didn't think that she'd go as far as to kidnap you, but when I got the video feed from d4rkn!te, I . . .' His voice trails off. 'I sent you that message to warn you. I let Tilman know what was happening. He was already almost there, too. I had the feed on my phone when he shot at you and saw where you were going. That's how I knew you were in the stairwell.' He pulls me closer and I can feel his heart beating fast as he kisses me, and for a moment everything slips away as I melt into him. He pulls away too quickly, and I reach for more. He puts his finger to my lips and smiles. 'There's a lot of time for that later,' he whispers.

I take a deep breath. 'I'm going to hold you to that.' But then, 'You said d4rkn!te sent the video feed to you? Where is he, anyway?'

Zeke shakes his head. 'No clue. He could be halfway across the world for all I know.' He stops for a second, then says, 'I approached him about the carding forum. He's the one who set up that kiddie porn site we found six months ago that we couldn't nail DeMarco on.'

'When did Adriana figure out that *you* were involved?'

'He told her he was working with Tracker.'

Ryan Whittier knows that he's a fed. He knows about me.

Zeke knows what I'm thinking. 'Don't worry. He's got a bigger agenda than you or me. He'll find something else. Some way other than Adriana to raise the money he needs.'

I pull away a little. 'I heard something about Spencer. That he's working with Ryan Whittier.'

Zeke's face clouds over. 'Spencer doesn't know him.' He says it so definitively.

Agent Tilman is walking over to us. He's shaking his head. 'You were just supposed to hack into the computer and find Ryan Whittier.' I think he's talking to me, but I realize he's talking to both of us. 'You'd better come with me. We need to debrief you.'

For a second, I can see that Zeke is considering arguing with him, but after a few seconds, he nods. He folds his hand around mine as we follow Agent Tilman. I have shut out the sounds and everyone else around me and move closer to Zeke, tightening my grip on his hand. He looks at me and gives me a small smile, squeezing my hand back. The adrenaline of the last hours has dissipated, leaving me exhausted.

I am about to ask Agent Tilman how long he thinks this debriefing will last when a French police officer approaches, a stern look on his face. He starts speaking rapidly in French. Agent Tilman and Zeke both wear frowns, because neither of them speak French. But I understand.

Adriana DeMarco has escaped.

EPILOGUE

Tony DeMarco is dead.

I read the story online and try to conjure some sympathetic feelings, but it's futile. He wanted *me* dead and tried to kill me up to the end of his own life.

You'd think that I'd feel relief, at least. But I'm still not safe. His daughter, my half-sister, Adriana, isn't letting go. She's vowed to exact revenge for her father. She's taken over his empire, and she's proving to be just as ruthless. And she's also proving to be as adept at hiding as I am. She's vanished. She was clever enough to have one of her lackeys pose as a French detective, The two of them drove away from the crime scene and haven't been seen since.

I feel his hands on my shoulders, and I shut the laptop cover. 'He's dead.'

Zeke nods. 'I know.'

Of course he does. He probably knew the second it happened. I stand up, and his arms encircle me, pulling me toward him.

'I thought I was keeping you safe,' he whispers.

I nestle deeper into Zeke's arms. 'I'm fine.' But am I? I don't know. Tony's death is the least of it. Everything that's happened in the last few days, the last week, has jolted me. I have discovered things about myself, about my sense of survival, about my loyalty to this man that I never realized before. I am willing to risk my life for him, just as he's willing to risk his life and career for me.

All those years sequestered on Block Island, daydreaming about my friend Tracker on the other side of the computer screen, always half in love with the idea of him. And now he's here. He's real, and I never want to let him go.

'None of this would have happened if I hadn't put that damn GPS into your phone.' He's angry with himself.

'None of what? You'd still have been compromised.'

'I'm talking about you. You could have been completely safe. No one would have known where you were.'

'Except for Madeline Whittier,' I remind him. 'She recognized me. And if it weren't her, it could've been someone else. Someone else my father ripped off. Someone else *I* ripped off.' I pause a second, then add, 'I didn't even know anyone was watching me. You were doing what they wanted, so I would've been OK.' But as I say it, I wonder. Would I have been? Or would killing me be the last thing Tony DeMarco did before he died?

I shift a little but he holds me tighter, as though I'm going to disappear again.

'What do we do now?' I ask.

He gives me a grin and kisses me. When I'm able to catch my breath, I pull away a little. 'You're distracting me.'

'That's the idea.' He runs his finger along my jawline and leans in again, but I try to keep my distance – as much as I'm able to. He gets the message this time. 'Let's get away.'

My whole life has been 'getting away.' I'm not quite sure what he means.

'Mallorca, a Greek island somewhere. French Riviera. Italian Riveria.' He smiles. 'Somewhere we can escape to.'

The idea of it appeals to me. Especially the islands. I have an affinity for islands, and he knows that. But we aren't exactly free and easy.

'You still have a job,' I remind him.

'For now.'

I let that hang between us for a few seconds. He's on thin ice with his people at the FBI. He went further than he was supposed to, and it doesn't matter that it was to keep me alive. It doesn't matter that he developed that software that would prevent the immediate transfer of information. We managed to keep some of it from being compromised, but not all of it. And d4rkn!te – Ryan Whittier – is still out there; he wasn't able to bring him in.

'Is he really a terrorist?' I ask.

'We've found communication between him and some radical groups. He went to Syria a year ago, was under the radar until he showed up in Paris and I hooked up with him about the carding forum.' He doesn't elaborate, which makes me think that there's more to it, but I'm not sure I want to press the issue.

'Do you think they'll fire you?'

'No. But the vacation? Let's say that it's not exactly my idea.'

So there *were* repercussions. That explains where he's been for the last two days. His debriefing lasted a lot longer than mine. I ignore the implication that he's on some sort of suspension or leave and say, 'How about going somewhere that doesn't have the Internet?'

He makes an exaggerated shocked expression. I lightly slap his arm. 'You can do it,' I promise.

'I know *you* can. Me, I don't think so.' I look for the teasing, but he's serious. 'We still have someone to track down.'

'He's gone,' I say. 'He's more used to being underground than I am. We won't find him.' I hate myself for doubting, for thinking that Spencer really is working with Ryan Whittier.

Zeke doesn't want to believe it. 'Nothing ever vanishes on the Internet.' He turns the laptop toward me and shows me what he'd been looking at while I was reading about Tony DeMarco. 'He's not as far away as we think.'

Spencer's still got my laptop, and he hasn't gotten rid of the remote access Trojan. He knows we're watching him. A photograph of a young man is on the screen. The image is a little fuzzy; it's been taken from a security camera outside an S-Bahn station. He's looking straight up at the camera with a defiant expression. There's no mistaking who it is. It's Ryan Whittier.

Zeke is already booking tickets.

So much for an island. I guess we're heading to Berlin.

ACKNOWLEDGMENTS

Writing a series about computer hackers means a lot of research hours online, but I am not a hacker or even as remotely computer literate as my characters. I try to be as realistic as possible, yet at the same time, I do make things up – this is a work of fiction, after all. If my characters do something online that isn't exactly possible right now, it might likely be possible sometime in the future, considering how quickly our Internet world evolves.

There are a couple of people I need to thank for their help with certain plot points in this book: Elizabeth Medcalf, one of my favorite partners in crime, for her extensive knowledge of Amtrak trains and railroad sidings. If it weren't for her, Tina and Spencer might still be riding the rails. And Joe Calamia, one of my colleagues at Yale University Press, for not freaking out too much when I asked him – perhaps a little too seriously – if an explosion would destroy a hard drive. I didn't even know that such a thing as a degausser even existed until he told me about it.

My editor, Kate Lyall Grant at Severn House, is wonderful to work with, and I have to thank the entire team in London for the amazing cover designs, great copyediting and overall support.

My agent Josh Getzler is a superstar.

I couldn't do any of this without my husband, Chris, daughter, Julia, and their support and patience when I have to sequester myself in order to get my word count for the day.

And finally, I want to thank all my readers and those fans of Annie Seymour and Brett Kavanaugh who have taken a chance on this new series. I'm so pleased you've come along on this new adventure. Without you, I'd just be writing for myself, and it's so much more fun this way.

Lightning Source UK Ltd.
Milton Keynes UK
UKHW011243110419
340873UK00001B/47/P

9 781847 518682